# The Waves at My Window

## Kristen Grafton

Cottage House Publishing

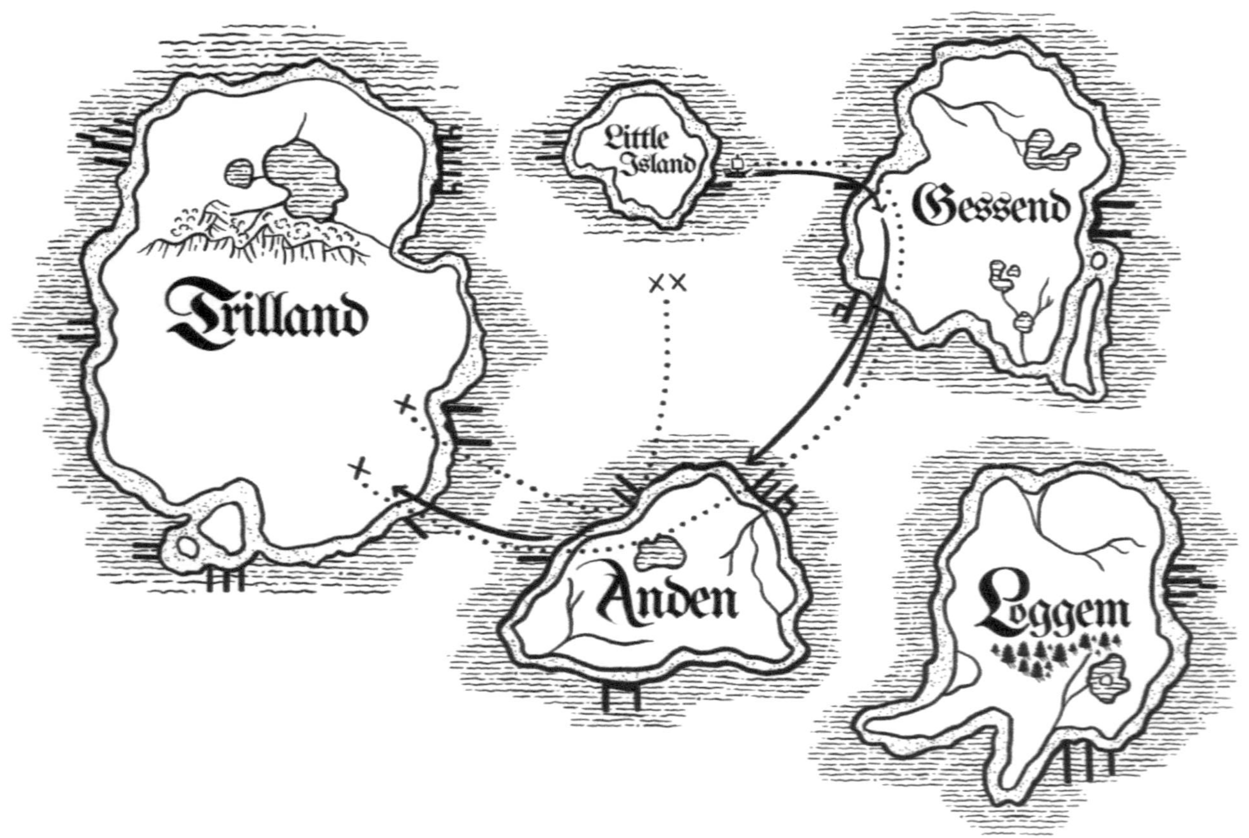
Trilland
Little Island
Gessend
Anden
Loggem

*For the younger me who didn't know if she could do it...*

# Chapter 1

The cool, glistening sand sifts through my fingers as I shove my fist into it and pull back up repeatedly. I love this part of the island. It's like my own private beach. It's isolated, and it requires a bit of a climb to get to. Few people in the village are able or even willing to scale the rocks. Sometimes, I wonder why no one else seems interested in this part of the island. Maybe, in a way, they've left it for me. Maybe they knew I needed it.

I hear the sand crunching behind me, and I know immediately it has to be Zane. He's pretty much the only person who ever seeks me out when I'm here. In fact, he's the one who first showed me this spot.

"Maris," Zane calls out behind me. "Did you hear the news?"

"No," I say. "I've been here all morning. What happened?"

"There's a ship passing by."

"So?" Merchant ships pass by all the time. In fact, they usually pull in for trade.

"*Passing by.*"

"What? Are they not coming in?"

"Doesn't look like it," Zane sits down next to me and runs his hand through his jet black hair. "I think they're just passing by over on the fishing side of the island."

"That's weird. Maybe they're circling back?"

He shrugs. "Yeah, maybe."

"What's up with you?"

He fidgets nervously, flicking his fingers against his palm. "Nothing. I just don't like it. Seems fishy to me."

"How ironic," I say, and he rolls his eyes. The only ships that come around are merchant ships, and they usually pull in, not pass by. A non-merchant ship hasn't passed this island in nearly a year. Not since I got here.

"Yeah." He shrugs and smiles. "So how much longer are you going to hide out over here?"

I feel the color rush into my cheeks. "I'm not hiding out!"

"Of course you are." He nudges my shoulder and laughs. "Since the day I met you, all you've wanted to do is hide out here. I think you'd live here if you could survive on your own."

I laugh. "I'd never survive by myself."

"Of course not. That's why you have me." Zane juts his chin up into the air with the utmost confidence and just a little bit of ego. "What would you ever do without me?"

"I don't know, Zane." I giggle. "I just don't know. Besides, shouldn't you be fishing?"

He shrugs. "No point hauling in more at this point if we can't sell it or consume it before it spoils."

"The catch is that good today?"

"Been that way for a few days. The new method is working—thanks to yours truly."

I scoff. "It's a good thing you're humble."

"By the way," he snaps his fingers, "before I forget, my mom wants to see you today. She asked me to tell you that."

"And you almost forgot? You are very unreliable."

"Hey, I remembered. I'm pretty sure she wants your help planning my surprise birthday party, but don't tell her that I know that."

"It's not a surprise if you know about it!" I playfully hit Zane on the arm, and he laughs.

"I'll act surprised. She'll never know the difference."

"You faked surprise last year."

"Just like I do every year."

"You don't think one day she is going to catch on?"

"I've been faking it since well before I knew you." Zane winks. "She hasn't caught on yet."

I roll my eyes. "Fine. You're impossible."

He laughs, but he sobers quickly, and I'm surprised by how serious he looks. It doesn't happen often. "I wish I could throw you a fake surprise birthday party."

I avoid his eyes. "You know how I feel about that."

"It doesn't have to be your actual birthday. We can just celebrate your existence."

"I wouldn't feel right celebrating my birthday without even knowing what day it is."

"I know, I know." Zane raises his hands in surrender. "But one day you will. And then you are getting a fake surprise birthday party, whether you want one or not."

I smile and look away. I hope he's right. I hope one day I will know what day it is.

"Well," Zane stands up and brushes the sand from his shorts, "I'm heading back into town. You coming, or are you gonna hide some more?"

I try to act outraged, but it's not very convincing. "I'm coming with you. Might as well go see your mom."

Zane holds out his hand to help me up. "Don't sound so excited."

~~~
~~~

Just as we reach town, we spot Zane's mom running toward us. It occurs to me that I don't think I've ever seen Harper run except for the one time she was chasing Zane's sister Daisy because she thought she'd lost her. She's breathing more heavily that seems necessary for the short distance she just ran, and her eyes are wild. Seeing Harper panicked—the one person who always seems calm, who calms *me* down when I feel panicked—makes me far more anxious than anything else. Before she reaches us, she reaches out her arm toward Zane.

"Mom." Zane catches her gently by the shoulders and brushes the hair from her eyes. "Mom, what's wrong?"

"The ship," she pants.

"What about the ship?"

"They dropped a lifeboat. It's coming to shore."

"What?" Zane and I say simultaneously. We both follow Zane's mom down to the shore.

Merchant ships don't drop lifeboats. They pull into the island. We row boats out to them sometimes. But they don't drop lifeboats and then just leave. As far as I know, this has only happened one other time: the day that they pulled in my lifeboat from a ship that passed by and didn't pull in to the island. A part of me that I'd rather not acknowledge wonders if there's some connection between that incident and this one, but I can't entertain those thoughts for too long; it can only lead to disappointment.

Almost the entire town is crowded around to see the lifeboat. The fishermen are still standing waist-deep in the water waiting for the lifeboat. Little kids are begging their parents to be lifted up so they can see. No one new ever comes to this town. Well, except for me.

This must be what the town looked like the day I came. I wish I remembered that day. Why on earth would someone abandon ship and paddle into this little, uncharted island? Why did *I* do it?

The boat is pretty close to shore and the guy paddling looks exhausted. Some of the younger men of the town swim out to help pull him to shore. Everyone races down to the beach to see the mysterious paddler, but Zane and I are some of the fastest runners in town, so we manage to get to the front of the crowd.

"Back up, back up," Tito calls out as he helps drag the boat up onto the beach. "Give us some space."

Zane runs over and helps Tito and the others pull in the boat. The paddler throws his arms over the edge of the boat and heaves violently in a display that nearly makes me the second person to vomit that day. Once he manages to compose himself, Zane helps him out of the boat and sits him down in the sand. He's very pale and looks like he could pass out or throw up again at any moment. One of the townspeople hands Zane a cup of water, who passes it on to the paddler, instructing him to drink slowly. He takes a few sips, but he doesn't look better.

"Hey man," Zane says. "You all right? What are you doing out here?"

"I—I was just—" the paddler wipes the sweat from his forehead. He looks up, and we make eye contact, but his eyes lock on mine and he looks excited. "Lorraine!"

It feels like my heart stops for a moment. I have a million questions I want to ask—*Who is Lorraine? Do you know who I am? Where are you from? Why did you come here? How did you find me?*—and yet, I feel incapable of uttering a single one. They all stick in my throat, threatening to choke me before I get a single answer. I can only manage one single syllable.

"What?" I say.

"Lorraine, it's you." He smiles softly. "I actually found you. I didn't think I would."

The entire town turns to stare at me, and suddenly, I feel very sweaty. I wish I could just vanish. "What are you talking about?" I whisper.

"I actually found you." He barely gets the sentence out before he passes out.

"Dang it," Tito grumbles. "He's got heat stroke. Let's get him inside."

Zane starts helping Tito lift him up from the sand, each supporting a shoulder, but I catch Zane staring at me. He mouths "what the heck?" to me, and I just shrug. Who is Lorraine, and why does he think I'm her?

Am I her? Am I Lorraine?

# Chapter 2

I wait outside of Ms. Flora's house, pacing back and forth, consistently fighting the urge to rub my arms. As the unofficial non-MD doctor of the town, the paddler was brought to her after he fainted. Most of the townspeople gave up waiting after a little while, but I, along with a few persistent others, are still here. Those who left made others promise to come get them if and when the paddler shared any information. Those who remain talk in whispers to each other now that they've exhausted the same old question: *Do you recognize him?* I can still feel all of their eyes on me, judging me, trying to see me through the paddler's eyes. I wish Zane and Ms. Flora would hurry up already. I so desperately want to get out from under the stares of everyone.

"He doesn't look at all familiar?" Daisy asks me out of the blue. Zane told me to watch his little sister, but honestly the last thing I want to deal with right now is Daisy's chatter.

"No, he doesn't."

"But he knew you."

I roll my eyes. "He called me Lorraine. That's not my name."

"That's not your name *now*." Daisy points at me. "Who knows what your name really is."

"Well he doesn't look familiar." I fold my arms, hoping to end the conversation. I think I've succeeded, but Daisy will not be deterred.

"Are you sure?"

"Yes, I'm sure."

"Are you *really* sure?"

"Daisy, please. Let's just wait for your brother to come back."

Daisy's questions have attracted attention, and I just wish everyone would stop staring at me. I don't know any more about this guy than they do, but they don't seem to believe that. I honestly wish that I did. I've imagined so many times what I would do in a situation like this. I'd hoped that if someone ever recognized me that I would immediately recognize them and some memory would come flooding back, but that didn't happen, and for that reason, it is hard to be optimistic that this guy actually knows who I am. Still, the hope nags at me anyway.

"Maris." Zane opens the door and beckons for me to come inside. Daisy follows closely, and Zane looks like he wants to tell her to wait outside, but it's useless to tell Daisy anything.

Zane closes the door and faces me. "He'll be okay. Just a bad case of heat stroke."

"Did he say anything else?" I say.

"No. He just kept muttering the same thing over and over, how he can't believe he actually found you—er, Lorraine—whoever."

"Do you think—"

He shakes his head. "He's pretty sick. He could be hallucinating. Or maybe you just look like someone, and he was so dizzy he couldn't tell the difference. I wouldn't take it seriously until we can really talk to him when he's feeling better."

"But if he knows something, even something small—"

"He's not even speaking in complete sentences, really. He needs a chance to recover."

I nod, but I'm not sure I'm as convinced as Zane is. This is the first hint at what might have been my former life. Is it foolish to hope that it's real?

"Is the ship gone?" he asks, and I nod.

"Didn't even wait for trade. Maybe we're not on its normal route."

"I guess."

I bite the side of my finger until it bleeds, silently admonishing myself for doing it. I try to hide the sliver of blood, but Zane spots it.

"Hey." He holds his arms out to me, and I fall into them, comforted by his presence. "Everything's going to be okay. We'll figure it out."

I press my face into his chest and cling to his back. Zane is safe. Zane is the only person not staring me down or assuming that I must know the mysterious paddler.

"Do you want me to walk you back to your place?" he asks, and I nod into his chest. "Come on then, let's go."

~~~

"Maris, is that you?" my roommate Elise calls out.

"Yes."

"What happened today? I saw everyone rush down to the beach."

I collapse onto the couch. "Some guy paddled in from a ship that passed by."

"What?" Elise perches on the couch next to me and leans toward me. "Who is he? Where's he from?"

I shrug. "We don't know. He has a bad case of heat stroke and seemed kind of out of it. He's at Ms. Flora's right now."

"That's so weird." Elise furrows her eyebrows. "That hasn't happened since—"

"Since I got here. Yeah, I know."

"Hey, you okay?"
~~~

I cover my face with my hands. "I'm sorry, I didn't mean to snap at you. It's just that that's all anyone has said today."

"It's just so unusual. I wonder if it was the same place you came from."

"That's the weird part." I pause, and Elise raises her eyebrows. "He recognized me."

"What?" Elise squeals. "Maris, that's the part of the story you *start* with. He knows you. That's so exciting."

"Sort of. He called me 'Lorraine.'"

"That's not weird. That might be your name. We don't know."

"It just sounded so wrong."

Elise smiles and rubs my arm. "You've just gotten used to Maris."

"But it's not my name," I say. "It's not anyone's name. It's just some name Zane came up with to call me. It doesn't mean anything."

"It means something to you."

"I guess." I hold the side of my head. "I hope he's feeling better tomorrow. I have to talk to him. Zane thinks he might have been hallucinating or dizzy or something, but he seemed so sure."

Elise rolls her eyes and chuckles. "Zane is such a skeptic. I don't think it's so outrageous to think this guy might actually know something."

I sigh and push myself up off of the couch. "Maybe. I'm going to bed. I'm exhausted."

"Goodnight."

I close the door to my small bedroom, but instead of climbing into bed, I head straight for my dresser and open the bottom drawer. The only thing I ever keep in this drawer is the outfit I was wearing the day I came to the island. I remember waking up in Ms. Flora's room and seeing it hanging on the back of the door. I guess Ms. Flora and Harper had changed me into some basic cotton clothing, but I remember thinking that the clothing hanging on the door that day looked so odd and foreign that I couldn't understand why the two women taking care of me would bring me clothing that seemed just a little too formal for a beach town. It was only after they told me that those were my clothes and they had washed them for me that I started to realize something was wrong.

Every so often, I like to take that outfit out, that black skirt, that pale green button-down shirt, and stare it, hoping that one day it will look familiar, but it always feels just as foreign as it did that day. Now that someone is here that might know who I am, I hoped the clothes would look different, but they don't. Still foreign. I inhale the smell of Harper's homemade laundry detergent that lingers on the shirt and find it at least somewhat encouraging that at least it smells familiar. I wonder if I'll ever look at this outfit and feel like the person who used to wear it.

~~~

The next morning, I make a beeline for Zane's house. There's one person that always makes me feel better to talk to, and that's Zane's mom, Harper. She's been like a mom to me when I have no one I really feel like I can trust. Zane, Daisy, and Harper have been my only family for a year now.

When I reach the familiar house, I stare at it a moment. When I first got here, I stayed at Ms. Flora's for a while so she could monitor my recovery. Then, I stayed here until I moved in with Elise. My stay with Harper was supposed to be temporary. Someone was supposed to show up for me. When no one did, the town found a more permanent solution. Still, this house feels like home in a weird way.

I walk up to the front door and knock. "Harper?" I'm about to call out again when I see her come around the corner through the glass pane.
~~~

"Hello, dear, what is it?" Harper smiles sweetly and wipes her hands on her apron that's permanently stained from all the delicious family meals she's cooked.

"Zane said you wanted to see me yesterday."

"Ah yes, so I did."

She opens the door, and I follow her to the living room. "I'm sorry I didn't come by yesterday. It was—kind of a weird day."

"Don't worry, dear. Have you gone to see the paddler yet?"

I shake my head.

Harper smiles sadly. "Well, you'll just have to try again later."

"Harper?"

"Yes, dear?"

"Will you tell me about the day I came?"

Harper laughs. "Now, how many times have I told you that story?"

"I want to hear it again. Maybe something will stand out now."

Harper beckons toward the couch, and we both sit down. "The day you came was a lot like yesterday. An odd, very official looking ship passed by, and they let down a lifeboat. The only differences were that it wasn't a merchant ship and you didn't paddle into shore. Zane and some of the other younger guys in the town swam out to get the boat.

"You looked healthy enough, but you had an ugly bump on your head. You must have hit it pretty hard. Ms. Flora treated you, but you didn't wake up for a couple of days. We were afraid you might never wake up. But you finally did, and, you poor thing, you were so confused. You couldn't tell us anything about yourself, not even your name, and you didn't have anything on you or in the boat that could identify you."

"Was I already unconscious when the lifeboat dropped?"

"We don't know. The ship was too far out to see anything like that. Plus, there was a storm that day."

"What kind of ship was it if not a merchant ship?" What other kind of ship would I have been on?

"Oh dear, I don't know. That was a year ago. Besides, those ships all look the same to me. Ask Zane. He might remember better. He saw it closer up than most of us."

I bite the inside of my cheek and try to think, try to remember. Nothing rings a bell.

I sigh. "Still nothing sounds familiar. I've heard that story so many times, and it never gets clearer."

Harper rubs my knee. "One day it will. One day it will all make sense."

"I just feel so useless here on this island. What am I supposed to be doing with my life?"

"What do you mean?"

"I must have been working toward something, wherever I was. I must have been *good* at something. But now, I'm here, and I'm just leeching off of all of you."

"Don't start with that," Harper says. "You are not leeching. We are happy to have you here. And besides, you're always welcome to come back to bake with me."

I laugh. "That's a terrible idea. I ruined all of your food."

"You did not."

"Zane nearly threw up when he tasted it. And he eats everything."

Harper cackles. "Okay, fair enough. Maybe you should stick to helping us all with our finances. I didn't think anyone would ever be able to balance Gus's budget."

"That's not hard, though."

"For you. Money and numbers come very naturally to you. That's what you're good at."

"Yeah, I guess so."

"I'm back, Ma," Zane shouts as he swings the front door open. "But I don't have any more coconuts. Gus said you always take all his stock, so he's cutting you off at 3 coconuts at a time." Zane leans around the corner and spots me. "Oh, Maris, I didn't know you were here."

"I came to talk to your mom. I was hoping she could give me some insight about what happened the day I came here."

"Look, just because some guy washed on shore and called you some name does not mean he knows you."

"Don't be so cynical, Zaney." Harper flits her hand and Zane's cheeks flush at his mom's nickname. "We don't know what this young man knows yet. We'll just have to wait until Ms. Flora's got him all fixed up. Now sit down and make yourself useful. Do you remember what the ship looked like the day Maris got here?"

Zane shrugs. "Wasn't really looking at it. I was paying attention to the floating lifeboat with an unconscious girl inside."

"But did it look like the ship yesterday?" I say.

"Wasn't a merchant ship."

"But was there anything familiar about it?"

"Not really."

"So maybe the paddler does know me," I say. "Maybe he knew where to find me and what route to take to get here."

"We don't know that," Zane says, rubbing his temple. "It's not that hard to bum a ride on a merchant ship."

"But you said it wasn't a merchant ship."

"I'm just saying that we have no idea what we're dealing with. He could be anyone. I'd wait until he wakes up. He looked delirious from sun exposure. Who knows what he was thinking."

I sigh. "Hopefully we'll know tomorrow."

# Chapter 3

The next morning, I can't wait for Zane to come by my house. I have to go see the paddler. I know Zane will be annoyed that I went without him, but I just can't stop myself from going to Ms. Flora's.

It's early, the sun still struggling to rise, so I sneak around the house as quietly as I can manage so I don't wake Elise. I consider eating something, but I can't cook without Elise sensing my messing with her oven settings. Besides, putting food in my stomach is probably a terrible idea considering how it's flip-flopping. The last thing I need is to fuel my nausea, so I decide I'll just pick something up later.

I start walking down the little gravel path from my house, enjoying the pink light from the sunrise. It's my favorite time of day. The island always looks so pretty in this light. Most of the town hasn't started the day yet, so the usually bustling town square is quiet and serene. I like walking through the town when it's like this. As much as I love the townspeople here, I love the solitude of my early mornings. Sometimes I just need the quiet.

I kick a rock down the path to the town square, unconcerned with the gentle clicking sounds it makes on the stone ground because I know it won't wake anyone. For some odd reason, everyone on this island sleeps like they're dead. I guess it's a side effect of living your entire life on an island, surrounded by the roaring and crashing of the waves and the squawking of the seagulls. I guess you get used to sleeping through the peaceful noise.

I've never been able to get used to it. The sound of the tumultuous waves at night have always bothered me. When I first got to the island and stayed with Zane and Harper, I had such a hard time sleeping through the night. The sound of the ocean would always give me nightmares. Feeling panic-stricken and afraid of drowning at sea or having your ship go down—those kinds of thoughts aren't exactly conducive to a good night's sleep. That's when Zane offered Elise as a potential roommate. She lives the furthest inland of anyone. It's much harder to hear the waves from our little bungalow tucked away in the palm trees. Much harder, but still possible. At least, for me.

I lose track of the stone I was kicking and start on another. This one doesn't bounce as well as the first, but it's louder. I kind of like that. I like having control over the noise I hear right now. It's so quiet early in the morning, so any noise I hear, I created. It's comforting somehow, having control over something so insignificant. Having control over anything, really.

I kick the stone a little too hard, and it ricochets off of a tree, and I lose that one too. I sigh and start looking for another when I'm startled by Gus clearing his throat behind me.

"Sorry, sweetie," Gus says with a cackle. "Didn't mean to startle ya. I was just getting my stand ready for the day."

"It's all right, I just didn't realize anyone else was up this early."

"I wanted to get a headstart today. I've got a good stock today, and I want to make sure I'm organized and got all my best fruits out front."

"Any mangoes?"

"It just so happens I've got several beauties." Gus beams with pride over his stand. "You want one?"

"Absolutely," I say, and Gus hands me a mango. "Can I swing by and grab another for Elise? She's been experimenting again."

"Of course. Tell her to put it in the fridge for at least an hour before cooking. Gets the best flavor that way."

I laugh. "Gus, you don't even chill your fruit."

He scoffs. "I don't like those crazy generator things."

I smile, but I keep fidgeting and looking around, and Gus notices.

"What's wrong, sweetie? Ya seem tense."

"I'm just a little anxious today, that's all."

"You worried about that paddler?" Gus asks, and I nod. "No need to worry. We'll sort it all out. It'll be fine."

"I just wish I could talk to him. Have you seen Ms. Flora yet today?"

"No, she's usually a late sleeper. Can't wake that woman up for anything." Gus laughs.

I laugh, too. "Oh, believe me, I know. When she had me staying there, I was awake and by myself for hours until she woke up."

Gus smiles and strokes my shoulder. "He might not even be awake either, ya know. That was a pretty serious case of sun sickness."

"I know. But I still want to check on him. I'll see you later, Gus. Don't forget to hold that mango for me."

"I'll save the best one for you," Gus calls out as I walk away.

I start down the cobblestone path again, almost wandering more than I'm walking with purpose toward Ms. Flora's. I want to get there. I want to talk to the paddler. I want to know what's going on. But at the same time, I don't. What if I don't find the answers I'm looking for? Maybe this paddler is only going to discourage me more.

After rushing to get there, I find myself at Ms. Flora's door sooner than I wanted. I take a few deep breaths before I push open the door, inducing a deafening creak. I don't bother to close the door behind me because the town square is quiet right now, and I don't want to make that obnoxious sound again. I risk a glance into the adjoining room where the paddler is, the same room Ms. Flora kept me in after I arrived, but I can only make out the outline of the paddler sleeping.

"Maris." Ms. Flora says, her voice scaring me so badly that I nearly jump off the ground. "What are you doing here, child?"

"I—I uh—I just came to see the paddler. How is he?"

"Not good, child, not good." Ms. Flora says as she wrings her hands nervously in her apron. "He's very sick. He'll make a full recovery, but he'll need to stay here for a few days to regain his strength. He's weak and worn out."

"But he'll be okay?" I ask. I can't tell if I'm actually concerned for his well-being or if I just don't want him dying on me before he can spill what he knows.

"Oh, no doubt. He'll bounce back. It just might take several days. I ran out of that good medicine I had when you first got here. Otherwise, he might get on faster."

"Can I see him?"

"Not now, child. He's still sleeping, and he needs his rest. Trust me, it would be better to talk to him when he feels better anyway. It won't do much to talk to him now."

"You're right. I'll come back later."

"Don't put too much pressure on him, child," Ms. Flora calls out as I leave. "He might know you, but he can't make you remember."

I nod and take off out the door. She's right. He can't make me remember. He could be my flesh and blood for all I know, and he still couldn't clear the fog in my mind. I have to remember on my own.

But still, this guy could know something about me, something that could jog my memory. That's worth something. It's so hard to believe in anything right now, but I can't let go of any hope of remembering who I am, no matter how small.

I find my feet carrying me to Zane's house, so I give in and decide to knock on the door. But it's Harper, not Zane, who opens the door.

"I hope I didn't wake you," I say.

"Oh no, dear, come on in." Harper says.

I follow her to the kitchen, and she pours me a cup of tea. It smells floral and delicious, and it reminds me that I still haven't eaten anything, so I pull out the mango from Gus and split it with Harper.

"Where's Zane?"

"You just missed him. He actually just went over to your house. He figured you'd be up early today."

I shrug. "Couldn't sleep."

"I don't blame you. The last couple of days have been insane for you. How are you feeling?"

"I don't know," I say. Harper stares at me, waiting for me to clarify that incredibly vague answer. "I just—I felt kind of happy yesterday when he called me Lorraine. Sure, that name meant nothing to me, and he was obviously ill, but I could see the recognition in his eyes. He genuinely believed that I was Lorraine. It gave me a kind of hope, but I feel like I just keeping running into roadblocks trying to get answers, and it feels like everyone is just staring at me all the time."

Harper takes my hand in hers. "We're just worried about you, dear, that's all. None of us knows what this means. It might be something, but it could easily mean nothing, too."

"But what if it wasn't nothing?" I say. "What if he really does know me?"

"Then we have good news. We just have to see what happens."

I stare into my teacup like it's somehow going to give me some answers. It's hard to understand how I could have spent a year hoping for someone to show up and give me answers and still feel like I don't know what I want to do when it actually happens.

"What is it, dear?" Harper asks.

"What if he does know me? What if he tells me all about who I am, and I still don't remember?"

"You can't think like that. You've got to let yourself relax. It'll come to you when you're ready."

I nod, but I suddenly remember Zane's mention of his not-so-surprising surprise party planning. "Oh no," I say. "My memory's getting worse. You wanted to talk to me yesterday, didn't you?"

Harper laughs. "Don't worry about that, dear. I just wanted to talk to you about Zane's birthday party, but we can do that later. You just try to relax today."

Before I can answer her, Zane throws the front door open and exhales dramatically. "There you are. I've been looking all over for you."

"I came here to talk to your mom—and you," I say.

"What, did you sneak through the trees? How did I not run into you?"

I shrug. I don't want to tell him that I went to Ms. Flora's without him.

"Well, do you want to take a walk and talk?" Zane offers.

"Sure," I say. I wave goodbye to Harper and follow Zane out the door. We don't get very far before he eyes me suspiciously.

"You went to Ms. Flora's already, didn't you?"

"N—no." Oh yeah, that was convincing.

"Maris, this town is ridiculously small. There's no way we wouldn't have passed each other unless you went inside somewhere, and it's too early for anything else. Why didn't you wait for me?"

"I was just so curious. I needed to see him, and I couldn't sleep anyway, so I came over here."

"More nightmares?" Zane asks. Zane is one of the only person I've told about those. Ms. Flora knows I used to get them, but I don't think she realizes I still have them.

I nod. "In the few hours I actually fell asleep. I was too riled up to sleep."

"Well, since you already went traipsing around town by yourself, what did Ms. Flora say?"

"He's still pretty sick. She told me to let him rest."

"So let him rest."

"I want to talk to him."

Zane rubs my shoulder and says, "It's gonna have to wait until he's actually conscious."

"I'm just so anxious to find out what he knows, or thinks he knows, I guess."

"I wouldn't get too excited yet," Zane says. "Maybe he just hallucinated from exposure."

I sigh. "Why are you trying to deter me from this? I've been living on this island for a year without a single clue about who I am. I don't even know my own name or how old I am. I don't know anything about myself, and yesterday, the first real clue paddled into shore, and all you've done is try to keep me from talking to him."

Zane jerks his head back at my outburst, and I think I blushed immediately after finishing it, but I'm glad I finally said it. I needed to say it.

"Look, you know the last thing I want is to upset you. Just give the guy some time to rehydrate, and then you can ask him all the questions you want."

"You don't understand. I just have to know."

"I know."

"I just have to know," I say again because it's the only thing I'm sure of. I have to know what he knows, and I have to know if it's true.

~~~

I spend the rest of the day hiding out on my "private beach." I desperately want to go see the paddler, but I know Ms. Flora won't let me, and Zane is busy all day today. A few times a week, he goes down to the other end of the island and helps out the guys with their fishing. Their catch is always better when Zane helps them. He's got a sixth sense when it comes to fish. He also helps them weave new nets and clean the fish they've already hauled.

A part of me wishes Zane didn't have to work today, but another, larger, part of me enjoys this solitude. I like being by myself, left alone with my own thoughts. Besides, I know if Zane were here right now, he'd be spending all of his energy trying to talk me out of speaking to the paddler.

I always thought that finding some kind of clue as to who I am would make things easier, but the paddler's arrival has only made things harder and more complicated. For months, I've been thinking that it would just be so easy if someone were just to show up on the island and tell me who I am, and then I'd remember and everything would be fine. But now, here is a guy who might actually be able to do that, and it isn't as relieving as I hoped it'd be.

From the edge of this cliff, you can see the ships way off in the distance. They're far off and hardly even visible at all, but you can just make out their outline from up here. They never come any closer. There's no reason for them to. This island is small and mostly self-sufficient, so it almost never has contact with the neighboring countries. In all the time I've been here, only two ships have ever come close to this island other than the merchant ships: the one I arrived on, and the one the paddler arrived on. I can't remember what the ship looked
~~~

like that day, and Zane doesn't seem sure of his memory either, but I can't help but feel like it has to be the same ship. Not necessarily the exact same vessel but from the same place. I wish I had some way of knowing if another ship would come any time soon, but considering that the first two were a year apart, my odds aren't good.

Against Zane's wishes, I am going to have to trust the paddler, if for no other reason than to find out where he's from. I don't have to trust him as far as I'm concerned, but at least he can tell me about where he's from. I need at least that much.

The walk back to my house is enjoyable. Suddenly, I don't feel so intimidated by the bustling town square. I feel somewhat empowered by my decision to trust the paddler, at least partially. I like knowing that I made this decision without the input, in fact in spite of the input, of the townspeople. I like feeling like I could be this bold and this confident in my own abilities. In a way, it feels very familiar and very comforting. I'm glad I finally feel at least a little better about the paddler even though his very presence still fills me with confusion and anxiety.

When I get back to the house, Elise is already cooking dinner. I love Elise's home cooked meals. She's an excellent cook, and she really maximizes the good food this island has to offer. She always talks about how one day she wants to be a chef, but there's really no chance of that happening as long as she stays on this island. I guess that's why she and I get along so well: neither one of us really belongs on this island, just for different reasons.

"Hey," Elise calls out cheerfully from the kitchen.

"Hi. It smells delicious in here."

"Thanks. I'm experimenting with coconut milk. So tell me," Elise says, wringing her hands in her apron. "How was the paddler? Did you hear what he had to say?"

"Never got the chance. Ms. Flora wouldn't let me see him. She said he needed more time to rest."

"Aw man, I'm sorry, Maris. I'm sure you'll get the chance soon. I hope he's as helpful as you want him to be."

"Me too," I say with a shrug. "It doesn't really matter. Even if he doesn't actually know me, anything he could tell me about himself or where he comes from might be useful."

"I'm glad you're staying positive about this. I was worried about you yesterday. You seemed so down."

"It was just a lot for one day, and seeing someone recognize me, whether he really did or not, just reminded me of how much I don't know about myself."

"You'll figure it out. I'm sure of it." Elise smiles wide and I return the favor. I like Elise. She always makes me feel better when I'm feeling down. She's a great friend. "Well," Elise says, standing up suddenly with a bounce in her step, "back to the kitchen for me. Hopefully this coconut concoction is good."

I laugh to myself a little. In the year I've lived with her, she's never once made anything that wasn't incredible.

# Chapter 4

The next morning, when I walk out my front door, I nearly crash into Zane who is lurking outside my house.

"What on earth are you doing?" I say.

"I knew you'd try to go over there early and I didn't want you to go without me... *again.*" Zane smirks.

"Fine. Are you ready?"

Zane nods, and we start walking toward Ms. Flora's.

"So, how did fishing go yesterday?" I ask, looking only at my feet or the path in front of us, not at Zane.

Zane shrugs. "We didn't really do much fishing. We had a lot of fish that we needed to clean, and a few of the nets got busted again, so I had to fix those."

"It seems like the nets are breaking really frequently."

"Yeah, we're not using the best material to make them. It works, but it doesn't last."

"Isn't there anything stronger we could use?"

"Not really," Zane says, kicking a particularly large pebble. "Coconut husks are strong, but they're too short to weave into nets. We just don't have many options here. The trees are limited in species. You know, one time years ago, I went with my dad on a merchant ship to nearby islands. It's pretty crazy how many different species of trees are out there. You wouldn't think that the islands near us would be so different from this one, but they are."

"Would those kinds of trees be better for weaving nets?"

"Yeah, maybe. I guess I should investigate that one day, but I don't know. We're hauling in plenty. I don't know if I see a reason to go looking for something else."

"Elise says that all the time," I say as we round a corner in the path. "She's so good at cooking, but she's limited in ingredients. I mean, last night she made this incredible coconut sauce, but she always wishes she could do more. She's always curious what's out there in other places."

Zane laughs. "Maybe Elise and I need to go exploring together."

"Maybe."

"You know, maybe you could give us a tour of some other beautiful island one day."

I laugh because the thought is so ridiculous. "Oh yeah, right. Like what island?"

Zane fidgets with the hem of his shirt. "Well, wherever you're from. Maybe one day you could show it to us."

It's only then that I realize that we'd both been avoiding talking about the massive elephant in the room. Zane and I used to speculate about this kind of stuff together, but it was never serious. We used to make up crazy, fanciful stories about where I must be from. Sometimes I was an alien, other times a mermaid. It was a fun game to play. Now that someone is on the island who claims to know me, it doesn't feel like a game anymore, and I kind of miss the levity of a childish game—it didn't feel so heavy.

Before I can answer him, we're standing outside of Ms. Flora's. Zane starts to open the door, but I stop him.

"Zane, listen," I say, and Zane raises an eyebrow. "I know you don't trust this guy, but I want to hear him out."

Zane rolls his eyes. "The whole thing just seems sketchy."

"Just give him a chance, please," I plead.

"Fine, fine," Zane says with a sigh.

We run into Ms. Flora on the way in, and she gives us the thumbs up to go see the paddler.

"Lorraine!" The paddler smiles and sits up straight when I walk in with Zane. "Finally, you came to see me."

"I came yesterday but Ms. Flora said you needed rest."

"Is that the older woman who lives here?" the paddler asks, and I nod. "Yeah, she won't let me do anything. She's afraid I'll pass out again."

"Well, you were in pretty rough shape, dude," Zane says. "Can't blame her."

I take a closer look at his face and find that he still looks like he's in pretty rough shape. His tan skin still somehow looks pale, and he seems to be really tired and fighting the exhaustion right now. His brown eyes look weary, but there's still a sparkle of excitement, and it's weird to think that I'm the cause for that excitement.

"No, of course not," the paddler says quickly. "I'm grateful for all of your help. I've just been dying to talk to you, Lorraine. I didn't mean to scare you the other day. I don't do well with sea travel, clearly."

"Why do you keep calling me 'Lorraine'?" All I can focus on is that name. It sounds so foreign, but he says it with such certainty.

The paddler looks at me confused. "I—I—What do you mean?"

"It's a simple question, buddy," Zane says.

"That's your name," the paddler says.

"How do you know?" I say.

"Because I was sent here to find you."

"So you keep saying." Zane rolls his eyes.

The paddler scans the room with his eyes before they land on a messenger bag on Ms. Flora's table. "My bag. Open the front pocket and take out the paper in it."

I hesitate, so Zane walks over to the table. He pulls out the paper and looks at it, but he doesn't say anything right away.

"Zane, what is it?"

Zane turns to face me slowly, his face very pale. "It—It's you."

Zane holds out the paper, and on it is a very faded picture of me. Granted, I'm younger in the picture, but it's clearly me. The jet black waves and dark blue eyes are unmistakable. I pore over every little detail: the tan skin, the handful of freckles on the nose, the slightly crooked smile, the cowlick in the side of the hair. It's me. About the age I was when I got to the town.

I take the picture from Zane and stare at it obsessively. I half expect it to somehow change before my eyes and morph into someone I don't know. The picture refuses to change, and I can't accept the reality of it. I flip it over and written in smudged pen is "Lorraine Everhart."

"Where did you even get this picture?" I ask.

"From a close friend. The captain of the ship—"

"How can this possibly be me?" I hold out the picture to the paddler.

"I don't understand." The paddler looks back and forth between me and Zane. "What do you mean?"

I look to Zane and beg him silently for help, and thankfully, he picks up on my cues. "Maris has no memories of life before she came to this island. She doesn't have any idea who you are or why you have a picture of her that claims she is 'Lorraine Everhart.'"

The paddler looks at me with wide eyes, and he looks nervous, almost panicky. "You don't remember anything? Nothing at all?"

I shake my head, and suddenly, the paddler looks very ill again.

"Well who are you?" Zane says. "Where are you from? Maybe something you say will mean something."

The paddler nods. "My name is Brent Grayson. I'm from a very small country called Trilland that isn't far from here. Our country is in great turmoil right now. Our queen has become a tyrant. The people of Trilland are suffering because of it." Brent pauses. "Is any of this sounding familiar?"

I shake my head. "So we don't actually know each other? You have just been following a picture of me?"

Brent looks confused, but shakes his head. "No, we don't know each other personally. But I know of you. Everyone in Trilland does. We think that you—"

"Wait, wait," Zane interrupts. "You mean you came here because you think Maris can save your dying country?"

Brent nods. "Yes, I think Lorraine is the only person who can."

"*Maris* isn't just going to take off with you. Your country's problems are your problem."

"It's *Lorraine's* country, too."

"Stop!" I yell and immediately regret it. "I can't take you two bickering back and forth." I hold my head in my hands, trying to sort through everything Brent has said, but none of it makes sense, and it only makes me feel more confused. "None of that sounds familiar."

"Lorraine, please, just give me a chance to explain. I'll tell you everything I know about you. Maybe something will click."

"You'll just confuse her further," Zane says through his teeth. "You're going back to Trilland."

"No," I say. "Let him stay. Let him tell me what he knows. If nothing is familiar, then he can leave."

"Maris." Zane beckons toward the door. "Can I have a moment?"

Zane and I step outside, and Zane closes Ms. Flora's door behind us.

"What are you doing?" Zane folds his arms. "Why are you letting him stay?"

"I want to hear what he has to say."

"He's insane. How do you know you can trust him?"

"He seems pretty sane to me," I say. "And you saw the picture. That's obviously me."

"That doesn't mean you are who he thinks you are. You heard him. His country's a mess. He could be pulling a con to try to spark a rebellion or something."

"Why would he do that?"

Zane throws up his hands in frustration. "I don't know. But maybe he saw a girl without a memory and thought he could insert whatever he wanted."

"He called me Lorraine long before he knew anything about me."

"I just think it could be dangerous. We don't know anything about this guy. He could be lying even about who he is."

"Which is why we should let him stay," I say. "The second he says or does something suspicious, he's gone. But regardless of his intentions, he might actually know who I am."

Zane sighs. "Fine. But I don't like it."

I smile. "I know. But you've been protecting me since the day I got here. You can't protect me forever."

"I can try." Zane wraps his arms around me and gives me a gentle squeeze. "Just be careful, okay? Don't get sucked in by whatever this guy says."

"I'll be careful. I promise."

I want to go back inside and hear more from the paddler, but I feel overwhelmed with the day's events already. As much as I want to continue talking to him, I just don't think I can handle it right now. I ask Ms. Flora to tell Brent that I'll see him tomorrow and walk absent-mindedly back to my house.

I spend the rest of the day in my room, my own seventeen year old face reappearing in my mind every time I close my eyes. I shut the picture away in a drawer hoping that would hide it from me, but I can't stop it from taking over my brain. I can't believe it. I even pull the picture out again, thinking that maybe if I look at it again, I'll be able to stop obsessing, but of course I just end of obsessing more. Now I notice the really pretty necklace I'm wearing in the picture. It looks expensive. I can't picture myself wearing a necklace like that now.

I can't believe he actually has a picture of me from a year ago. He must know me somehow even though he claims he doesn't really. Maybe we're just acquaintances or maybe distant relatives. Maybe we knew each other as kids or something. There has to be a connection between the two of us. Who just randomly has pictures of someone they don't actually know?

~~~

I spent the whole night tossing and turning. Sleep was basically impossible. I couldn't get my mind to shut off, which is ironic, considering I've felt like it was shut down for a year. I ended up giving up on the venture of sleep and just staring out my window at the night sky, watched as it turned pink, then orange, as the sun rose. Very distantly, I can see the waves down on the beach. They're calm today, which seems paradoxical. Shouldn't the waves be turbulent today? Shouldn't everything be chaotic if I feel this chaotic?

The sun is still struggling to push past the horizon when I hear what can only be described as a cheerful knock. Elise always knocks like it's the best day of her life. I've always kind of liked that.
~~~

"Yoo hoo!" Elise calls from the other side of my door. "Rise and shine, I made pancakes for breakfast."

I open the door and hastily clump my hair up into a messy bun. "You hate pancakes."

Elise rolls her eyes. "I don't *hate* them, I just—I—"

"You *hate* them." I chuckle. "You always have."

"Okay, maybe I'm not the biggest fan of them, but you like them, so I made them for you." Elise smiles brightly.

I squint at her. "We've been roommates for a year, and you've never made me pancakes."

Elise flings her arms out by her side dramatically and sighs. "Fine. Zane told me what happened yesterday, and I thought you might need some cheering up. I got up early and made the first batch of pancakes, but since I never eat them, they were a complete disaster. I went and got a recipe from Harper and now they look good—well, as good as pancakes can look."

I laugh, but my laugh fades quickly as I think about what Zane must have told Elise, and probably Harper, about the paddler. *Hey everybody, turns out Maris is from some country she's never heard of, and she's supposed to save it, all according to some random guy following her picture like a stalker.* Of course I know that Zane is much more sensitive than that, but in my mind, that's how I feel.

Elise sees the despair on my face and holds out her arms for a hug. I hesitatingly accept and let Elise scratch my back and try to comfort me. It helps a little, but nothing could really console me right now except the miraculous return of my memory.

I let go, and Elise fixes my hair like only a best friend can. "So," I say, "there are pancakes?"

Elise smirks. "Mm-hmm. And some fresh oranges and coconuts from Gus because I know there are few things you like more than fresh orange juice and coconut milk."

I let myself smile. "Then what are we waiting for?"

Elise breaks into a smile so big that I think it's going to break her face with happiness. "Well let's go then!" Elise grabs my hand and practically skips to the kitchen, forcing me to keep pace with someone who has far more energy than me. She's probably caffeinated too, which is even more lethal.

The pancakes smell divine, and I smile when I see that Elise has strained the pulp out of the orange juice. She never strains the pulp, even though she knows I like it that way, because she prefers to ingest large clumps of orangey gunk. The fact that she strained it shows just how dedicated she is to making me feel better.

We start eating, and I can definitely tell that these are Harper's pancakes. They taste very familiar. When I first got here and stayed with them, Harper made them every day, trying to make me feel secure and comfortable. Zane loved it at first, and so did I, but we both reached a point where we couldn't even think about eating another pancake. We just didn't know how to tell Harper that. She seemed so happy to make them for me that I didn't want to crush her spirit. She had already done so much for me; could I really complain about pancakes? Zane's the one who finally cracked, screaming in horror one morning when he saw pancakes on the table. He begged his mother to make something, anything else, even oatmeal which he hates, just to get a change from the never-ending daily pancakes.

Elise lets me happily eat a few pancakes and down a few glasses of orange juice before she starts the conversation we both know is inevitable.

"So Zane says the paddler has a picture of you?"

I nod. "From before I got to the island. Around that time."

"And it's really you?"

"It sure looks like me."

"Can I see it?"

I hop off the barstool at our counter and grab the picture from my room. I hand it to Elise, and she trades me with a glass of sweet coconut milk. I drink eagerly, feeling comforted by the silky liquid.

Elise's eyes grow wide, and she looks back and forth from the picture to me, trying to accept what she thinks her eyes see. "Wow," she says after a while. "It's really you."

I chuckle. "That was pretty much my and Zane's reaction."

Elise flips it over and squints. "Lorraine Everhart?"

I shrug. "Brent says that's my name. He kept calling me Lorraine."

"Brent?" Elise asks. "That's his name?"

"Yeah."

Elise slides the picture across the counter to me. "So Zane said that this guy—Brent—doesn't actually know you? He just knows of you?"

I sigh. "It doesn't make any sense. He calls me by name—well, he calls me Lorraine—so confidently, like he's totally positive about who I am. And obviously this is me," I say, holding up the picture. "But how does he know who I am if we supposedly don't know each other?"

"Maybe you're famous, like a celebrity or something."

I laugh. "That's unlikely. You've heard me sing in the shower. I'm terrible."

"True." Elise giggles. "Well, maybe you're a famous actress. Maybe you're a movie star or a theater star or something."

"Yeah right, like *I* could ever get up in front of people and perform."

"Maybe you're royalty. Like a princess or a duchess or something crazy like that."

"I can't even picture that."

Elise and I both laugh, and for a minute, it's like everything is normal, except it's not. "Well, I can't think of any other explanation for why this guy knows who you are."

I bury my face in my arms on the counter. "I have to go back and talk to him to find out, don't I?"

"Don't you want to find out?" Elise jumps up and starts French braiding my long, black hair. She's always been jealous of my long hair. She keeps hers short since she cooks all the time, but she misses all the hairstyles for which long hair allows.

"Of course I want to find out, but I wish I just remembered. It'd be so much easier than trying to get information out of this random guy."

"Sounds like he'd tell you willingly," Elise says, twisting her fingers in and out of my hair, crafting a structured braid. "And I think you'll remember a lot faster if you have some kind of information to go off of. This might be exactly what you're looking for."

"I sure hope so."

"Hair tie," Elise says, and I hold up my hand, letting her pull one off my wrist. I always have at least three on each wrist. At any given time, this thick hair might have to be corralled, and sometimes one just doesn't cut it.

Elise wraps the end of my hair tightly with the hair tie before gently fingering the braid, admiring her handiwork. "Are you going to go see him today?"

"I don't know if I'm up to it today."

"Then do I have an idea for you." Elise clasps her hands together happily. "Harper is trying to plan Zane's 'surprise' birthday party." Elise air quotes "surprise," just like Zane did the other day, because we all know he knows every single year. "The paddler coming to the island kind of distracted from that, but what do you say we head over and help her out? Zane will be out all day today helping the fishermen."

I allow a small smile to form on my face. "Sure, that sounds great."

"Fantastic." Elise gently pushes me toward my room. "Now get dressed, something pretty to match that gorgeous hair I just braided."

I throw on the first thing I see in my closet, but Elise apparently doesn't consider it on the same fashion level as her braid, so she changes me into a light yellow sleeveless button down shirt, tying the ends into a knot, and lets me borrow a pair of white shorts. When she forces me to look in the mirror, I'm surprised to find that I really do look very pretty. I don't usually spend a lot of time on my appearance because what difference does it make if I don't know who I am? Besides, living on an island like this, physical glamour isn't exactly at the top of anyone's list. Well, except maybe Elise's.

Elise is one of the most beautiful women on this island. Even though she keeps her curly blonde hair short, it's always styled to perfection. She wears makeup, a very unusual practice in this village, but she keeps it to a minimum, sticking only to a small amount of lipstick and mascara. She's tall and thin, taller than I but somehow the same proportions as I. Sometimes I'm jealous of her beauty, but then she does something like this, where she obsesses over my thick, wavy, black hair and reminds me of how beautiful I can be, even on a day when that's the last thing on my mind. Elise always knows exactly how to help me. She is an expert at making me feel better and encouraging me. When Zane and Harper first tried to find me a place to live and a roommate, I was scared, but Elise is the least frightening person I know. It's so hard for me to imagine my life without her anymore.

Elise and I pass Zane leaving to go help the fishermen as we get to his house. He waves goodbye as he heads out. He's shirtless, which he always is when he fishes, but I catch myself noticing more than usual.

I don't usually see him before he goes, only after he gets back, when he reeks of rotten fish and is coated in a thick layer of ocean grime. He looks different now. Attractive. Of course, I've always known that Zane is attractive, but I've tried not to let myself notice it too much. I've tried not to get romantically involved. Other guys in the village have asked me out before, but I've always turned them down. How can I date someone right now? I need to focus on myself and knowing myself.

But Zane sure does look good shirtless. I stare for an abnormal amount of time, and I think Zane catches me, because I catch him staring at me, too. We both exchange awkward clearings of the throat before Zane heads on his way. Elise smiles at me in a way that suggests that I should be able to read her thoughts in her eyes and her expression, but I've never been good at that, so I mostly just try to ignore her, and thankfully, Harper swings the door open.

"Girls, so glad you could come by," Harper says, welcoming us inside. "Everything has been so crazy lately, I haven't had time to get myself together. Sit down, girls. Okay, first things first. We need to talk food. Elise?"

"I figured I'd make the same cake as last year. He really enjoyed that coconut glaze paired with the pineapple cake."

"Well, that coconut glaze was to die for," Harper gushes, writing down the cake choice in a notebook. "What about snacks?"

"Well the food I made last year was good, but it didn't do well out in the heat. We either need to be indoors or switch to heat-friendly food."

"I don't know. Maris?" Harper turns to me.

"Uh- I don't know. I think Zane would prefer to be outside. So, hot food, I guess. Maybe kabobs or something? He likes grilled food."

Elise lights up. "Maris, you're a genius. Why haven't we thought of that before? Okay, I'll put in an order for fruit from Gus and some meat and fish from Tito pronto. These will be the best kabobs ever."

"Kabobs." Harper scribbles in her notebook. "So, I guess food is settled. Party activity?"

"Dancing?" Elise suggests.

Harper raises her eyebrows skeptically. "Can you picture my son dancing?"

"Good point." Elise giggles. "But we have to do *something*."

"Do we?" I say, then immediately regret it because both Elise and Harper's eyes lock on me. "I mean, Zane is a laid back kind of guy. Couldn't we just serve food, play some music, and hang out? I think he'd like that better than something more elaborate."

"Hmm." Harper rubs the side of her face, and I find myself sweating bullets. Does she like the idea? Does she hate it? Does she hate me for saying it? "I love it. Maris is right. Zane would much rather just chill and hang out."

Exhale of relief. "I just thought, you know, he loves the people in this village more than anything."

"Definitely." Harper scribbles in her notepad. "I love it."

Elise says, "Okay, I'll get working on the food. I'll let you both know if I think of anything else."

"Thank you girls for helping plan this," Harper says as Elise and I head out. "Zane will love it. And I bet this year he'll be the most surprised yet."

Elise and I smile, but the second Harper closes the door behind us, we both crack up laughing. Everyone in town knows Zane is never surprised except Harper. We all just let her think she succeeds every year because we all love her too much.

"You know," Elise says as we walk back to our house, "Planning Zane's birthday parties is so much easier with you here."

"I doubt that's true."

"It is. Harper still thinks of him as her little boy, and I don't know him well enough to plan a party for him. I just cook."

"And you cook very well," I say.

"Obviously." Elise flips her hair. "But you know him so well. You're his closest friend. A town get-together was a brilliant idea. And night fishing last year? Genius."

"I just suggest things he likes."

"But that's the thing. You're the only one who knows that stuff. You're the only one he opens up to."

"You're ridiculous."

"I am not," she says. "Did you see the way he just looked at you?"

"I knew you'd say something about that."

"Well of course," she says. "I've known Zane my whole life, and I've never seen him look at anyone the way he looks at you. He's into you."

"He is not," I say, feeling heat in my face.

"He so is. He has been since the day he met you."

"You don't know what you're talking about."

"Look, you can continue in purposeful ignorance, but mark my words, Zane likes you."

I shrug because I don't trust my voice not to shake right now. Zane likes me? Why would Elise think that? I think she's making stuff up. Zane is my friend. He's always been my friend. Nothing more. Elise is just imagining things.

Really, I've never let myself think about Zane as anything more than a friend. I don't feel right getting involved with anyone when I don't know who I am or where I'm supposed to be. Zane is no exception. If anything, Zane is the most important reason I shouldn't get involved.

Zane is too important to me to ruin our friendship. There's so little in my life that I'm absolutely sure of, and wanting Zane in my life is one of those things. I would never compromise that.

Elise breaks the silence. "So, are you going to see the paddler again today?"

"Maybe. I was thinking of asking Zane to go with me after he gets back from the beach. I don't really want to go alone."

"That's probably a good idea. I'd go with you, but I have to do some trial cooking for Zane's party."

"Good luck."

"You too."

# Chapter 5

I don't think I've ever waited for Zane like this. I feel so uncomfortable just standing here, leaning up against a palm tree because I'm trying to look casual but sweating bullets, until I see the fishermen coming up the beach. Is he going to think I'm weird or clingy or something? Why am I just standing here like an idiot? I could have gone to his house and waited for him there, maybe talked to Harper or something. But no. Instead, I'm here, in my self-inflicted anxiety. I silently curse Elise for making me overthink this.

Every few seconds I consider leaving, but the need to see the paddler—what's his name, Brent?—keeps my feet in their place. He has a picture of me. He knows my supposed name. He thinks I am some kind of hero who will fix his country.

He has a picture of me.

That's the thing I can never get past. That's what makes his story sound credible. But if we don't know each other personally, how did he even come by a picture of me?

I'm startled out of thought by the sound of the approaching fishermen. They're laughing and playfully jeering at each other, and they sound truly happy. Life is so simple for them. Looking back, my life was simple, too, before Brent got here. I thought finding someone who knew me would bring clarity, but now I think I had more clarity when I was utterly confused.

"Maris," Zane says, and I practically jump three feet in the air. "Geez, sorry, didn't mean to scare you."

"Really? You snuck up behind me. How did you think you wouldn't startle me?"

"You're the one standing here, looking like you're waiting for me," Zane says, then holds up the net full of fish. "Besides, I reek. You should have smelled me coming. So why are you here?"

"I want to go see the paddler—Brent."

"So go see him," Zane says. The fishermen have since passed us by, so we start walking slowly in their path.

"I don't want to go alone. I was hoping you would come with me."

"Hey, you're the one who wanted him here. I wanted to kick him off the island."

"I still think that what he has to say might have some merit. I want to hear him out. I just—"

"You just don't want to hear him out by yourself," Zane says, and I nod. "I still don't like it."

"Please just come with me."

Zane feigns annoyance. "Fine. I'll drop off the fish and meet you at Ms. Flora's."

~~~

"Brent?" I knock on the door and open hesitantly. "Are you awake?"

"Yes, please come in," Brent says, and Zane and I step inside. "I'm glad you're here. I didn't know what happened yesterday. Is everything okay?"

"I just got a little overwhelmed, that's all."

"That's completely reasonable. I shouldn't have hit you all at once with so much information."

"No, you shouldn't have," Zane says, his arms folded.
~~~

"Zane, right? Good to see you again as well." Brent forces a smile. "What, did you just get in from fishing or something?"

"Actually yes," Zane says. "I was helping out the guys who do all the fishing. Hauled in quite a catch today. Sorry about the smell. We do things the old-fashioned way around here, and it's not the most glamorous, but Maris really wanted to come over tonight."

"It's quite all right. I'm glad you came. And I am sorry for freaking you out. I just got a little overly excited about you."

"Let's not talk about that," I say. "You said you know about me?"

"Yes."

"Then tell me what you know. Let's start there."

Zane and I sit down, I set the picture of me on the table in front of us and in front of Brent, and Brent looks like he's searching for where to begin. After opening his mouth and then closing it again a few times, he finally begins.

"How much do you know?"

"Seriously dude?" Zane says. "She's told you she doesn't know anything. At all."

"Only what you've said so far," I say, trying to diffuse Zane.

"Which isn't much."

"Okay, okay," Brent says. "You got to this island a year ago, right?"

"More or less," I say.

"Okay. That means that you are eighteen years old. You left Trilland when you were seventeen."

"Do you know her birthday?" Zane says eagerly.

"I'm sorry, I don't. I think it's in the fall? Maybe winter."

"Please, just continue," I say. "So I'm eighteen?"

"Yes. When you were seventeen, you left the country to visit the outer provinces of Trilland. Your ship went into a storm when you were lost to us and ended up here."

"Wait," I say. "What do you mean I was lost to you? You said you don't actually know me."

"Yes, that's true. I tried to tell you the other day, but you left so suddenly that I didn't get the chance."

"Yeah, well, you started saying something about how Maris was, like, your hero or something weird like that," Zane says. "That's a lot to put on someone."

"I understand, but I didn't say that lightly. Lorraine, you are the princess of Trilland."

"What?" I say. I think of Elise's joke this morning. She was kidding when she said I could be a princess. I never thought she'd be right.

"That doesn't make any sense," Zane says.

"Sure it does," Brent says. "You come from a long line of royal blood. The Everhart family has been ruling Trilland for centuries. That's why Trilland desperately needs you to return."

"Why?" Zane and I say simultaneously.

"After you disappeared, a tyrant took over. Her name is Cassandra, and she's your cousin. She's been gunning for your throne for several years now, but your family and the rest of the government wouldn't stand for it. She had no chance as long as you were alive. Once you were gone, she saw her opportunity and took it. She promised to help the country through a difficult time and swore she would try to find you, but she doesn't want you found. She wants you gone forever. If you came back, she would get thrown out. Everyone adores you. Everyone wants you as their ruler. If you just came back and confronted Cassandra—"

"Wait, wait, hold on," Zane sneers. "There's a flaw in your story. If Maris is really the rightful ruler of the country, then how did this girl take over? Why didn't Trilland just try to find Maris?"

"The people think Lorraine is dead," Brent says softly, his eyes filled with pain. "The ship you were on," Brent says to me, "was lost at sea. There was a big storm, and the ship was wrecked."

"And yet Maris is here," Zane says.

Brent nods. "Well, yes. The captain of the ship—Captain Wilson—he knew the storm was coming. He wanted to turn back and return to Trilland so that Lorraine wouldn't be hurt. But the crew wouldn't let him. They mutinied and took control of the ship, and—" Brent hesitates.

"And what?" I say.

"I don't want to upset you."

I take a deep breath. "Please tell me."

"They tried to kill you," Brent says all at once, so quickly I barely understand it, barely have time to process it. "They succeeded in knocking you unconscious, but the captain managed to get you on the lifeboat and steer you near one of the islands over here. I guess they assumed you would just die either on the boat or on the islands, so they left."

My chest feels too tight for my lungs, and I struggle to maintain a calm appearance. How could I not remember any of this?

"So how do you know all of this if the ship wrecked?" Zane leans back and folds his arms.

"The captain survived the shipwreck. After the mutiny, they locked him in a cabin in the bottom of the boat. They got very close to Trilland before the storm hit, and when the ship started to fall apart, he escaped and floated on some driftwood to Gessend where I'm from. It's a small island owned by Trilland but mostly left to itself. It's basically a province. Captain Wilson told us all what happened. He held onto the hope that maybe you survived. Most of the people in Gessend doubted him, but he was right. Here you are." Brent smiles.

"So, you want us to believe that this guy survived a mutiny and a shipwreck?" Zane says.

"Is it any more outrageous than Lorraine surviving an attack and floating unconscious in the open ocean?" Brent says.

"Maris survived because *I* rescued her," Zane growls. "Not because some imaginary captain did some heroic act."

"I'm grateful that you helped Lorraine, but that doesn't minimize the captain's actions."

Zane jumps to his feet. "It most certainly does. I'm real, and I'm right here to tell you my story. Anyone in the town can confirm it. Where is this captain? Why didn't he come himself? Who can verify your story? You're just some political phony trying to take advantage of a girl with amnesia." Zane storms out of the house, slamming the door behind him.

Between everything that Brent has said and Zane's strong reaction, I feel my head spinning violently. It feels exactly like it did a year ago when I woke up in Ms. Flora's, in this very room, and felt my head spin from all the questions Zane and Harper asked and my lack of answers to them. It occurs to me that I don't think I've been in this room since I moved out of it into Harper's house. There's something kind of poetic about having this discovery in the room where I first woke up, but it also feels a little bit like the walls are closing in around me.

"I'm sorry," Brent says after a few moments. "I didn't mean to upset your boyfriend."

Heat immediately rushes to my face. "He—he's not—"

Brent chuckles. "Are you sure? It sure looks like it to me."

"He's not my boyfriend. And it wasn't you, he's just protective."

"I'm not trying to take advantage of you or anyone else, I promise. I hope you know that."

I hold the side of my head. "I don't know what to think. I have no way to know who to listen to."

"Please consider this then," Brent says. "If I'm lying, if I'm making this whole thing up like he seems to think, what could I possibly gain? The people of Trilland know the princess Lorraine Everhart. If I brought back a different girl, they would know. I'd probably get arrested, either by Cassandra for threatening her rule, or by the government for faking your return. I have nothing to gain by bringing back anyone who isn't the real Lorraine Everhart. I'm totally sure of what I'm doing. I'm sure it's you. I am not trying to trick you."

What Brent says makes sense, but I have far more reason to trust Zane. But what if Zane is being irrational? He always ends up storming out of the room when we talk to Brent. Maybe he's just paranoid. And if I listen to Zane's paranoia, I could miss my chance to figure out who I am.

But a princess? I definitely can't picture myself as a princess. There's no way that could possibly be true. Being a princess is far more than I'm capable of. And besides, this is starting to sound like a fairytale. Girl with amnesia discovers she's a princess? That's a little too fantastical for me. Just this morning, that was nothing more than a joke between Elise and me.

But Brent does have that picture of me. If he doesn't know me, it would make sense that he could come by a picture of me if I'm a princess. That's equatable to being famous. Ugh, that's uncomfortable even to think about. I don't want to be famous.

"I feel like I've overwhelmed you," Brent says, and I realize that I haven't been looking at him but rather staring off into space. "Why don't you go home? Take a break and come back to see me when you feel better."

"Maybe that's a good idea," I say, standing up, pocketing the creepy picture of me. "Thank you for talking to me."

"Happy to." Brent smiles. He's finally starting to look better. The color is returning to his face and he looks less tired. He almost looks attractive now, despite how disheveled he still is. His blonde hair is all messed up, and his brown eyes still look tired, but he's looking better, like the life is coming back into him. I guess Ms. Flora's treatments are doing him some good. I can only hope that I'll start to feel better, too.

# Chapter 6

"Just wear the green romper," Elise calls from my bed. I stare at the green romper sitting on the bathroom counter with disdain.

"I hate the green romper," I say.

"You look amazing in it. Green is your best color."

"It's too formal."

"It's a romper, Maris," Elise says. "It's the epitome of casual. Stop overreacting."

"I don't want to look like I spent all day getting ready for Zane's birthday dinner. You already did my hair."

"Don't be so dramatic. All I did was braid your bangs back so they don't hang in your face. It's hardly a royal hairstyle."

"Please don't say the word 'royal.'"

"Still freaking out about what Brent said?"

I sigh, giving up, and throw on the stupid romper, and it makes me angry to see that it does look good on me. "How can I not freak out?"

"This is, like, every girl's dream. You're a princess. That's so glamorous."

"It's not glamorous. Supposedly I have to save a dying country. And besides, that isn't every girl's dream. I never wanted to be a princess."

"You don't know that," Elise says. "Maybe you used to love being a princess. Who knows?"

"Exactly," I say, sitting down next to Elise and tying the strings of my sandals. "Who knows? Because I certainly don't. Maybe this guy is making all this up."

"My gosh, Zane's gotten to you."

"So what if he has?" I say, feeling a bit defensive. "Zane has always been there for me. This guy hasn't. I don't know anything about him."

"Except that he knows *you*," Elise says. "This is what you wanted, and now you've got it. Stop questioning it."

I half mutter something under my breath, but it isn't really coherent, and thankfully, Elise doesn't press it. Why is it that when I want someone to believe in Brent they don't, but when I want someone to be skeptical of Brent, they aren't?

"Look, just forget about all of that for now," Elise says, and I roll my eyes. "Sorry, bad choice of words. Tonight is Zane's fake birthday dinner so that he won't suspect the surprise party that Harper throws every single year. Let's just enjoy it."

"Deal," I say, and Elise and I head out the door to Zane's.

It doesn't take us long to walk to Zane's, and it's almost like Harper senses our presence because she swings the door open before we have a chance to knock.

"Girls, lovely to see you." Harper smiles wide when she opens the door. "Come in, please, come in. My famous pineapple upside down cake is in the oven right now. Should be nice and fresh by the time we finish dinner."

"It smells fantastic in here," Elise says. "Here, I brought some lemon cookies. I accidentally made too many."

"Thank you dear," Harper says as she takes the cookies. Elise never messes up a recipe, but Harper refuses to take food from people when she cooks dinner, so Elise always has to lie and claim she accidentally made too many. Of course, Harper knows that, but no one questions it. We all just go along with it. It's a nice kind of tradition the people on this island have, and I kind of like it. It's sweet in its own way.

"Zane," Harper shouts. "Come down, the girls are here."

"What's he doing holed up in his room?" Elise asks.

"Oh, who knows? Honestly, I've been calling him for at least fifteen minutes, but he still hasn't come down."

"Maris, why don't you go see if you can get him?" Elise says, and when I try to protest, she nudges me with her elbow. "Go on, see what you can do."

There's no use arguing with Elise at this point, so I reluctantly go upstairs. I've only been in Zane's room a handful of times, mostly when I was living here. It's small, much like the rest of the house, and completely void of decoration, very unlike the rest of the house. He only has a bed, a desk and chair, and a small bookshelf with a limited library on it. Over the years, Zane has collected a few books here and there. He's quite the bookworm when he can get his hands on books, but that's usually only when the traders come by selling them. He always buys a few when they come.

"Hey," I say, knocking on the door. "Your mom claims she's been calling you for fifteen minutes."

"Zane looks up with a smirk from his desk. "You and I both know that means she's been calling me for about five."

"Well, sure, but still. Elise brought lemon cookies."

"That's great. I love those cookies."

I can't think of anything else to say, and it seems like Zane can't either. Well, we've officially run out of conversation topics. This is weird. I don't like when it's awkward between us. How do I fix it? How do I return our relationship to the time before he blew up at Brent for calling me a princess and stormed out?

"This is weird," Zane says, echoing my thoughts.

"It is," I say.

"I'm sorry. I shouldn't have stormed out like that."

"It's okay."

"That all just sounded so crazy to me. You, a princess?"

"Gee, thanks."

Zane laughs. "No, no. You know what I mean. That's crazy."

"It is crazy," I say. "I don't really know what to think."

"Have you talked to him again?" Zane asks, and I shake my head. "What did he say after I left?"

"Nothing really. Nothing new."

"Zane," Harper calls out again. "I swear, it's been at least an hour."

Zane and I both laugh. "I guess we should go down," Zane says.

"Yeah."

"So, we're good?"

"Of course," I say. "Always."

"Good." Zane smiles. "You, uh, you—I mean that, uh—you look—"

"Oh, Elise made me wear this thing. I kind of hate it."

"It, uh, it suits you," Zane says, scratching the back of his neck. "Let's go downstairs."

"Yes."

Zane and I walk down the stairs, me in front of him, and I can't help but obsess over what he just said. Did Zane just give me a compliment? Like, a sincere compliment based on my appearance? I don't think that's ever happened before. I can't believe it. Could Elise be right? Does Zane like me?

No way. Not a chance. There's no way Zane likes me. He just saw what I saw. The green suits me. Not the romper. The green. Zane doesn't like me. He can't.

~~~
~~~

"Well, that was fun," Elise says, pulling a leftover lemon cookie out and handing it to me before taking one for herself.

"Harper's dinners always are," I say.

"You and Zane were upstairs for a while. Good talk?"

"Yeah, I guess." I can't stop thinking about what Brent said earlier. I tried not to, like Elise said, but I just can't stop thinking about it. How am I supposed to be a princess? How could I not remember something that monumental?

"I was thinking about changing the glaze on these cookies to a vanilla flavor. What do you think?"

"Sounds great," I say. And besides, if I'm as important and beloved as people say, why isn't anyone looking for me? I mean sure, this Cassandra chick told everyone I'm dead, but really, did everyone beside Brent and some captain believe that? Shouldn't someone be looking? Wasn't there anyone close to me who would have known something was wrong, or at least tried out of desperation to find me?

"You're still thinking about Brent, aren't you?" Elise says.

"What?"

"You've been spacey all night. You're still obsessing over what Brent said."

I sigh. "I tried not to."

"I know you did."

"But I just can't help it."

"Think of it this way," Elise says. "This can only be good. Personally, I think Brent is telling the truth, but even if he's not, this can only lead to further discovery. You'll figure out the truth, you'll go home, find your family, and feel better about this whole thing. You'll forget how worried you were."

Find your family? Family? "Wait, what did you say?"

"Which thing?"

"About family."

"Oh, you'll find them," Elise says. "Once you get back to wherever you're from, whether that's Trilland or somewhere else, you'll find the family that's been worrying about you. You'll be reunited with them."

Family. Family. That word bothers me. "I'll see you at home, Elise."

"What?"

"I'll see you at home," I say again, taking off running into the town square.

Family. Family. That word bothers me. The concept bothers me. As I run to Ms. Flora's my mind buzzes with the word. Then other words start buzzing: father, mother, sibling, grandparent, aunt, uncle, cousin. The words jumble in my head, and they all bother me.

By the time I reach Ms. Flora's front door, I'm panting hard. Family. Something's missing. Something's wrong. Where are they?

"You left something out the other day," I say to Brent as I throw the door to Ms. Flora's open.

Brent looks up from the book he's reading, startled. "What do you mean?"

"You want me to believe that I am the rightful heir to the throne."

"You are. The Everhart family has ruled Trilland for centuries."

"Then where are my parents?" I say. "I got to this island a year ago when I was seventeen. There's no way I was nearly old enough to be queen back then. And you said something about how everyone loves them. Where are they?"

Brent hesitates, and I know the answer. I knew the answer before I came here, but I hoped that I might be wrong. I hoped that Brent would deny it, but he doesn't. He just shakes his head. I feel the air around me get heavy.

"How?"

"They died many years ago," Brent says softly. "Your father died when you were young, I think twelve years old, maybe thirteen, of pneumonia. Your mother died only a year or two after. They say she died of grief."

I sit down on the couch and stare intently at the rug. My parents are dead. That's why no one is looking for me. That's why no one found me. No one is there to look. If they were alive, I probably wouldn't have been on this island for a year. They would have found me. They died long ago while I was still with them, and I don't even remember it. It makes me sad, mostly because I don't even remember them. I can't even honor their memory because that memory is not there.

"I realize this is hard for you," Brent says as he leans in, "but if it's any consolation, they cared deeply for you. They were confident in your ability to rule Trilland."

A single tear trickles down my cheek. "How can I rule a country I don't remember with the inspiration of the parents I also don't remember?"

"You will remember." Brent takes my hand. "I'll make sure of it."

# Chapter 7

The sun pierces into my eyes, demanding me to wake up. I forgot to close my curtains last night, and now I'm paying for it. I get up, close the blinds, and immediately collapse back into bed, pulling the covers around me. It's got to be after noon if it's that bright outside. But who cares? I wasn't planning on going anywhere today anyway.

I grab the photo of me off my nightstand and stare at it, still waiting for it to change into someone else, but it never obliges me. It's always the same face, my face, staring back at me, mocking me. I hate it. A picture of my dead parents would almost be less offensive.

Some part of my brain wonders if I should even be upset. After all, maybe Brent is wrong about me or is lying like Zane thinks. If that's the case, then I have no reason to believe him about my parents. But oddly, some part of me deep down knows it's true, and that's almost more upsetting. Why does it feel like my very bones remember their loss but my mind doesn't?

"Maris?" Elise knocks on my door as she opens it slowly. "Are you okay? It's after one."

"I'm fine."

"You didn't say anything when you got home last night. I was worried about you. Where did you go after dinner?"

"To see Brent."

"What did he say?"

"It doesn't matter."

"Sure it does." Elise sits on the side of my bed and sets a cup of tea on the nightstand.

"No, it doesn't," I say, pulling the covers up to my mouth. "I'm sorry, could you just leave me to myself for a little while? I don't feel well."

"Of course. Feel better," Elise says, closing the door quietly behind her.

~~~

I think I fell asleep again. I feel weird, but it's still daylight outside. I know because those stupid curtains are open again. Did Elise open them? I feel like I would have noticed if she had. Did she come back in while I was asleep and open them?

It requires too much energy to get up and shut them again, so I just roll over and try to face away from the window, but when I roll over, I see Zane sitting at my desk, reading his latest book find. He smiles at me when he sees me, finishes the page he was on, and then shuts the book and leans forward.

"Elise says you're not feeling well?"

"Yes."

"She thinks you're sick," Zane says. I don't answer. "But you're not sick. You and I both know that. When you're sick, you get so whiny. And you're not whiny." I can't help but smile at least a little. "Ah, there we go, I got a smile out of you. Now why don't you tell me what's really going on?"

"Why are you even here?" I say, sitting up a little.

"Didn't I tell you? Elise told me you were sick. I came over to make sure you were okay. So, what's up with you?"

I shrug. "Talked to Brent last night."
~~~

"He didn't upset you, did he?"

"No," I say. "Well, not directly. I realized that it was kind of weird that my parents, the supposed king and queen of Trilland, weren't out looking for their lost daughter. Brent says they're dead. Died when I was little. And I don't even remember them."

"Oh Maris," Zane says, moving to my bedside. "I'm sorry."

"You don't sound surprised."

"The thought had crossed my mind," Zane says. "I didn't want to say anything until I could be sure. Didn't want to upset you for no reason."

"My parents are dead, Zane, and I can't even remember them. I can't even remember them."

I start to cry and I can't seem to stop it, so I just sit there and let the tears stream down my face. Zane slides over closer to me and puts his arm around me and pulls me into his chest. I let him, partly because I don't have the energy to resist and partly because I desperately want the comfort. Zane feels warm and safe, and I let myself cry all over his shirt even though I know I'll be embarrassed about the tear stains later. Zane holds on tight and rubs my back, and it feels good.

"I'm sorry," I say, sniffling into my hand.

"For what?" Zane says while he strokes my hair. "It's okay to be upset about this."

"But I can't remember them."

"You will."

"How do you know?"

"I just do," Zane says, and for whatever reason, I choose to believe him. Maybe because I have to just to keep my sanity. It occurs to me that Zane hasn't tried to refute Brent either. I wonder if that means he finally believes him.

I stop crying and just let Zane rub my back, keeping my head on his shoulder.

Being here with Zane feels so natural. I don't ever want to move from this position. I like being this close to Zane. But how can I be this close to Zane? He seems calm enough about it, but he's probably just tolerating it because he knows I'm upset. He's too nice for his own good. What on earth am I doing? Does liking being this close to Zane mean I like him? Who says I should be able to be this close to Zane? Suddenly Zane's arm around me is making me very claustrophobic because I feel like maybe it shouldn't be there. And am I a terrible person for enjoying this moment with Zane right after finding out my parents are dead? Has my memory loss made me calloused?

I bolt upright, and Zane pulls back suddenly as well. "Is everything okay?"

"Yes, I'm fine. I just need to get up. Go for a walk or something," I say, jumping off the bed.

"That's a good idea," Zane says, smoothing the wrinkles in my sheets I created with my scrambling to get off the bed. He looks almost—almost handsome sitting there on my bed, smoothing the ridiculously frilly pink sheets Harper gave me. "Do you want me to go with you?"

No. Stop that. Stop thinking about Zane like that. "No, I'm fine. I'm just going to take a walk over by the cliff. I haven't really been over there since Brent got here."

"Okay, well enjoy your weird little isolated hideout." Zane winks and elbows me playfully, and it's really hard for me not to think about how good he looks when he winks.

"I will."

"See you later?"

"Of course."

Zane heads out of the house, and I take my time getting ready to leave so that we won't have to awkwardly walk the same direction without going to the same place. I grab a swimsuit and add some shorts and twist my hair into a messy knot. My hair's just going to get wet anyway, so why bother?

I take the short walk over to the base of where the climbing starts to get to my little cliff, but instead, I hang a right and head for the sea. There's a really nice inlet where the waves slow down and create a little pool that I love to swim in.

It only takes me a few minutes to reach the pool. I toss my shorts to the side and jump in, letting the gentle waves undo my sloppy hairstyle. I float on my back and watch the waves mimic the blue wave design on my bikini and stick my ears under the water so that all I hear is the sound of my own heartbeat. It's comforting. I like the silence, even if it is manufactured. And I like this little pool. I really like swimming, but the water makes me nervous. Probably for the same reason the roar of the waves keeps me up at night. I just can't sleep when I hear those waves beating the shore. It creeps me out.

But here, in this little inlet, the waves are so gentle that they actually relax me. The water is just a little warm from the sun hitting this shallow spot, but it retains some of its ocean chill so that it is always the perfect temperature. I let myself sink under the surface and swim the short distance down to the bottom. There are lots of little minnows and starfish living at the bottom and I like to swim down and poke a few starfish, watching them move their legs in defiance, and swirl my hand around, sending the minnows darting all around me. The life they exude gives me life, or at least that's how it feels. Sometimes I wish I could stay down here, just me and the minnows. Down here, there's no Brent, no lost memory, no confusing thoughts about Zane, just water, just silence. But eventually my lungs demand that I surface.

I come up out of the water and shake my hair, sending water flying all over the place. My eyes burn a little from the saltwater, but it's a good kind of burning, a clean kind of feeling. I rub my eyes, give my hair another shake, and start to drift onto my back again.

"Hey, watch where you shake your hair."

I spin around, probably showering the speaker in more water, and make eye contact with Brent.

"You scared me," I say.

"Sorry."

"You're up and about. Feeling better, I guess?"

"Much better. Ms. Flora thought I would benefit from a walk in the sun."

"And you walked out this far? Ambitious."

"I got lost in my thoughts and just kind of wound up here."

"That's how I found my cliff," I say.

"Your what?"

"My cliff," I say, pointing up to the edge. "Around the corner there's a climbing path that leads to a really pretty cliff. A little while after I got here, I found it. It's kind of an oasis."

"You sure?" Brent says. "Because this right here looks like an oasis. That water is beautiful."

"It's a close second."

Brent sits down in the sand and takes off his shoes and rolls up his pant legs. He sticks his feet in the water and smiles, closing his eyes with relaxation. He swirls his feet around a little and stretches his arms, letting his biceps ripple.

"So, what do you say we shoot the elephant in the room?" he says.

"What?"

"You okay? I'm sorry, I really didn't want to upset you yesterday."

"It's not your fault," I say. "Besides, you would have had to tell me eventually."

"I kind of hoped you'd remember something first. Something to lift your spirits."

"Nothing I can do about it now."

"Ocean's good therapy?" Brent smiles.

"Yeah, I guess so. I like watching the fish."

"Fish?"

"Yes. There are minnows in here. See?" I say, pointing to a cluster that darts around my leg.

"Cool," Brent says, but he sounds a little tired.

"I like watching them. They remind me that life goes on, with or without me, so I might as well suck it up and join in."

Brent smiles again. "That was so insightful, so—so inspirational. You sounded like—" Brent stops suddenly and looks away, staring intently at the water.

"Like who?" I say, but Brent just shakes his head. "Who?"

"Your father," Brent says. "I remember the speeches he used to give. That's exactly how he sounded."

"Really?"

"Yes. I'm sorry to bring him up, but you really sounded like him."

"Don't be sorry," I say. "I'm glad to know some part of me still remembers them and remembers me."

Brent digs his heels into the sand at the edge of the water and forms little ditches where his feet rest. He very purposefully avoids eye contact, and it seems like he might even be blushing a little bit.

"What?" I say.

Brent looks startled, but he answers. "I hope you don't think I'm pressuring you or anything. I know I got pretty energetic when I realized it was you, and I kind of laid a lot on you, but you have to know how exciting this is for me. I didn't know if I'd ever find you."

"What do you mean? Isn't that why you came out here?"

"Most people just assumed you died. The few who held out hope that maybe you survived gave up months ago. Captain Wilson is basically the only one left who's still convinced you'd be out there somewhere. He had so much faith that you survived. I wanted to believe him, but it just didn't seem likely, you know?"

I twist my mouth a little. He's right: it doesn't seem likely. I probably wouldn't believe Captain Wilson either. It's quite a stretch to assume someone would survive drifting unconscious like that in the middle of nowhere. "Why did you come then, if you didn't believe him?"

"I just couldn't disappoint him. We became pretty close during this past year, and the only time he seemed truly happy was when he was talking about you." Brent smiles just slightly. "I figured you were a lot more to him than just a royal figure. He was never going to give up, and I felt like I just couldn't say no to helping him. I'm sure glad now that he didn't give up."

"I don't know, you didn't exactly find what you were looking for. I'm not really what you wanted."

"You are absolutely what I wanted," Brent says, making eye contact for the first time in a while. "I found exactly what I was searching for."

Suddenly I become very aware of the fact that now I'm the one who's blushing. He and Captain Wilson are putting so much stock into me that I hardly feel like I can live up to expectations, but somehow the way Brent is looking at me right now makes me feel like maybe I haven't totally let them down. At least not yet.

Brent sighs and rubs his face. His eyes look swollen, and he just seems totally exhausted. I don't think Ms. Flora intended for him to walk this far.

"Hey, you okay?"

"Just tired," Brent says. "Maybe I took on more than I was ready for."

"You should probably head back to Ms. Flora's. I'll walk you over."

"You don't have to," Brent says, standing up in the sand.

"I think I should. Don't want you passing out in the sand somewhere," I say as I get out and put my shorts back on, wishing I had brought a shirt as well.

# Chapter 8

B rent and I have been talking a lot lately, but not about my memory. We talk more about Trilland and Gessend and other stuff. Brent thinks that if we avoid the topic of me for a while, I'll relax, and my mind can clear up.

"So, Cassandra's been trying to take power for a while?" I ask.

"Yeah, pretty much since your parents died. The only reason she couldn't is because you were still there."

"But I was so young."

"Didn't matter. You existed. The parliament could basically run the country until you were of age. It was like an interim, a waiting period. She couldn't touch it."

"Until I died." I air-quote "died."

"Exactly."

It seems wild to know that someone had been after me for years, yet I can't remember it. To make matters worse, she was my cousin. I kind of wish that Brent had a picture of her, too, because I almost feel like that would be easier to recognize than myself. I don't even know why I feel that way, but a picture of anyone else—my parents, Captain Wilson, even Cassandra—feels like it would hold more weight in my mind than my own year-ago face. Maybe even a picture of Trilland would help.

Brent and I sit in silence for a few minutes before I work up the nerve to ask a question I've been wondering about for a while.

"Who is this Captain Wilson? He seems like he was more than just a loyal captain."

"He's worked as a royal ship captain basically since your parents got married," Brent says. "They always talked about how he was their most loyal employee. I don't know why, but he definitely was more than just a ship captain."

"I wish I knew more about him."

Brent's eyes light up. "Wait a second, I forgot. I can't believe I forgot about this until now. I have a letter from the captain." Brent rummages around in his bag and hands me a yellow envelope.

I open the letter and look at the words, but I can't bring myself to actually read them. I examine the signature, as if I would be able to tell if it's fake or not, and I notice a paperclip at the bottom of the page. A picture has been attached to the other side. As soon as I flip the picture over and see the captain's face, I feel a strange sense of clarity, just for a moment. My mind surges with a strange but clear picture in my head. A memory.

*It's raining hard, and I can remember feeling seasick even though I have no memory of the ship itself. The captain's face, dripping wet, looks panicked.*

*"This isn't good, Lorraine," he says to me as quietly as he can over the roar of the waves. "My crew has never acted like this before. I think it's Cassandra."*

*"What do you mean?"*

*"I think she's trying to get rid of us." The captain's face quivers.*

*"She wouldn't—she—"*

*"Trust me, I've got a bad feeling. We've got to get you out of here."*

*"How?" I shout, feeling my stomach flipflop. "We're in the middle of nowhere."*

*"No, we're not." The captain points over the port side. "There are many tiny islands around here. Little ones that don't make the maps of Trilland. You can make it to one of them."*

*"You can't be serious."*

*"It's your best chance. You have to take the risk."*

*"Please, no—" I start to argue, but the captain takes both of my hands in his.*

*"I'm afraid they'll hurt you, Lorraine. I'll come back for you, I promise. You have to trust me."*

*"But—but—I—"*

*"Just stay safe. I'll be back. I'll come for you. Just don't forget what your father taught you, and you'll be fine."*

No sooner than I remember it does it already feel fleeting. But this is the first memory I've ever had of my past life, and I refuse to let it slip away that easily. I feel the cloudiness coming back, so I grab a pencil and paper and start scribbling down every little detail I can remember.

"Hey, what happened? What are you doing?" Brent waves his hand in front of my face, but I ignore him. I don't want to lose this. "Lorraine, are you okay?"

"Shh. I'm fine," I say. "Just give me a second."

I take a few more minutes to write down everything I can and reread it to make sure I didn't miss anything, but when I finally look up at Brent, he's staring at me with his jaw dropped and tears studding his eyes.

"What?"

"It's just—" Brent's voice shakes a little with emotion. "That's the first time you've actually responded to me calling you Lorraine.

Every time I say it, you look at me strangely. But you just answered to Lorraine."

"I remember him," I say with glee, unable to suppress my smile. "I remember the captain."

"You what?" Brent sits straight up. "You do? You really do?"

"Yes. Well, sort of. I can remember him warning me about Cassandra when we were on the ship."

"That's fantastic." Brent grins. "I knew it would come back to you."

"It's certainly not everything, but it's the first memory I've had in a year."

"It is everything. This is the first step to getting it all back."

"Thank you for this letter." I hug Brent without thinking, and I'm kind of embarrassed, but he hugs me firmly right back.

"Thank the captain. I'm just his messenger."

"You have no idea what this means to me." I clutch the letter and my own handwritten transcript of my memory to my chest, afraid that if I let them go, I'll lose the memory, too.

Brent notices my obsessive hold on the letter and smiles. "Hey, you keep that. He wrote it for you anyway."

"Thank you."

"My pleasure." Brent leans in, and his gaze slowly drops from my eyes to my lips. It makes me a little uncomfortable, but what makes me more uncomfortable is that I find myself leaning in, too. Brent slowly strokes my arm, and I suddenly don't feel so shy. I pull Brent in and kiss him gently. I don't know what's come over me, but I like the way Brent's lips feel on mine.

When we both pull back, Brent has the faintest smile on his face, and it's cute. He looks so happy. But his face drops suddenly when he looks behind me. I turn around to see Zane standing in the doorway, completely stunned by what he just saw. What on earth could he be thinking?

Brent coughs awkwardly, and Zane drops the bag he was carrying. "Didn't mean to interrupt," Zane says. "Ms. Flora asked me to bring you some food."

With that, Zane doesn't bother to look at me but just walks away, and it hurts me more than I thought it would. Why am I so bothered that Zane is upset that I kissed someone else?

I take off out the door, leaving Brent standing alone in the room, and try to catch up with Zane.

"Zane. Zane, wait." Zane stops, but he doesn't turn to face me. "Zane, please."

Zane spins around, his eyes filled with fire. "What was that?"

"It was nothing," I lie. "I was just excited and got carried away."

Zane shakes his head. "You don't just get a little excited and kiss someone, Maris. I know you. You're too shy to do something so bold."

"I am not."

Zane scoffs. "Yeah you are. My mother and I took care of you in our home for weeks before you ever spoke to either one of us."

"I was scared, Zane. I couldn't remember anything, not even my own name, and you expected me to carry on conversation with two people I'd never met before?"

"Nothing's changed since then. So, why is this guy different?"

I raise my voice. "Things *have* changed. Something Brent said triggered something. I remember something."

Zane's eyes widen. "Really? What?"

"The captain. I remember the captain."

Zane rolls his eyes. "The captain? Really?"

"What does that mean?" I fold my arms.

"I mean that this guy has gotten in your head. You want so badly to believe him, and he tells these stories with great detail, and you just think it's a memory."

My eyes sting with tears. "How can you say that? I do remember. I remembered a conversation Brent never told me about."

"I think you're letting this guy play games with your mind."

"You know what I think?" I yell. "I think you just don't want me to remember because you think I'd go back to my life and leave you, and you don't want that."

"Well, wouldn't you?" Zane's eyes look simultaneously angry and sad under furrowed eyebrows. "I've been protecting you for a while now. I'm not going to stop now just because some guy we know nothing about has romanced you."

"Is that all you care about? That kiss? Is that all you can think about?"

"Yes, it is," Zane says, oddly quietly.

"Why?"

Zane laughs cynically. "Geez, Maris, I thought I'd made myself clear."

"Made what clear?" My hands are shaking, and I suddenly feel a little faint.

Zane takes my face into his hands and kisses me, so suddenly, I nearly fall over. His hands feel hot on my cheeks. Or maybe that's the flushing of my own face. When he releases, I'm surprised at how sad I feel not to have his lips on mine, like I didn't know what I was missing until it wasn't there.

"That," Zane says sadly. "I thought I had made that clear, but apparently not. I hope it's obvious now."

Zane walks away, and I want so desperately to run after him, but I can't seem to move my feet. The pounding of my heartbeat seems to immobilize me. What would I even say if I did go after him? What would I do?

I look back at Ms. Flora's. I can't go back to Brent right now either. I know even less about what I'd say to him.

Part of me is angry at both Brent and Zane. I finally remember *something,* and it feels like they've both made it about them. I shouldn't be kissing anyone right now, and I hate that I've gotten distracted from what really matters right now.

I start down the path to my house. I've had too much excitement today. I need to be alone, away from people for a while.

# Chapter 9

"Hey," I say to Elise as I walk in the door.

"Hello," Elise calls cheerfully from the kitchen. "I'm making this new mango salsa to go with dinner tonight. I got the recipe from Harper, but who knows if it'll be good. And who knows if it will even go with the fish. Does mango go with tuna? Does anything go with tuna? Maybe tuna is one of those things that doesn't go with anything…"

Elise keeps babbling on about tuna and it's many complexities, but I just can't muster up the energy to maintain conversation with her right now. I walk right past the kitchen into my room and collapse face first onto the bed. A few moments later, Elise knocks on the door.

"Are you okay?"

"Not really," I mumble into my pillow.

"What happened?" Elise sits next to me and strokes my hair.

I roll over to face her. "I kissed Brent."

"What?" Elise squeals. "How did it happen? Wait, did you kiss him, or did he kiss you? Does Zane know?"

"Why would you say that?"

"Say what?"

"About Zane," I say. "Why does that immediately come to your mind when I say that I kissed someone else?"

"What do you mean?" Elise furrows her eyebrows. "It's Zane. Zane has always—" Elise hesitates, realizing what I mean. "You mean you really didn't know?"

I press my face into my pillow again. "No, I didn't know."

"Oh, Maris. I tried to tell you."

"I thought you were kidding."

"I thought you understood that I wasn't kidding."

"Was it really that obvious?"

Elise chuckles. "Yeah, it's always been obvious. Ever since the day he pulled your lifeboat in."

"Why am I so stupid? How did I not know?"

"Maris, you're not stupid. You've had a million other things going on ever since the day you met Zane. It's not unreasonable that you weren't guy watching."

"It's just that the more I think about it now, the more signs I see of his feelings for me. Why couldn't I see them before? It's been so obvious for so long."

"Wait, wait." Elise waves her hands. "Backtrack for a second. What happened with Brent?"

I sigh and roll onto my back. "I don't know. I didn't think I thought of him that way, but I got caught up in the moment. I didn't even realize what I was doing until after it was done."

"What do you mean you got caught up in the moment?"

I smile for the first time since my argument with Zane. "I—I remember something."

What?" Elise screams and throws her arms around my neck. "Maris, that's amazing. What did you remember? How did it happen?"

"It still feels kind of vague. In the moment, everything felt clear, but now I feel confused again. Brent showed me a picture of the captain he's always talking about, and I had a flash of a conversation I had with him."

"That's so exciting. So, is Brent telling the truth? Do you know?"

"He's telling the truth about the captain and the mutiny. I can't guarantee anything beyond that."

"Still, that's something. That's more verification than we've had this whole time. What did Zane say? You told him, right?"

I cover my face. "Zane found out because he walked in just as I kissed Brent. So, he didn't exactly have the best reaction."

"Oh no." Elise covers her mouth. "Zane saw you?"

I nod.

"What did he do?"

"What do you think? He freaked out. He yelled at me, called Brent a liar, yelled some more, kissed me, then walked away."

"Whoa, whoa, whoa." Elise flails her arms frantically. "Okay, when you walked in the door, your first words should have been, 'Hey Elise, guess what? Today, I remembered something from my past, and I kissed Brent, so Zane kissed me.'"

"It's more complicated than that."

"But those are the most important details."

"Elise, what do I do?"

"Well, who is it that you really have feelings for?"

"I don't know," I whine and roll my eyes. "I don't even know who I am. How am I supposed to know who I like?"

"Okay, okay, one thing at a time. You need to try to remember more. Now that something came back, it should be easier to remember more."

"But that means going back to Brent. What am I supposed to say to him?"

Elise shrugs.

"And what am I supposed to say to Zane?"

Elise shrugs again. "I don't know. But figure it out fast," she says before returning to the kitchen.

I know Elise is right. I need to figure out what is happening, I just don't know how. Nothing seems sure anymore. I still don't know who I am. I acted irrationally today and kissed Brent. Zane, the person who means the most to me, is angry with me.

First things first, if I'm going to figure out what to do about Zane and Brent, then I need to figure out who I am. The only way to do that is to work on my memory. Maybe I can work backwards from the only memory I have.

I reread the notes I wrote of my own memory, but it doesn't jog anything else like I hoped it would. Still, I'm glad I wrote it down in case the memory fades again. I pull Brent's letter from the captain out of my bag and hold the envelope carefully, afraid of its contents. It takes several moments to work up the nerve to open it again and when I do, I set his picture aside.

*My dear Princess Lorraine,*

*I realize you probably don't understand my actions. I must have seemed idiotic that day when I suggested that you escape to an unmarked island, but you have to trust me when I tell you that I did what I needed to do to protect you.*

*I don't know what happened to you or why you never returned to Trilland. I certainly hope that you are all right. I'm hopeful that Brent will find you in good health. I wouldn't be able to forgive myself if you were injured in my attempts to keep you safe. I wish I could have come to find you myself, but I'm older now, and the mutiny was rough, and I can't manage a trip myself when I don't know how long I'd be gone.*

*Besides, the people of Gessend need me here. They are in chaos without a leader. A leader like you.*

*Lorraine, whatever happened, you need to return to your country. Trilland needs you now more than ever. Cassandra's reign has all but destroyed the country and its provinces. She's wreaking havoc, and you can fix it. You're the only one who can return Trilland to its former glory.*

*It won't be easy. Cassandra won't give up easily. But the people of Trilland will rejoice when they find out that you're alive. They always loved you, and they will love you again.*

*I don't know what's keeping you away, but I truly believe that you can come back from whatever it is and take over your rightful place. You need to hurry. Overcome, Lorraine. Overcome for Trilland. Remember what your father taught you, and you can do it.*

*I hope to see you again soon,*
*Lawrence Wilson*

I had hoped that reading this letter would help me. I thought that maybe I would remember something else or that the captain would give me some kind of insight, but this letter only worries me more. He seems so confident that I can overcome whatever has been keeping me away from Trilland, but what if that struggle is that I don't know who I am? How can I be the strong person he thinks I am if I'm not that strong person anymore?

And what did my father teach me? The captain seemed to think that whatever it was, it could get me through anything, but I can't remember it. I wonder if it was common knowledge. Maybe Brent knows. It's a long shot, but I need all the help I can get.

But that means going back to Brent, which scares me to death. How can I face him again?

I flop onto my stomach and groan. I didn't think it was possible for my life to get any more complicated, but here I am.

I toss and turn for hours, trying to figure out some plan of action before exhaustion wins out and I finally drift to sleep.

# Chapter 10

I hate being nervous. Standing outside of Ms. Flora's makes me nervous, and I hate it. But I have to accept my fate and go talk to Brent, as much as I want to and don't want to all at the same time.

I push the door open slowly, trying in vain to minimize the creaking of that ever noisy slab of wood. I can't decide if the door groans more when I open it or when I close it. It feels like the door is mocking me, judging me for being so stupid as to kiss or be kissed by two different boys in the span of about fifteen minutes. Each moan of the old, rotting wood pains me and makes me feel lightheaded.

"Lorraine!" Brent jumps up from the desk excitedly. He looks happy to see me, which is good, I guess. But he also looks nervous. He runs a hand through his hair, trying to smooth the blonde curls that are expressing their dislike for the humid island air by frizzing uncontrollably.

I glance over at the desk to see that Brent was in the middle of writing some kind of letter. "I didn't interrupt anything, did I?"

"No, no, please, sit down." Brent gestures toward the chair. "I was just writing to Captain Wilson to update him. I was hoping you would come by."

"You were?" I ask.

"Of course." Brent sits on the edge of the desk, and I hate myself for thinking that he looks kind of attractive like that. "I felt bad about the way we left things the other day."

"It's not your fault."

"It is, in a way," Brent says with a shrug. "I let you take full responsibility for what happened when it was both of us."

"That's not really what I came here about." I pull the captain's letter from my bag and hand it to Brent. "Will you read this?"

Brent takes it hesitantly. "Are you sure you want me to?"

"There's nothing personal in it. Besides, right now, it might make more sense to you."

Brent looks confused by me but opens the letter anyway and reads slowly, taking in every word. I watch his eyes scan over certain parts of it multiple times, and when he finally feels like has absorbed the letter fully, he looks back up at me.

"He's right, Lorraine. Cassandra's reign has to come to an end."

"The part I was hoping you could help me with is the note at the end. Do you know what my dad taught me?"

Brent shakes his head. "How would I know that?"

I sigh. "I was hoping that maybe it was common knowledge. The captain seems to think that, if I could just follow my dad's advice, I could be successful. I remember him telling me that on the ship when it was raining, too. Maybe my dad's advice is the key to everything, but I just can't remember it."

"It might not be what you think it is. Maybe it was just like survival information or something about government."

"It doesn't matter what it was. My dad thought it was important, and Captain Wilson thought it was important for me to remember, so I have to figure out a way to remember it."

"How are you going to remember such a random piece of information?"

"Isn't that what you're here for?" I say. "Captain Wilson sent you here to help me come back, so help me."

Brent sighs and rubs his temples. "He could be referencing any number of things. There's no way for me to know every little thing your father ever said to you."

"Then I need Captain Wilson."

"Look, eventually we will go back to Gessend and see Captain Wilson, but you really should regain at least some of your memory before that. Those people, that island, it's all part of Trilland. They'll recognize you."

"But what if my dad's advice is the key to jogging my memory?"

"We'll figure something out."

I collapse onto the bed. "How am I supposed to do this?"

"Lorraine," Brent says, taking both of my hands into his. "It's going to be okay. I know you can do this."

"But what if I can't?"

"You can."

"No," I cry. "And I made a huge mistake. I shouldn't have kissed you. I shouldn't have kissed anybody."

I run out the door and into the town square.

Talking to Brent didn't help me at all. I feel like this guy doesn't know nearly enough to be at all helpful. I need Captain Wilson. His words in that letter are the only thing that have jogged any kind of memory.

I wander through the town square, casually kicking at the gravel as I shuffle along. I have to find some way to get to Captain Wilson. I know Brent is just trying to protect me by telling me to wait to go to Gessend, but I need someone who can actually help me remember.

I'm sure Captain Wilson would help me if he were here. I need to get to him. I'm so lost in my thoughts that I don't even really notice the people around me, and I slam straight into someone.

Oh, hey," Zane says as I so gracefully walk straight into him.

"Sorry, I wasn't paying attention."

"I know."

"Listen, Zane, I—"

"Sorry, I've got to get going. Tito's waiting for me at the docks," Zane says, stepping to the side of me.

"Oh, of course. See you later?"

"Yeah, maybe." Zane shrugs.

"I'm serious, Zane. We need to talk about my memory, about Brent—"

"Later, Maris."

And without another word, he walks off.

I desperately want to follow him, but I just can't. I just can't deal with another encounter with Zane like that. Zane has never been so cold with me. Is he really that hurt by my kissing Brent? I didn't think he cared that much. Or, at least, I didn't think he cared *like that*.

He didn't even say anything about my memory. Not before, not now. He doesn't seem happy at all for me. For a year that's all I've talked about. For a year he has told me repeatedly that one day I'd remember, and now that I have, even if it's just a little bit, he completely ignores it and brushes past it? Even if he's mad, I thought he cared more about me than that.

Well, just because Zane doesn't care doesn't mean I shouldn't. I need answers even if Zane thinks I'm imagining things. I'm not going to let him stop me from regaining my memory. I never thought I'd have to go against Zane to do so, but I guess that's the way it is. That's the way Zane wants it.

I spin around on my heel and walk right back into Ms. Flora's. I fling Brent's door open, much to his surprise, and sit down in the chair across from him.

"All right, let's do this. How do you think I can get my memory back?"

Brent smiles. "I've got a few ideas. You sure you want to start right now?"

"I've been waiting long enough. Time to figure this out."

"Okay, let's start with Captain Wilson since that's the only thing you remember so far," Brent says.

"Okay."

"Do you remember your relationship with him? Like, how did you meet him? How do you know him?"

"I don't know," I say.

"How long have you known him? A couple of years? Your whole life?"

"I don't know," I say again. Doesn't this guy understand amnesia?

"Is he family? Friend?"

"Brent, literally all I know is that one flash of memory. I don't know anything else about him. Right now, you probably know him better than I do."

"You're right," Brent says. "Let's focus on the memory then. What was the weather like?"

"It was raining."

"Sprinkling or torrential downpour?"

"Heavy, but not torrential," I say. "It was raining hard, and the waters were choppy. I was pretty much soaked through."

"Okay, good," Brent says. "What time of day?"

"Early morning. I remember that Captain Wilson had to wake me up. Plus, I got here early in the morning. The fishermen found me when they went down to the beach."

"What's the last thing you remember before waking up in Ms. Flora's?"

I can't answer Brent's question right away. The memory of Captain Wilson gets fuzzy toward the end, like a bad photograph that has damaged edges. I think hard, but I'm having trouble getting past the moment when Captain Wilson tells me to remember my father's advice. Maybe I won't be able to get past that without remembering my father's advice.

"Hey, you know from the people here that you arrived in a lifeboat, right?" Brent asks.

"Yeah."

"How did you get into the boat?"

"Captain Wilson," I say automatically before really thinking it through. But when I really think about it, I find that I'm not lying. I do remember that. It was Captain Wilson's idea. He warned me, but not in enough time. We tried to pack some of my stuff and sneak out, but the crew caught us. I remember getting hit. Getting hit in the head. I remember falling to the deck. I remember hearing shouting, but I also remember having trouble seeing. I remember Captain Wilson picking me up.

"Captain Wilson convinced them I was dead," I say. "I got hit in the head and he told them he at least wanted the right to send my body off to sea. They let him put me in the boat and send me in the direction of this island. I was barely conscious, so everything at this point is really blurry. But they believed him. They thought I was dead."

"Did Captain Wilson say anything to you when he sent you off?"

"I don't think so," I say, "but of course I could be wrong. I don't think he would have been able to with everyone watching."

I stop and rub the side of my head. A sharp pain has inhabited my temples. I don't remember when it started, but it's really bad now.

"You okay?" Brent asks.

"Yeah, I just have a headache. Strained my brain, I guess."

"Take a quick break. This is good. You've remembered a lot. Everything you said matches what Captain Wilson told me."

"He told you that? Why didn't you tell me?"

"I would've eventually, but I wanted to see if I could get you to remember it after reading that letter."

"Well it worked," I say, but I'm still a little annoyed that Brent kept that from me. The last thing I need is information withheld from me.

"Maybe working backwards from there will be most effective. Now we have the last memory from before the amnesia struck. If we go backwards, maybe eventually we'll get to childhood."

"That seems impossible."

"You'll get there," Brent says with a smile.

"Do you have any communication with him?" I ask. "With Captain Wilson?"

"I've sent a few letters, but I'm sure they'll take a long time to reach him."

"What did he say about my amnesia?"

"I haven't received a reply yet."

"Oh."

"Do you want to write him?"

"No," I say quickly. "I wouldn't know what to say."

"I'm sure he'll be glad to know you're okay whenever he gets my letter. He's very worried about you. You're all he talks about."

"He must be more to me than a ship captain," I say. "Did he ever tell you how he knew me?"

"He just said he was a family friend. I don't know how close of a relationship that is or how long he's known you."

I sigh and slide down in the chair, rubbing my forehead.

Brent asks, "Ready to keep going?"

I shake my head. "I've got a headache. I think I need to stop for the day."

"But you're making such good progress. You can't quit now."

"I'm not quitting, I'm taking a break."

"We don't have time to take a break," Brent snaps and then suddenly drops his head in his hands. "I didn't mean to bite your head off."

"Why don't we have time?"

"It's fine."

"It's not fine," I say. "Why don't we have time?"

Brent sighs. "We just can't stay here forever, you know? We have to get back at some point."

"*You* have to get back at some point. I haven't said anything about going to Trilland."

"Lorraine, Trilland is in danger."

"Isn't it more important that I get my memory back before I try to do anything for Trilland?"

Brent takes a deep breath but avoids eye contact. I move to get in his line of sight, forcing him to look at me. "What are you not telling me?"

"This is kind of a time sensitive issue."

"What does that mean?"

"Trilland law states that if the heir to the throne is unable to take the throne for whatever reason, then after twelve month's time, someone else may try to lay claim to it. That's what Cassandra is trying to do now."

"What happens when that time is up?"

"Cassandra can legally become queen."

My head is spinning. I feel like I should care more about this, but it's hard to care about a country I can't remember. "How much time do we have?"

"I'm not sure exactly, but it's not a lot of time. A few weeks."

"You should have told me this sooner."

"I was trying not to put pressure on you."

"Everything you've said since you got here has put pressure on me, so that ship has sailed."

Brent suddenly seems very small, and he starts fidgeting with his fingers. Weeks. I haven't been able to remember anything for a year, and now I've got weeks to piece it together. It seems that every word that Brent speaks now causes my head to pound harder.

"I know you can do it."

I cover my ears and shut my eyes as tightly as possible. "You don't know that. You don't know anything about me. Maybe I'm not cut out to be a princess. Maybe I would cause Trilland more harm than good. Maybe—maybe I just can't do it."

Brent doesn't say anything for a while. I think he might be afraid to. But when he finally does, it's not as comforting as I'd like it to be.

"Captain Wilson and your father both believed in you. And I believe in you too. I wish this situation were different than it is."

"Look," I say, "it's not your fault that I'm under pressure, but it is what it is."

"I just—after everything Captain Wilson and I did, after all you've done to remember, I just couldn't take seeing you be too late. You're

Trilland's last hope, and I never thought I'd find you, and now I did, so I need this to work. I need you."

"I get it," I say. I slump further down into the chair and let my head fall onto my hand with a thud. Weeks. *Weeks.*

"Why don't you go home?" Brent says. "Get some rest."

"Okay," I say, getting up and grabbing my shoes that I had kicked off earlier. Brent takes my hand and kisses it lightly, and I don't really know what to say, so I opt for saying nothing at all.

"See you soon," Brent says.

I force a smile in response and kind of meander out the door. Putting so much effort into remembering has completely worn me out. If I didn't know the walk to my house so well, I might get lost because I'm not paying attention to my route at all. My legs feel heavy—really my whole body feels heavy—and it feels like it takes abnormal effort to keep moving. I'm so distracted by my own thoughts that I practically walk straight into Gus with all my stumbling about.

"Careful there," Gus says with a laugh. "You gotta watch where you're going. Wouldn't want you to get hurt."

"Sorry, Gus," I say. "I'm not feeling well, that's all. Just wasn't paying attention."

"What's wrong?"

"Just a headache."

"Well here." Gus pulls a mango off the back of his cart and hands it to me. "I got more of these in, and they're just as pretty as the last batch. I thought you might like one."

"Thanks Gus." I take the mango and sniff it. Gus is right. It smells amazing.

"And hey, tell Elise I've got her pineapple and kiwi ready for her," Gus says, patting a box on the cart.

"Already? You're quick."

Gus shrugs. "Not many big orders this time of year. I tried selling to some of the merchants, but they didn't go for it. Couldn't convince them to spend a little extra for quality. No accounting for taste, I guess."

"Having money flow issues?"

"Not since you helped me out. I just wish I had a bigger market. Elise's recipe experiments keep me going, but I know my fruit is the best around."

"You're not wrong."

Gus sighs. "Anyway, just tell Elise I'll bring her stuff by later."

"I can just take it to her."

"Oh no, you ain't feeling well. I don't want you to worry about it."

"I'm okay, really. And that's a small box anyway. I can carry it."

"If you're sure."

"I'm sure."

Gus hands me the box, and it's a little heavier than I expected, but I'm grateful for the distraction. This way, I'll be focused on the heavy box instead of my own thoughts.

"What's she need all this fruit for anyway?" Gus asks. "Is she trying out a new recipe or something?"

"No, it's for Zane's surprise party. She's making kabobs."

"Harper still insists it's a surprise, huh?" Gus laughs. "Well, sign me up. I love Elise's cooking."

"We couldn't have the party without you," I say. "Well, have a good night. I'm headed home."

"Get some rest, dear."

~~~

"I've got your fruit from Gus," I say as I set the box down on the kitchen counter.
~~~

"Yes." Elise claps her hands and happily rips the lid off the box, picking up different fruits and smelling them. "They look fantastic. Just in time, too. I want to make a practice batch."

"I'm sure your kabobs will be fine."

"They will be if I do a practice batch," Elise says. "So how was your time with Brent today?"

"It went well. I remember more."

"Really?" Elise says excitedly. "What else do you remember?"

"I remember everything from the first memory of Captain Wilson up until I got here."

"That's fantastic."

"I guess so."

"You're not excited?"

"It was just so hard," I say, dropping on to the sofa. "I've got an awful headache now. It took way too much out of me. Is it really going to be this hard?"

"Not necessarily." Elise sits down on the couch next to me. "Maybe it was just hard because you're just getting started. It doesn't have to be hard forever."

"I'm just so worn out. I don't think I can handle this every single time I try to remember something. I can't even enjoy it and be happy because I'm too exhausted."

"So take it slow."

"I can't." I explain everything to Elise about the law and Cassandra's plan, and the weeks, the measly weeks I have to somehow repair all the pieces of my destroyed life. She listens carefully, more carefully than I've ever seen her listen to me, and waits until I'm thoroughly finished explaining and even listens to a little bit of ranting.

"Can I suggest something crazy?" Elise says after a moment's pause.

"Don't you always?"

"You know what you need to do."

"Oh I do, do I?"

"Yes," Elise says. "You do."

I sigh and close my eyes. "I was hoping you wouldn't say it."

"Maybe you need to go to Trilland."

"And you said it."

"Don't tell me you haven't been thinking it."

"Of course I've been thinking it," I say. "But I don't want to go to Trilland. I don't remember anything."

"That's not true."

"I don't remember *most* things."

"It would help you remember. It's a familiar place."

"What?"

"I'm serious. The letter from the captain is what first jogged a memory. Maybe that's what you need. Maybe seeing the country, meeting people you know, maybe even the captain, will help. It's just an accident you ended up here. Maybe if you were there, you wouldn't be struggling as much."

"That's crazy."

Elise hops up onto the kitchen counter. "I told you it was. But you were thinking it, too, so you must also be crazy."

"I need Captain Wilson. Not all of Trilland."

"Then go find him."

"Finding him means finding Trilland."

"Maybe seeing Trilland would help."

"I couldn't go even if I wanted to."

"But you want to?" Elise asks, and I glare at her. "Look, I never thought Brent was planning on staying here forever, and now you know you're under a time crunch. It's the best idea."

"If I go to Trilland, and I don't know who I am, it'll be a disaster. If Brent is right, and these people need me that badly, I can't show up unable to help them."

"Well, it's the best idea I've got, and I've had it for a while, and clearly so have you. I just haven't wanted to suggest it yet. I wanted you to be more comfortable with yourself, but here we are. I really think this would help you. The plan is not without its flaws, but I think it's what you need."

"I don't know."

"Yes you do."

"Elise."

"Just ask Brent about it. See what he thinks. Maybe talk to Zane, too."

I scoff. "Zane has barely spoken to me since—since everything happened. He's been avoiding me."

"Well he's going to have to get over it, especially if you suggest the idea of your leaving to him. He's still your best friend, and you care about his opinion, right?"

"Right."

"Then talk to him. You guys will get over this hump."

"I can't deal with this right now," I say, getting up off the couch. "I'm going to take a nap. Wake me for dinner?"

"Of course."

I practically slam the door behind me. Elise wasn't supposed to say what I was already thinking. I was hoping she would tell me that idea was crazy. Now I'm left with the realization that I have to go to Trilland, and that is a terrifying idea.

# Chapter 11

I've been avoiding Brent the past few days. I'm glad he was able to piece together a memory, but I'm still exhausted from it. I haven't worked up the energy to go back yet and really try again. Is this how it's going to be to recover my entire memory? Because I just don't know if I'm up to that.

I decided that I needed a break. Maybe spending some time on the island just hanging out again like I used to will help me relax. Harper asked me if I would be willing to take Daisy down to the beach. She doesn't like letting Daisy go alone. I thought about turning her down the other day because I was so tired, but I think this is going to be good for me. It'll give me a chance to have a break and do the things I used to do before Brent arrived. Spending a day with Daisy is an easy, enjoyable, typical activity.

By the time Daisy and I reach the beach, I'm already feeling better. It's a beautiful day, Daisy is chatting on about some boy she thinks is cute, and I feel more at peace than I have in weeks.

"He's just so cute, you know?" Daisy prattles on. "I mean, it's weird because Amy thinks that he likes Chloe, but Francie says that Renee says that Chloe asked his friend Luke, and he said that he doesn't like her, but he wouldn't tell her who he does like. I guess it could be me, but Deena told me that Gina told her that last year he liked Betty, and I don't know if that changed."

"He probably doesn't like the same girl he liked a year ago," I say. "Besides, isn't Betty with Eric?"

"Yeah, but he could be pining. I asked Zane for his opinion, and he told me to just ask him. Can you believe that? Like, I'm just supposed to walk up to Tyler Cochran, of all people, and ask him if he likes me? He's crazy."

"Of course you can't just ask him," I say cheerfully, but my stomach sinks a little at Zane's name.

"Exactly," Daisy says triumphantly. "Boys are so stupid about this stuff."

I can't help but laugh. It seems Daisy and I are both playing our own games of romantic politics.

We reach the beach, and Daisy runs straight for the tide pools, and I spread a blanket on the sand and lie down. The sun feels so good today. It's hot, but there's a nice breeze so it doesn't get too hot. I rub some sunscreen on my arms and a little on my face, the only parts of me that are really prone to burning, and sprawl out, enjoying the smell of the ocean.

Daisy runs back and forth from tide pool to tide pool, looking for something interesting. If you really look, you can find some cool stuff in the tide pools here. Maybe it's because the island is so small, but sea creatures really don't mind coming up pretty far. They slip into the tide pools, and you can see them pretty well since the water is so clear.

This was a good idea. This is a good break from everything. Today, I don't have to think about my memory or Brent or Trilland or Captain Wilson, or anything. I can just focus on having a good day with Daisy.

"There's a cool looking crab in this one," Daisy calls out. "I think it's looking at me."

"Be careful not to touch it. It might pinch you."

"I won't. Ooh, that's a cool looking fish."

Daisy runs to the neighboring tide pool to see what exciting sights await her there, and I sit up and watch the waves. The ocean is fairly calm today. It's a little choppy, but not too bad. I think I'll go for a swim a little later.

"Maris! Come look at this."

I walk over the tide pool where Daisy is crouched over and staring intently at something. When I bend over, mimicking Daisy's position, I see a starfish clinging to the side. It's a really cool looking one. It's kind of orange, but the center is bright purple. I don't think I've ever seen one like this.

"Wow, that's really cool," I say.

"I've never seen a purple starfish before," Daisy says, a huge smile on her face.

"It's a pretty color."

"Did you know that starfish can regrow their legs if they get broken off?" Daisy says.

"Yeah. Pretty neat, right?"

"My mom told me that. When I was eight, Tiny Tommy Pearson cut off a starfish leg, and my mom told me about that so I would stop crying over the starfish."

I smile. "My mom told me about that, too."

"What?" Daisy says excitedly, and it isn't until Daisy points it out that I realize I've just recalled another memory.


*I actually do remember my mother and I talking about starfish. I think I was maybe eleven years old or so. I'm not sure about my age, but I remember that day clearly. I had given a small speech for a charity event, and it had gone badly. My stage fright had taken over, and I flubbed the speech. I ended up running off stage in tears and running straight home. My mom found me on the beach outside the palace. I can't remember the palace, but I remember that beach perfectly. It has little tide pools, just like this.*

*And I remember my mother perfectly. Her black hair, just like mine, was curled to perfection but fell over her shoulders with a life that my hair has never had. Her blue eyes sparkled even when she wasn't doing anything special. They just always sparkled. She always sparkled. Her dress was baby blue, flowy, and made her look angelic, which she kind of was. Her earrings were little roses. She smelled like roses, too. She always smelled like roses because Dad liked roses.*

*I was sitting there in tears watching the fish in the tide pools dart back and forth. My mom came up behind me, practically floating like she always did because she was so graceful, and didn't say anything right away. I remember being grateful that she didn't try to console me or lecture me for leaving or anything like that. She just sat down next to me. After a few minutes of silence, she pointed to a starfish at the edge of the tide pool. It wasn't as pretty as this purple one here today. It was just a plain orange starfish. But I remember exactly what it looked like.*

*"Do you know how strong starfish are?" my mother asked, her voice soft but pretty, like a soft ocean wind through rocks. I shook my head and sniffled. "They are very strong. They are some of the strongest creatures on earth."*

*"That is one of the strongest creatures on earth?" I pointed at the squishy, stationary star and wondered how that thing could possibly be strong at all.*

*"Oh yes," my mother said. "They're practically unbreakable."*

*"But they're so soft and squishy."*

*"That's their secret. They look fragile, but they're not. Let me tell you something really interesting about starfish. If you break a leg off of a starfish, not only will that starfish grow its leg back, but that broken leg will grow a whole new starfish."*

*"What?"*

*"Isn't that cool?" my mother said. "Fishermen used to break starfish because they thought it would kill them, but it didn't. All they did was make more starfish."*

*I sniffled again and avoided eye contact with my mom. I was still upset over what had happened, but my mother knew me well enough to know that a cool story about a starfish would distract me.*

*"You, my dear, are like a starfish. If someone tries to break you, all they'll end up doing is spreading more of your greatness around. It won't be the end of you. It's only the beginning of what you can do."*

It was such a simple analogy, but it made all the difference that day. She not only made me feel better about the botched speech, but she also inspired me for years to come. I never thought the starfish story my mom told me one day to comfort me would be so important to me later.

"Maris." Daisy snaps me back to reality. "Did you just remember something?"

"Yes. I remember something my mom told me once about starfish."

"That's so exciting!"

"It is," I say, smiling to myself. I feel like I did after the first memory I recovered. I feel happy, encouraged, relieved. This is different from my sessions with Brent. I don't feel exhausted or like I don't want to keep trying. This is the way I need to remember things. When I remember naturally, it's exciting.

Maybe Elise is right about Trilland. Maybe Trilland would be an organic method of memory recall. Maybe if I went, I could remember everything this easily. Maybe it really would all come back to me if I saw my home, my country, my people.

But a small, or rather large, part of my brain keeps saying, *But what if it doesn't?* What if going to Trilland doesn't fix my memory, and then I'm stuck there in a position I'm not prepared for? What if it makes things worse? Then I'll be under pressure to remember.

Elise is right. I should ask Brent what he thinks. He'll be able to give me more clarity.

I should ask Zane, too. If he'll even talk to me.

~~~

I drop Daisy off at her house and head straight for Ms. Flora's. When I get there, I don't even stop to talk to her. I go straight to the guest room and swing the door open.

"So I want to ask you something."

"Go for it," Brent says.

"My roommate Elise said something kind of crazy to me the other day."

"Okay. What do you mean?"

"She thinks she has the answer to my memory problem."

"Yeah?"

"Yeah."

"Well?" Brent says. "What is it? What did she say?"

I hesitate before answering. I still think Elise is kind of crazy. Honestly, I still think *I* might be crazy for thinking it, too. "She thinks I need to go to Trilland."

"Go to Trilland?"

"Yes," I say. "She thinks that if I go to Trilland and see everything there and see the people I used to know, then I'll remember. Since the letter from Captain Wilson is what first jogged a memory, she thinks seeing Trilland will act like a bigger, stronger version of the letter."

"Hmm," Brent says, tapping his finger on his knee slowly.

"What do you think?"
~~~

"I like it," Brent says far more enthusiastically than I expected him to. "I agree."

"You agree?"

"Yeah, I think it'll work."

"What?"

"Maybe Trilland *is* the key. It makes sense. They say amnesia patients are supposed to keep everything about their lives the same because the consistency is what recovers their memory. You've had a disadvantage in that regard."

"But—but I can't go to Trilland."

"Why not?"

"I don't remember anything." I thought Brent was going to argue with me. He was so set on my remembering more before doing anything. I think I was hoping he'd say no so that I could back out of the idea.

"That's not true."

"You know what I mean," I say. "If I go back there now, I'll get recognized. People will expect me to be me. I mean, they'll expect me to fix everything and remember everything. I can't do that right now."

"But what if seeing Trilland fixes your memory?"

"But what if it doesn't?"

Brent doesn't answer me right away. I must have gotten to him. He must know I have a really valid point there. He furrows his brow for a few moments before answering me. "I can't guarantee that seeing Trilland will be the answer, but I also can't say that it won't. I think your roommate is right that this has a really good chance of working. I know it's scary, but this could be the answer you've been looking for."

"I guess I'm not as optimistic as you."

He chuckles. "You brought it up."

"I didn't think you'd agree."

"It's worth a shot, isn't it?"

I twist the corner of my mouth. It might be worth a shot, but it could also end really badly. That's why I never said it out loud. I didn't want to make this plan a reality. There are so many ways this could end abysmally and very few ways it ends well.

"How about this?" I say. "You know where Captain Wilson is since he sent you. Why don't we go back to him first? We can go to Gessend and meet up with Captain Wilson first. Then I can spend some time with him. He actually knows me personally, so he can probably do much more for me than I can. Then maybe I'll feel more comfortable about Trilland, and we can go from there with the aid of the captain."

"I don't know about that."

"Why? You think going to Trilland is a good idea but not going to see Captain Wilson? He's the one trying to find me."

"Gessend isn't as familiar to you. It might be more upsetting than going to Trilland."

"How? Trilland will devolve into chaos if I show up."

"So will Gessend."

"But the captain is there, not Trilland." I squint at Brent, and he folds his arms and starts pacing. "Why don't you want me to go meet the captain?"

Brent huffs. "That's not what I'm saying. I'm just worried going to Gessend would mean biting off more than you can chew. Besides, do we really have time to go out of our way when we need to get back to Trilland immediately?"

"Well, going to Gessend makes much more sense to me than Trilland right now."

Brent heaves a long sigh. "We can go to Gessend if you really want to. But I still think Trilland is a good idea. Why did you bring it up if you didn't want to go?"

"I just don't know. I guess I half-expected you to say that Elise was wrong. I didn't think what I would do if you agreed with her."

"Ultimately, it's your choice, but Trilland needs you to make a decision sooner rather than later."

"That's just great."

"We don't have to leave tomorrow. Talk to your friends. But don't wait too long."

"Okay."

"Yeah?"

"Yeah."

"Okay then," Brent says with a smile. "Do you want to get started?"

I nod, but I feel very uneasy about the whole thing, somehow more uneasy than I already felt. Brent has talked of little else than the captain, and now it seems like he wants to keep me away from him. I know he said that's not the reason, but I can't help but feel like Brent isn't being totally honest. I already know he kept information from me. What is he not telling me about Captain Wilson?

# Chapter 12

"**I**'m exhausted," I say.

"Well, we've been at this for hours," Brent says. He delicately avoids saying that this is the fifth day in a row that we've been "at it for hours." Five days and still no progress.

"I feel like I've put in a ton of work, and I only remember a couple of things."

"Hey, that's more than you remembered a few days ago," Brent says. "Don't worry about it. The rest will come."

I collapse in the chair, holding my head in my hands on the desk. I can't keep doing this, but I can't stop. I need to remember. I need to remember more than I've ever needed anything. Brent has been so patient with me, more patient than I've been with myself, but I feel like I'm wasting his time.

"Is that music?" Brent says.

I lift my head and recognize the song playing. It's from the list of songs I gave Harper to have played because they're Zane's favorites. Zane's party is starting, and I completely forgot about it. Maybe Zane's right. Maybe I have been self-absorbed lately.

"It's Zane's birthday party," I say, jumping up and hastily strapping on my shoes. "I have to go."

"Have fun," Brent says, but something about the tone of his voice tells me he's feeling uncomfortable but doesn't want to say anything. It's a feeling I'm well-acquainted with.

"Why don't you come with me," I say. "Everyone's welcome."

"Really? You sure?"

"Yeah. It's going to be a casual party. You should come."

"Sure, that'd be great," Brent says, his smile wide.

Brent and I walk the short distance to the town square, the sound of the music and the laughter of the town intensifying. There are lights hung above the square, and everyone is dancing and celebrating. Luckily, it looks like I didn't miss Zane's entrance. He would have been furious if I had, and I don't need anything else making it awkward between us.

"Hurry, get over here," Elise calls us over. "Tito is bringing Zane up from the beach now."

"Everyone get ready to yell 'surprise,'" Harper says, and everyone nods in agreement and gets ready.

Brent leans in and whispers to me, "Won't he see the lights and hear the music?"

"Of course," I whisper back. "Zane always knows about this party. He just pretends to be surprised to make his mom happy."

"That's sweet."

"It is," I say, and something inside me feels unsteady. I've always thought it was nice the way Zane lets Harper think she's successful. But what is it about Brent saying that that gets to me?

"He's coming! I see them," Harper shouts before crouching down, as if she is actually hiding while standing in plain sight.

We all mimic Harper's pose and jump up and yell "surprise" when Zane and Tito walk up. Zane feigns surprise, just like he always does, and hugs his mom.

"Mom, you didn't have to throw me a party again," Zane says.

"Nonsense," Harper says, waving her arms in her son's face. "You are my only son. I have to celebrate you. It's my duty as your mother."

"Well, you got me there." Zane hugs his mom again. "You pulled off quite the event here."

"I went all out." Harper grabs her son's arm and starts leading him around the party. He spots me and we exchange a quick awkward hold of eye contact before Harper pulls him away. "Elise made kabobs, and they smell delicious. I got Tito to help me hang the lights, Tiana offered to play guitar, and she's got a whole list of songs picked out by Maris."

Zane whips his head around and stares me in the eye. "You picked the music?"

"Yes."

"It's good stuff."

"It's all stuff I know you like."

"Well, then I have good taste," Zane says, and he and I both force a laugh. That's the first light-hearted moment we've had in a while, and yet, it feels extraordinarily heavy.

Zane smiles, and I'm about to say something else, anything else, to keep the good mood going, but Zane looks at Brent, and I see the light go out of his eyes. He puts his hand out to Brent, and Brent shakes it.

"Thanks for coming," Zane says.

"Happy to be here," Brent says.

Zane and Brent stare at each other for a moment before Daisy grabs her brother's arm and leads him off, and he starts shaking hands of all the people who came to celebrate another year of Zane.

"Did you tell him about going to Trilland?" Brent says abruptly.

"No. Why?"

"He seems weird. I thought maybe you had told him, and he was upset."

"I haven't said anything yet. I've only talked to you and Elise."

"Have you decided about Trilland?"

"No. I still don't know if it would help. Besides, I've remembered more. Maybe I just have to be diligent, and more will come."

"Maybe," Brent says. "I still think going would help you."

"I'm still not sure."

"I know," Brent says solemnly and forces a smile. "Just let me know when you decide. And let Zane know, too."

I nod, and Brent wanders off to talk to the few people he's actually met on the island. I stand in the center of town, people celebrating all around me, unable to stop the avalanche of emotions and thoughts that are threatening to crush me. I know why I'm still not sure about Trilland. Aside from my fears about my still faulty memory, I know it's because I haven't talked to Zane yet. I need his opinion even if he's mad at me. I need to know what he thinks. If he thinks it's a good idea, I'll go. If he thinks it's a bad idea, I'll stay. It's that simple. Talking to Zane, however, is not simple. I almost wonder if maybe now is not the time when we're supposed to be celebrating his birthday, but suddenly, it feels like I can't possibly put it off another moment longer.

I weave through the crowd, awkwardly bumping into a few people along the way, and make my way over to the grill where Zane is eating kabobs by biting the entire skewer of fruit and meat off in one bite. Elise smiles at me, and Zane notices, so he turns around to see the recipient of Elise's grin, and he almost looks disappointed when he sees me.

"Enjoying the kabobs?" I ask.

Zane nods, his mouth still stuffed with food. He chews quickly and swallows hard. "Elise's food is the best."

"Hey, can we talk?"

"Right now?"

"It won't take long. Please?"

"Okay," Zane says. "Let's go over there."

I follow Zane out of town square and down the path to my house a little ways. We get far enough that the music is a little less oppressive, and we're far from the lights, so long shadows from the sun setting reach across Zane's face. I take a few deep breaths, careful not to make them too deep that it's noticeable, and prepare myself to look Zane straight in the eye.

"Thanks for helping my mom by picking music," Zane says abruptly.

"What?"

"I just didn't want to forget to thank you for that. My mom has terrible taste in music. Left to her own devices, we'd be listening to bluegrass right now or something weird like that."

I let myself laugh a little. "You're welcome."

"So, you came with Brent, huh?"

"What?"

"Brent," Zane says. "He's obviously with you. You brought him?"

"Well, yeah, sort of. I was with him just before the party, so I just invited him. I figured you wouldn't mind if he came."

"I don't."

"We were just talking. He's been helping me with my memory."

"I know."

"We've made really good progress."

"That's great."

Zane's words are not particularly emotional, and he doesn't say anything hostile, but the tone of his voice and the half-angry half-indifferent look on his face tells me a different story than his words do.

I miss Zane. I feel like the person standing in front of me is just not him.

"I didn't come with him," I say, trying to reassure him. "I just invited him."

"Does he know that?" Zane asks, and I raise my eyebrows in response. "I mean, he's hanging all over you."

"He doesn't really know anyone else."

"He's gotten to know you pretty well."

"I told you, it's not like that."

"You kissed him," Zane hisses. "That means something."

"No it doesn't," I say. "I wasn't thinking. I was excited. It didn't mean anything."

"It meant something to me. You spend all your time with this guy. I never see you anymore. No one does. My mom, Elise, Daisy—no one sees you anymore. You spend every free minute with him."

"Regaining my memory is important to me. You know that."

"This isn't about your memory anymore. That's obvious. This is about him."

"No it's not," I say. "He's helping me."

"He's not your memory, Maris! He's just a guy. By his own admission, he doesn't even know you. He's just some random guy who claims he knows your life story."

"He does know my life story. I remember some of it now."

"That's not because of him."

"You're not going to let this go, are you?"

"Why should I?" Zane says. "You're not letting it go."

"Zane, I didn't want to talk about this," I say, remembering why I dragged him out here in the first place. I don't want to argue with Zane. I need to know if he thinks I should go to Trilland. Sure, he's angry, but he'll still be honest with me. "I wanted to ask for your advice."

"Since when do you care?"

"I've always cared. Your opinion means everything to me."

"Just ask what Brent thinks. That's all you care about anyway."

Zane's words hurt, but what hurts more is his expression. I've never seen his eyes so vacant, so void of any kind of concern or sympathy. He's looking at me like he's never cared about me at all. I'd almost rather see some kind of hurt in his eyes because at least that would mean he cares, but his anger clouds them, and I can't see anything else. Maybe there is nothing else.

"I'm going to Trilland," I say suddenly, and I'm surprised I blurted it out like that.

"What?" Zane says.

"I'm going to Trilland. Brent thinks it'll help my memory. Plus, we'll be able to see Captain Wilson. I think it just might help."

"So go then," Zane says, walking past me toward the party. "Good luck."

Zane walks back to the square without looking back at me even though I watch him and desperately hope he does. I thought he would try to stop me. I thought he would say it was a stupid idea. The way he was acting during that whole conversation, I even could have expected him to tell me that I'm just falling for Brent's lies or something. But not a single scenario I thought up included Zane telling me to go. And it certainly didn't involve him telling me to go *like that.*

I think I wanted him to try to stop me. I think I was hoping that if Zane said I shouldn't go like I thought he would, I could justify my own fear about going. But I guess that's not how it's going to be.

I turn my back on the party when I can no longer see Zane. I start the walk toward my house instead of returning to the square. I wonder if Elise has any bags I could borrow to pack my stuff into.

I guess I'm going to Trilland.

<h1 style="text-align:center">Chapter 13</h1>

E lise can't understand how I packed so lightly. I only borrowed one bag from her, and it's not very big. But what do I really need to take? I've got clothes, shoes, and minimal toiletries. What else could I possibly pack?

"Do you want to borrow some sunglasses?" Elise calls from her room.

"No."

"Are you sure you won't want them in Trilland?"

"If I don't use them here, then I don't think I'll use them there."

"What about your green skirt? You look great in it."

"Elise, that's *your* skirt," I say. "Besides, I've got enough clothing already. I kind of feel like I've packed too much, actually."

"That's impossible. All you've got is that teeny tiny bag."

"That's all I need."

"Fine." Elise sighs. "There's nothing more I can do here."

Elise is definitely overestimating how much clothing I'll need to take with me, but her mention of her green skirt reminds me that there is something else I could bring. I go to the dresser, open that bottom drawer, and grab the green shirt and black skirt from when I arrived. They're not as nice as they once were, but they're still the nicest clothing I own. Who knows? A nice outfit might come in handy.

As I shove the folded clothes into my bag, Elise walks into my room and smiles, but she looks a little down.

"Hey, don't be sad. I'm not leaving forever."

"You might be," Elise says. "If you go there and remember everything, you'll probably stay. You'll want to stay so you can help Trilland if it's as bad as Brent says."

I hadn't thought about that. I hadn't considered what would happen if I got my memory back. I've been so focused on just getting it back that I didn't think about what I would do if it happened. Will I come back here? Will I stay in Trilland? Which outcome am I even hoping for at this point?

"We'll see each other again," I say, and I do believe at least that. Even if I decide to stay in Trilland, I'll have to come back to get the rest of my stuff and to say goodbye to everyone. That seems like a weird outcome to consider.

"Soon, I hope," Elise says, putting her arms around me and giving me a firm hug.

"Me, too."

"Ready?"

I nod, and Elise grabs my bag, despite my protests, and we head out the door and start toward town square.

Elise and I don't say much during the walk to the town square. I think we're both trying to keep it together at least until I board the ship. Brent managed to get in contact with a friend from Gessend who has a ship and crew. I'm not sure why Captain Wilson didn't come himself. He never did reply to any of Brent's letters. Maybe he never got them.

I can see the ship in the distance. It's exciting to see, but it's also kind of ominous. I don't remember much about anything that isn't this island. The little I remember about Trilland is patchy and scattered at best. And that doesn't even account for the stop in Gessend we have to make to pick up Captain Wilson. As far as I know or can remember, I've never been to Gessend. It's owned by Trilland, but I don't know what to expect.

When we reach the town square, I see that the entire town has gathered to see me off. I smile a little to myself. It's nice knowing that everyone is so concerned about me that they came out so early in the morning to see me go.

Brent walks up beside me carrying his own bag. "Hey. You ready? You got everything?"

"Sort of," Elise says with a smirk.

"I'm ready," I say. "I just want to say goodbye to everyone first."

Brent takes my bag from Elise. "Of course. I'll be down at the beach when you're ready."

Brent shakes a couple of hands before heading down to the beach. I scan the crowd, but I don't see Zane. I know we had a fight at his party last week, but it's been a while. I'm sure he'll show up to say goodbye. He's probably just helping the fishermen or something.

"Good luck." Elise gives me one last hug. "Everything will turn out great."

"Thank you."

Elise gives my back a quick rub before stepping aside and absorbing into the crowd. Ms. Flora steps up next and gives me a gentle hug.

"Have a good trip," she says. "I hope everything works out for you."

"Thanks," I say. "And thank you for all your help. I'd probably be much worse off if it weren't for you."

"You are very welcome. I'm glad I could help."

Tito steps up behind Ms. Flora and smiles. "Hope it works out."

"Me too," Gus says, pushing Tito aside. "You're gonna be great, sweetheart." Gus hands me a mango. "One for the trip."

"Thanks Gus. It smells great."

I shake a few more hands and hug a few more necks before I'm practically tackled by Daisy who wraps her arms around my neck and giggles.

"Good luck, Maris," she says. "If you are a princess, you have to promise to let me see your tiara."

I laugh. "I promise, Daisy. Are you here alone?"

"No." Daisy points behind her at her mother, but I don't see the person I was hoping Daisy would point to. Zane isn't anywhere near his mother.

"Good luck, honey." Harper hugs me and strokes my hair. "And keep in touch."

"Oh, I'll be back," I say. "Thank you for everything you've done for me. You can't know what it means to me."

"You've been a wonderful friend, dear. Not just to me."

Harper smiles, and something in her eye tells me she's talking about her son.

"Zane?" I ask tentatively. I'm afraid of asking, but I'm more afraid of not knowing.

Harper shakes her head slowly. "He left early this morning. He said he didn't want to come."

"You're sure?"

"I'm sorry, dear." Harper rubs my arm. "He's being stupid, if you ask me."

"Thank you, Harper."

"Have fun, sweetie."

I walk through the crowd, wave to a few kids, and make my way to the beach with the entire town following. Brent helps me board the ship, and I wave goodbye to the townspeople from the railing of the ship. As soon as the sails are let down and the wind starts propelling the ship forward, I feel an uneasiness. What really awaits me in Trilland?

# Chapter 14

Being on this ship is bringing back a lot of memories, and even though it's nice to remember things again, I could do without remembering the mutiny right now. It's making me really seasick and uncomfortable with sailing. I didn't used to be. I remember that. I used to even like sailing. But now, it just reminds me of the day the crew mutinied. My stomach is in knots, and I can't seem to relax.

That also might be because of the way I left things with Zane. I didn't want to have that fight with him. I didn't want to leave while he was still angry with me, but he left me no choice. I had to leave. I have to get to Trilland. I have to see things for myself. My memory has come back to me in pieces, and going to Trilland might be the final piece. I need this to finally understand.

I cling to the wall of the cabin and try to keep from hurling for the second time since I got on the ship. I don't like this captain. I remember liking the way Captain Wilson handled his ships. He steered with such precision and skill that the effects of the waves were minimized. This captain doesn't have such aptitude. I can't wait until we get to Gessend and get him back. Maybe he can stabilize this thing and therefore my stomach.

Plus, I'm dying to see him. I feel like he will be able to help me more than anyone else. This stupid, nauseating, naval journey is worth it just to see Captain Wilson again.

I risk a glance out the window, but I can't look for long before the movement starts to make me ill. It's pretty foggy outside, so it's not like I can see waves sloshing around or anything, but I can see the ship moving up and down.

Normally I like the fog. I don't know if I've always liked the fog, but there's something relaxing about it. I kind of like knowing that sometimes, even just for a few minutes, the rest of the world is as confused as I am. Being unable to see what's right in front of you somehow makes the darkness in your mind a little less unsettling.

"Hey." Brent opens the cabin door, and I try to stand up straight and appear not ill. "Still feeling sick?"

"I'll be all right," I lie, both to Brent and myself. "How far are we?"

"Not far," Brent says. "We should be there within the hour. Nervous?"

"Not about Captain Wilson. I'm excited to see him. I'm nervous about getting back to Trilland."

"It'll be fine." Brent puts his arms around me and holds me close. "Once we pick up Captain Wilson and get over to Trilland, you'll feel much better. It's just the anticipation, the not knowing what's going to happen."

"You're probably right," I say. I wish Zane were here. He'd make me feel so much better about this. "But I still don't remember everything. What if I get there, and the people think I've come to save them, and I just can't?"

"You might just have to be honest with them about how you're feeling right now," Brent says. "But I wouldn't worry about that just yet. Just take this one step at a time. First, Captain Wilson. Then we'll worry about what you do and don't remember."

"Deal." I smile, and Brent hugs me again. I choke back the nausea that's still filling the back of my throat and try not to think too much.

Brent is right. I need to focus on Captain Wilson right now. I can't think about Trilland or Cassandra or Zane right now, even though that's basically impossible. I'll drive myself crazy if I think about everything all at once.

~~~

I sleep for the rest of the trip to Gessend because I just can't take the sea sickness anymore. Brent wakes me up when we reach Gessend, and I scramble to look presentable after sleeping and vomiting the whole way here. I haven't seen Captain Wilson in a year, and everything is so different now. I don't want to add "looks terrible" to the list of things I've become since he last saw me. I pull my hair back into a ponytail and borrow some makeup from the ship captain's daughter in hopes of making myself look less sick. I don't know when I last wore makeup that Elise didn't force on me, or if I ever have, but it feels so natural to put on.

I decide to bite the bullet and put on the green shirt, the one I grabbed last minute that used to be mine, and wear it with an old pair of jeans. I can remember wearing it the day of the mutiny, and even though it still doesn't feel like me, it's a nice shirt, and maybe wearing green will distract from how green my face must be.

"You ready?" Brent knocks on the cabin door. "The boat is waiting."

"Yeah, I'm good." I throw open the door in a hurry, nearly hitting Brent in the face. I tug on my ponytail to make sure it's secure, smooth my shirt, and start forward, but Brent is just staring at me. "What?"

"You just—you look beautiful," he says, eyes wide.

"Really? I was just trying not to look seasick."

"You don't look seasick. You look—uh—"

"I look what?"

Brent shakes his head. "Nothing. Ready?"
~~~

Brent holds out his arm, and I take it as he helps me into the boat we're taking to shore. It's a short paddle to the island, which is great because I still don't feel comfortable on the waves.

We reach the shore, and I'm startled to find that Gessend is a much more populated island than my little one. The shore is buzzing with people, unlike my sleepy little town, and suddenly, after days wishing I could reach land and get off the boat, I'm terrified to step on shore. Somewhere in that crowd of people might be Captain Wilson, probably the only person left that can really tell me about myself because he knew me. I've been waiting for this for so long, and now I'm terrified to see it through.

The entire group we brought ashore gets off the boat before I even realize what's happening, leaving only me and Brent left. Brent nudges me gently and rubs my back.

"Hey," he says softly, so only I can hear. "You okay?"

I nod, but I feel excessively panicky. I feel like I might be sick again even though the boat's not moving.

"It's going to be all right." Brent takes my hand and kisses it. "Remember, this is a good thing."

"I know, I know." I wave my hand at him and try to make myself believe it.

"Come on." Brent nods toward the crowd. "Let's go. My house isn't far from here."

"Your house?" I ask. "Aren't we looking for Captain Wilson?"

"Of course," Brent says. "But it's already getting late. I think it'll be best just to rest tonight, get some dinner, that kind of thing. You'll be better prepared to see Captain Wilson tomorrow."

"But—"

"Trust me, Lorraine." Brent takes my hand and helps me get out of the boat. Did we really travel all this way just to wait?

We start walking toward the crowd. I feel kind of disconnected from my body, like I'm aware that I'm walking, but somehow, I don't feel my legs actually moving. My vision is distorted, like the colors aren't as vivid as they should be. Is your vision going black and white a sign of a heart attack or a stroke?

I guess I look as bad as I feel because Brent gives my hand a squeeze, trying to reassure me. The closer we get to the crowd, the weirder I'm feeling. Several people are staring at me like their long lost friend who has finally come home. *People recognize me.* They all seem so excited. They don't even know me. At least, I'm pretty sure they don't. To them, I'm just some political figure. Why do they care so much about someone who is basically a politician? More importantly, why do they care so much about a politician who can't even *remember* them?

"Brent—" I clutch Brent's arm, and he turns and smiles at me.

"It's fine. Just keep walking."

The crowd parts a little, and most people stop staring at me. There's one older woman whose eyes seem like they're trying to bore straight into my brain, but otherwise, everyone else has let it go. Brent pulls me to the left very suddenly, and I'm grateful to find that we're on an isolated gravel road.

Once I'm sure we're out of earshot from anyone, I say, "They were all staring at me."

"They know who you are."

"How can you say that so calmly?"

Brent sighs. "They don't think they're looking at the princess of Trilland. You've been missing for a year. Everyone thinks you're dead. Most of them probably think you just bear a striking resemblance to her. That's why they're staring."

"And if they figure out who I am? What do I say?"

"You're not going to be giving a press conference. Trust me, people in Gessend aren't as nosy as the people on your island. They'll leave you alone."

I'm not happy with Brent's answer, but what can I do at this point? I'll just have to wait until tomorrow. Maybe it is better to meet Captain Wilson when I'm not still seasick.

Of course, I'm not really meeting him per se, but still.

Brent pushes open the door to a little beach bungalow, and a little bit of dust floats through the air. He flips on the lights, and I have to stifle a laugh. Brent's interior decorating skills are atrocious. He's got one really ugly dark brown sofa, a wooden stool, and no other furniture or decor. He clearly lives alone, and no one helped him decorate.

"Sorry, it's a little dusty," Brent says. "Obviously, I haven't been home in a while."

I wander around the room, which is basically just one giant living room with a wall that acts as a kitchen, and I'm kind of surprised to find that, despite the hideous furniture, it's not all that different from my house that I share with Elise. It's little and homey and beachy. That's comforting, at least. Something familiar.

"Here," Brent says, taking my bag from me. "I'll put your bag in my room. I'll sleep on the couch."

"You don't have to do that. I can sleep on the couch."

"Don't be silly. It's fine."

I follow Brent into his room and find it's pretty similar to the main space: just a plain wooden frame bed with black sheets and a small desk in the corner. Strangely, the room is a little reminiscent of his room at Ms. Flora's. I guess that explains why he was so comfortable there. Frankly, I'm glad for that.

"The sheets are clean, I promise," Brent says. "I cleaned before I left."

"You were that sure you'd find me?"

Brent shrugs. "Well, I just wanted it to be clean, but yeah. Captain Wilson was so sure that I had no choice but to be also."

"Where is his house, by the way? If it's close, I see no reason why we can't go over tonight, even just briefly."

"It's not close," Brent says a little too loudly. "Look, it's late, and he goes to sleep really early. We'll catch him first thing in the morning. Besides, there will be fewer people out in the morning. Trust me. Are you okay with halibut for dinner? My neighbor is a fisherman, and he always sells me fish for a good price."

"Sure."

"Be right back."

Brent leaves, and I poke around his room a little. I don't know why he's being so hostile about Captain Wilson. Isn't that the whole reason we came here? A part of me has the urge to just walk outside, ask someone for directions to his house, and go there myself. But of course, the larger part of me stays put. If I've waited a year, I can wait a few more hours.

Brent has several pictures of me on his desk, which is kind of creepy, but I figure Captain Wilson would've given him several pictures if he wanted him to find me. What's even creepier is that all of the pictures of me show me wearing a lot of jewelry and nice clothing. They're all headshots, so I can't see the whole outfit, but what I can see looks nice. I've never seen myself wearing anything other than tank tops, shorts, and swimsuits. At least, I haven't in the last year. There's also a few old newspapers sitting underneath the pictures of me. I pull one out and start reading. It's the newspaper from when I went missing.

The headline reads "Princess Lorraine Lost at Sea: Trilland Mourns." I skim the article, and it's just a summary of the fake storm story.

Obviously, this is completely impossible, but I wish I could have been there, in Trilland, when I went missing. I want to know how people reacted. Other than Brent's story, which may or may not be reliable, this newspaper is the closest I've ever come to knowing what it was like. It's comforting and also terrifying to think that the country was this upset. I'm glad to know I mean so much, but can I really handle meaning that much to an entire country?

Brent bursts through the front door and scares me half to death. "I'm back. Are you ready for dinner?"

"Yeah." I set the newspaper down and head out to Brent's kitchen, itching to get out of here as soon as possible.

~~~

The waves don't crash against the shore quite the same way here as they do back home. They seem louder, harsher. I always thought the waves were too loud outside Elise's cottage, but I think they're actually louder here. I hope they're not louder still in Trilland.

I shuffle through my bag and silently curse at realizing that Elise was right: I have nothing to wear to meet Captain Wilson. I should have packed something nicer, or at least not worn the one nice thing I have yesterday. She'll never let me hear the end of it. I guess cream linen pants will have to do. They look kind of good on me even though they are crazy wrinkled from being shoved in a bag in a hurry. I throw on a royal blue tee that looks good with the loose pants, and royal blue seems appropriate right now.

"Hey," Brent says as I walk out. "I made pancakes."

I smile to myself. The last time I ate pancakes was when Elise made them for me after Brent got here. But just as quickly as I smile at one memory, I feel sad at another, remembering Zane. I still can't believe
~~~

he didn't say goodbye, even though we were fighting. The Zane I thought I knew would never have done that.

"Are pancakes okay?"

"Yeah, they're fine, but it's like, noon."

"So?"

"It's lunch time."

"You're telling me you don't eat pancakes all day?"

"Well, no, I do. I don't know, I guess I'm just still asleep."

Brent laughs and keeps cooking. I'm surprised that he didn't wake me up. I would have liked to get an early start. What if Captain Wilson is busy? I mean, I'm sure he made time to see me, but it's stressing me out to keep delaying this.

"So, I was thinking we could go over to the beach today. It's nothing like your beach, but it's still really pretty."

"I don't know, maybe. Depends on what happens with Captain Wilson."

"Oh no, I was thinking we could go now. It's perfect weather."

"Now?"

"Yeah," Brent says. "Trust me, it's really pretty."

"I believe you, but we came here for Captain Wilson."

"We'll see him. I just don't want to bombard him."

"Well I kind of do," I say. "I didn't really come here as a tourist."

"Doesn't mean you can't see the sights."

"Brent."

"Captain Wilson won't mind."

"I do mind," I say. "I'm getting increasingly irritated with you. Is there a reason you don't want me to see Captain Wilson?"

"Lorraine, of course not," Brent says, but something about his body language suggests otherwise. He keeps shifting back and forth and fidgeting with his fingers. "I just don't want you to rush things.

Besides, he's not expecting us until tonight. The trip was faster than I thought it would be."

"Really?"

"Yes. He's expecting us tonight. He's meeting us in the square."

I sigh loudly. "Fine. Beach?"

You'll love it, I promise."

Brent and I eat an awkward breakfast. Well, awkward for me. Brent's totally oblivious to how awkward this is. He just keeps talking about how great the beach is and all the different things he loves about Gessend, but I couldn't care less. I don't think I'll be able to care about any of it until after I meet Captain Wilson. Maybe not even then.

~~~

Usually I like the beach, but the sand here is coarse, and it's irritating me almost as much as Brent is. I've just been lying on the beach for hours. I'm tired of being here, but every time I suggest leaving, Brent shoots me down.

"Hey," Brent says suddenly, "want to go swimming?"

I shake my head. "No. I don't really like swimming."

"I caught you swimming at the inlet on your island."

"That's different. It's not the ocean."

"It is."

"It's not," I say. "There're no waves there. It's not at all the same."

"Fair enough."

Brent runs off to the water and dives in, and I'm left on the beach once again. I think in any other circumstance I might have enjoyed today, but right now, I'm just irritated by everything. I can't focus on anything else, and I don't want to focus on anything else. Somewhere on this island is Captain Wilson, waiting to see me. If I knew this island better, and if I weren't afraid to be recognized by someone, I might
~~~

wander and try to find him. Yet here I sit, waiting for Brent to want to go see Captain Wilson.

Brent comes back from the water with a smile. "You sure you don't want a swim?" Brent asks, shaking his hair and scattering water all over me. "The water is the perfect temperature."

"I'm sure."

Brent sits down and starts towel drying. This is it. We are going now. I'm going to make this happen.

"Brent."

"Hmm?"

"We need to go. Now."

"Lorraine—"

"No. You have officially put this off for an entire day, and I'm tired of it. I want to go now."

"There's no need to rush."

"You've been rushing me for weeks. I'm fine. I want to see him."

Brent sighs. "Fine. We'll go see if we can find him, but it's still too early."

Brent reluctantly grabs his stuff and I follow, happy that I was finally assertive for once in my life.

"But Lorraine, I think we—"

"No, Brent. We are going now."

"I was just going to say that we should go home and change."

I stay quiet for a minute. That's a good point. "Fine. We have to be fast though."

"Yeah, I got it."

We go home, I change quickly, but Brent takes forever. I put on the same outfit I had on this morning and wait impatiently for Brent. When he finally emerges, he looks irritated, and it bothers me, but I'm almost beyond caring.

"Okay, we're going to have to go to the square, and it's going to be crowded this late. People might recognize you."

I take a deep, shaky breath. "That's fine." It is, in fact, not fine, but I can't let Brent know that now. He might try to delay again.

"Just stay close."

I nod, and we head to the square. It's not a long walk since the island is so small. There are no people around us at all until we hit the square, and then suddenly there's a massive crowd. People are looking at me kind of strangely, and it freaks me out, but I try not to think about it.

The deeper we walk into the square, the more people stare. They seem obsessed with me. People are staring a lot. Some people are smiling, and others look concerned, but all of them look at least somewhat excited, which is absolutely terrifying.

Suddenly, the crowd starts to part as Captain Wilson pushes his way through. I guess he spotted me. He's got a bad limp, and it seems like every step is a struggle. I don't remember him having a limp, but that probably doesn't mean much considering my recent mental history.

When Captain Wilson reaches us, he barely glances at Brent before throwing his arms around me in a tight embrace. Being hugged by Captain Wilson is comforting and familiar. Even though he's hugging more tightly than I would prefer, and I still feel way too nauseous for that, it feels nice to find something that feels familiar. I think I can hear him crying into my shoulder, but I don't call him on it. It's nice to know someone outside of the tiny village I've been living in for a year cares about me.

When Captain Wilson finally releases, he moves his hands down to hold each of my hands in his and smiles wide. "Lorraine, I'm so glad that you're okay. I was worried I'd never see you again."

I nod and smile, but I don't know what to say, and it's really awkward. I want to say something, I want to reciprocate, but I just can't. I look to Brent for help, and he steps forward.

"Captain, can we go somewhere private and talk?" Brent says, and Captain Wilson nods, so we both follow him into the village, leaving the crowd behind on the beach.

Captain Wilson leads us to a small little beach bungalow, lights a few lanterns, and gestures for us to sit down. He doesn't really have much furniture, but Brent and I manage to find a couple wooden stools tucked under the counter to sit on. Captain Wilson pulls up his desk chair and stares admiringly at me.

"Sorry for the excitement on the beach, but everyone in the village was so excited to see you again. How are you? How did you like the townspeople? It's a nice little village, isn't it?"

Captain Wilson keeps firing questions, and something strikes me as weird about the way he's talking to me. I look at Brent, who's the only one who's had contact with him this whole time, and he seems uncomfortable. He's been so calm this whole time. What shook him up?

"I'm sorry, I'm babbling." Captain Wilson chuckles. "It must be overwhelming."

"What do you mean?" I ask.

"Well, I mean coming back after all this time. It's been so long since you've seen any of the kingdom. It's a lot to reacclimate yourself to."

"It's more so the fact that I don't know any of this that is overwhelming me right now," I say.

"What do you mean?" Captain Wilson leans in, looking very confused.

"What do *you* mean?" I say.

"I know this island isn't part of the mainland kingdom, but you visited it many times when you were little. You know all about it. Don't you remember?"

"No, I don't," I say. Suddenly it's starting to click. "Captain Wilson, do you know why I haven't come back for a year?" Captain Wilson shakes his head with a confused look on his face. "I've had amnesia for a year, ever since the mutiny when you sent me to that island."

"You *what*?" Captain Wilson shakes his head in disbelief. "Brent, why didn't you tell me that in your letters?"

"Yes, Brent, why?" I say. I can't believe he didn't tell Captain Wilson about my amnesia. What has the Captain been thinking all this time about why I never came back?

"I was so sure that I could help you get your memory back before you would ever see Captain Wilson. I didn't want to worry him by telling him if I was just going to fix it."

"Well you didn't *fix it*," I snap. "You just lied to me and Captain Wilson this whole time. You know I've been struggling with this, and you knew I was worried about coming back to Trilland, and you lied to me. What about all those people on the beach? Do they know?"

"They know only what I've told them," Captain Wilson says quietly. "So no."

"I really thought it would be for the best," Brent says. "I really thought you'd remember by now. I didn't mean to be deceptive, but I hoped it would all work out."

"But it didn't," I say. "All that happened is that you lied to us."

"Lorraine, please, I—"

"Stop," Captain Wilson stands. "Maybe you should just go home. We'll talk tomorrow. Lorraine can stay here with me."

Brent nods solemnly and walks out the door, taking just a moment to look back at me, but I purposefully avoid eye contact. When the door finally closes, I hear Captain Wilson sigh with relief.

"I'm sorry, I had no idea what was happening," he says.

"It's not your fault."

"Are you okay? This whole thing must be terribly overwhelming for you. Do you remember anything at all?"

"Bits and pieces have come back to me in recent days, but I don't remember everything. I spent the last year not knowing anything. Not even my name."

"My goodness, that's terrible." Captain Wilson shakes his head. "How did you start to remember?"

"Actually, your letter jogged the first memory," I say. "When I read your letter and saw your picture, I remembered our conversation just before you put me in the lifeboat. That was the first thing to come back."

"Glad I could help." Captain Wilson smiles. "So you didn't remember anything until then?"

I shake my head. "And I've only remembered pieces since then. I was hopeful that coming back to Trilland would jog the rest of it."

"Well, I certainly hope so. But if you go over to the mainland, and you don't remember everything, or at least enough, you're going to feel completely consumed by the people there. They've all missed you for so long."

I hold my head in my hands. "That's so much pressure. I'm so afraid of letting everyone down."

"You just being alive is enough. You won't let anyone down."

Tears stream down my face. "Yes, I will. If I can't remember anything, how am I supposed to help these people?"

Captain Wilson pats my knee gently. "Just because you can't remember who you were doesn't mean you're not still that person. You can still be the leader you were destined to be even if you only have a patchy memory. And I will help you," he says, and I nod slowly, still hiding behind my hands. "You don't have anything to fear. It will all be okay. You won't be alone."

"It's just all so scary," I whisper. "And I thought I'd have Brent's help, and now I don't know if I want it."

Captain Wilson smiles and takes my hand. "We can worry about Brent tomorrow. You need to rest tonight. Take the cot in my room. I'll sleep out here."

"Oh no, I don't want to put you out." I wipe a tear from my cheek. "Besides, there's no furniture out here."

Captain Wilson waves his hand dismissively. "I'll be fine. I've got a hammock somewhere. Worse comes to worse, I'll borrow something from the neighbors. Don't you worry about anything except getting some sleep."

Captain Wilson pushes up from the chair with a groan and starts limping across the room. Obviously my memory cannot be trusted, but I'm so sure that he didn't have a limp before.

"Captain Wilson?"

"Yes?"

"What happened to your leg?"

Captain Wilson looks down at his leg like he wasn't aware there was a problem. He rubs his thigh and chuckles a little.

"Injury from the mutiny," he says. "I broke my leg. It was pretty ugly and I didn't get medical attention until much later, after I got to Gessend. Plus, I had to try to swim on it. It's just sore and kind of arthritic."

"That's terrible."

Captain Wilson shrugs. "It honestly could've been worse. But it took me a while to get back on my feet. Literally." He laughs. "The only thing I'm sorry about is the time I lost while recovering that I could have been trying to get to you."

"You did everything you could." I look at his leg, and my own starts to fidget. "Do you think it'll ever be the same again? Your leg, I mean."

"Don't worry about it. I'm okay. Get some sleep now."

I nod and head into the small bedroom. It's a tiny room, probably originally a closet or something, and it doesn't even have a door. I let my hair down and shake it out, letting the slight curl from having the ponytail all day wrap around my shoulders. I sit down on the bed and sigh. I wish I could talk to Zane. He's been my best friend for a year. I could really use him right now.

But he's not here, and I can't reach him. Even if I could, I doubt he'd talk to me. I feel so terrible about what happened. I don't even care who was in the wrong anymore, I just wish we could pretend it never happened and go back to the way things were. Or maybe I wish things were different between us. I just don't know. I don't feel much like Lorraine Everhart right now, and I wish I could just be Maris for a moment, but without Zane, I feel like Maris is lost, and if I'm not Maris and I'm not Lorraine, then who am I?

I wish my parents weren't dead. I still can't remember them except for vague, blurry memories of them, but I can't help but feel like they would be able to help me right now. Isn't that what parents do? Maybe my mom would give me a comforting hug and stroke my hair or something. Maybe my dad would offer some advice—

My dad's advice! I almost forgot. Maybe Captain Wilson remembers what that advice was. Maybe it will help.

I tiptoe out into the living room, calling softly for Captain Wilson. When I turn the corner, however, I see Captain Wilson laying on the floor. I guess he gave up on the idea of getting the hammock and decided just to sprawl out on the floor. He's snoring pretty loudly, I don't know how I didn't notice it before. How did he even fall asleep that fast?

I creep back into the bedroom and lie down on the scratchy cot. No advice from my parents, no Zane, no Brent. What am I supposed to do? How on earth am I supposed to go to Trilland like this? I can't even ask Elise for her opinion because she's not here either. I just wish someone would tell me what to do.

# Chapter 15

When I wake up the next morning, I feel like I haven't slept at all. I'm exhausted by the day before it's even begun. I climb off the cot, and my back is pretty sore. How has Captain Wilson been sleeping on this for a year? No wonder he didn't seem to care about sleeping on the floor.

I walk over to the window and push the linen curtain back and let the sun in. The sun makes this room seem less dreary and makes me feel at least a little bit better. As long as the sun continues to rise, life can't be too bad, right?.

I guess either Brent or Captain Wilson brought my luggage over because it's sitting neatly on the floor by the cot. I grab some shorts and a tank from my bag and get dressed, pulling my hair back into a ponytail. It's still really early, and if this village is anything like my town back home, no one will be up this early, so I shouldn't have to worry about my appearance. It's weird having to think about stuff like that, but these people are expecting a princess, not an island girl with a messed up head.

Captain Wilson is still asleep in the living room, so I leave him to sleep in. He probably needs the rest anyway. I need him feeling his best when we go to Trilland.

I don't know this island well, and I probably shouldn't be wandering around by myself, but taking walks early in the morning is the only time I feel like I can think clearly. This island is fairly similar to my own anyway, just rockier. My island is sandy and tropical, but this island is rocky and rugged.

I decide it's probably best to stick to some kind of trail since I'm not used to the landscape here. I follow the trail into town and observe all the little shops and homes, just like my own town. The sound of the gravelly path underneath my bare feet is strangely satisfying. It's like when I kick pebbles around at home. It makes a delightful crunch with each step I take, and I feel in control.

I hear a rustling sound in the trees to my left, so I stop and listen, hoping it's not some kind of animal. Animals never disturb the town back home, but what if it's different here? I take a step closer, and I hear giggling, and I relax. It's just a couple of kids.

"Hello?" I call out. A little girl about six years old peeks around the wide trunk of a palm tree. "You're up awfully early."

"So are you," the little girl says, and her friend giggles from behind the tree.

I walk up to the tree slowly so I don't spook them. I put my hands on my hips and mock surprise. "Are you two spying on me?"

An explosion of giggles. "No!" the girl behind the tree shouts.

"We just wanted to see you," the other says. "Up close."

I kneel in the grass next to them. "Yesterday was pretty crazy wasn't it?" I say, and they nod. "There are a lot of people in this village."

"Well, you're back." The first girl smiles brightly. "We wanted to see you."

I force a half-hearted smile. "Do you remember me?"

The first shakes her head, tossing what was clearly her mother's hairstyle all over the place. "I was too little. But I've seen pictures. And I've heard stories. You're the best princess ever."

The two little girls smile wide and stare at me like I'm the greatest thing ever to happen to them, like I am a real princess. I guess I am, but I still don't feel like one. Did I ever feel like one? I wish I could remember.

"Are you going to make everyone happy again?" The second girl stares up at me with her big, brown eyes. "My mommy says you will make everything happy again."

Tears sting my eyes, but I force them back so I don't upset them. What if I let them down? "I'm going to do my best," I say with a smile. "I'm going to go for a walk now. Stay out of trouble." I wink, and the girls giggle wildly.

I manage to find my way back to the beach where we arrived. Since I can't go to my usual cliff to be alone and think, I figure this will be a good substitute. There is a group of men getting some fishing in early in the morning off to my left, but I'm far enough away that we shouldn't bother each other. Besides, I like seeing them fish. It reminds me of home.

I sit down in the sand, stretching my legs out so the waves just reach my feet when they climb up the shore. The water is a little bit cold, but it feels good after walking down that gravel path. I shove my hand into the sand and pull out a fistful, watching it slip through my fingers, the way I do at home. The sand here is coarser and darker, but the effect is the same: it relaxes me. Watching the sand slowly drift away is kind of therapeutic.

I watch the fishermen for a few minutes, and I can appreciate their work. It's slow, quiet, but so very important to this village. They seem comfortable with their jobs, only occasionally talking to each other, but always smiling or whistling. They notice me, one or two of them wave, but they don't bother me, and I don't bother them. We have an unspoken understanding, both parties agreeing that solitude is necessary at this moment.

But I'm not alone. I was so wrapped up in watching the fishermen that I didn't hear someone come up behind me. Now that they tap me on the shoulder, I jump badly. I wonder if maybe the girls followed me, but when I turn around, I see someone I simultaneously want to see and don't want to see: Brent.

"Don't scare me like that," I say.

"Sorry." Brent takes a step back. "I didn't mean to startle you. What are you doing up so early?"

"I'm always up early." I face the ocean again and fold my arms around my knees. "I like the solitude," I say, hoping he'll get the hint, but he either doesn't understand or doesn't care.

"You could've gotten lost wandering around by yourself." Brent sits down in the sand next to me, and I scoot away. "Lorraine, can't we just talk?"

I hug my knees closer to me. "I don't want to talk."

"You and I both know that's a lie."

"No, it's not," I say forcefully. "If I tell you that I don't want to talk, then I don't want to talk. Don't think that just because I'm a girl or that I'm quiet that you can just ignore me. What do I have to do to get you to listen to me?"

I didn't look at Brent the whole time I sputtered that out, but now that I do risk a glance over at him, I'm startled by his expression. I guess I expected to see anger, defiance, maybe even a smirk of disbelief. But I see none of those expressions. What I do see is a look of pure awe and almost excitement. He seems somewhat elated that I just yelled at him.

"What?" I snap, feeling kind of irritated at his response.

"That—that was amazing. It was just like you used to be."

Well that was unexpected. "What do you mean?"

"You just—you told me off. You just sat there and—you just let me have it."

"And that makes you happy?" I say in disbelief, irritation still creeping into my voice.

Brent nods. "Yes, it does. I knew you could be yourself again. Take that attitude with you to Trilland, and Cassandra will have to fold."

I push myself to my feet and brush the sand from my shorts in defiance. "Well, I'm glad you're so happy, but I still have a problem. I still don't know who I am, I have a whole country depending on me, and the person who I thought would help me lied to me and is now happy that he ticked me off."

I start to walk away, but Brent chases me. "Lorraine, please. I didn't mean to upset you, and I didn't lie to you. I really do want to help you. Please let me help you."

Brent grabs my arm, and I wrench it away. "Help me by leaving me alone."

"Lorraine, please," Brent calls.

"And stop calling me that," I yell loudly enough that even the fishermen turn their heads, so I lower my voice. "Stop calling me Lorraine. My name is Maris now."

I fume the entire walk back to Captain Wilson's place. I want Brent's help—maybe I even *need* Brent's help—but he can't even bother to apologize for lying to me and Captain Wilson, so I guess I'll have to do without him.

I practically throw the door open, startling Captain Wilson, who was just cooking breakfast, out of his wits.

"What's wrong, dear?" Captain Wilson holds out his hand, and I run into his arms. He holds me tight, and I feel comforted by his presence and warmth. It occurs to me that I should feel strange about so implicitly trusting a man I hardly remember, but something about him is so warmly familiar, and even if I can't remember much about him, my heart seems to remember him, almost like muscle memory. "Talk to me," he says.

"I can't do this," I mutter into his shirt, my face pressed into his chest, hiding any tears that would dare escape. "I just can't be the leader all of Trilland wants me to be."

Captain Wilson hugs tighter, and I start to cry. "I know this is stressful, and I know you're in way over your head here. But I really do believe in you. You just need to believe in yourself."

I feel a small smile force its way onto my lips, and I hold on tight to Captain Wilson. I can remember why I always liked him so much. He's so warm and comforting. He feels like family.

And right now, I really need family.

"Captain Wilson," I say, still stretching my arms around his waist, "what did my father say to me? What was his advice?"

Captain Wilson pulls back and looks sad. He tucks a stray piece of hair behind my ear. "You don't remember?"

I shake my head. "I remember you telling me to remember what he said, but I can't."

Captain Wilson gestures toward his living room, and we both sit down on his makeshift barstools. He takes a deep breath before he begins.

"My dear, do you remember how I met your father?" I shake my head, and he sighs. "Your mother and I were very good friends growing up. We were practically like brother and sister. We grew up together. So when she met your father and was seriously talking about marrying him, I insisted on meeting him, even though he was the prince. I figured if he was serious about her, he'd be okay with meeting me.

"I guess your mother mentioned this to him because before I could even try to contact him, he called me personally and invited me over for lunch, just the two of us. We talked for hours, and I knew that he really loved your mother. But what struck me most about him was what he told me when we first met. He said to me, 'Life can either be a series of mistakes, worries, and regrets, or a series of successes, achievements, and unexpected accomplishments.' He told me that that is how he operated his life. He never wanted to have any regrets because he was too scared to attempt something. And that was his mantra for you."

While Captain Wilson talks, I feel a bit hazy. His words sound familiar, and I'm sure I've heard this story before since it seems significant to my parents' relationship, but I can't quite grasp it. It isn't until he repeats my father's mantra that my mind clears. I find myself saying the words along with Captain Wilson in my mind. As soon as he said the first word, the entire proverb came to me. Suddenly it's like I can't understand how I ever could have forgotten his words. He's said this to me ever since I was a small child. I can almost see his face when I say the words to myself, and I try to grab hold of it, but it slips out of my mind as quickly as it came.

"Lorraine?" Captain Wilson says, confusion slipping into his voice. I get the impression that this isn't the first thing he has said since he told that story.

"What?"

"Are you okay? You seemed kind of dazed."

I smile. "I'm fine. That story sounds familiar. I remember my father's words now."

Captain Wilson smiles and exhales with relief. "I'm so glad. He meant every word, you know. The day of the mutiny, the last thing I wanted to do was separate from you, but I hoped his words would remind you to make the best of it. It never occurred to me that you wouldn't remember."

I take his strong hand in both of mine and give him what I feel like is a firm squeeze, but it seems to register only barely on his tough hands. "You had no way of knowing what would happen to me."

He smiles. "But I knew you'd be okay. I knew that somehow you'd pull through. I just wish I had known what happened."

"Why didn't you ever go back to Trilland?"

"Cassandra blamed the whole thing on me. If I had gone back, I would have gotten arrested, and then I never would have been able to find you. Besides, I gave the people here hope. They believed we'd find you because I did."

I nod slowly, but I break eye contact with Captain Wilson. This isn't what I wanted. I didn't want to be someone important. I wanted to figure out who I was. I don't want to be a princess. I don't want to save a dying country. I don't want any of this.

"Are you okay?"

I shake my head. "No, not really. When I agreed to let Brent bring me here, I just wanted to see you. I feel like everyone wants me to be someone I'm not."

"But you are. You are that person."

"I'm not. Not anymore. And I don't know how to be her or how to save Trilland or how to stop Cassandra. She'll know."

"She'll know what?"

"She'll know that I can't remember."

"How would she know that?"

"I don't know, I just know she will. And then I'll fail, and it'll be too late, and Trilland will hate me."

"Lorraine, dear," Captain Wilson says, wrapping an arm around me, "no one is going to hate you. Everyone hates Cassandra because she's vicious and manipulative and has ruined the country. Anyone who even attempts to stop her will be celebrated. And you're more than that. You're the person they have hoped, only in their wildest dreams, would come back. Even if you don't remember, you're still the same person."

Captain Wilson's speech is encouraging until that last sentence. The words sound eerily similar to things both Brent and Zane said to me, each with entirely different meanings. And neither one was helpful.

Captain Wilson continues, "Your presence alone will strengthen Trilland. Did you see the reaction people had to you yesterday? They're just excited about you."

"But I can't face Cassandra. I agreed to come here because I wanted you. I was hoping that seeing you would jog more of my memory, but it hasn't. Just a random thing my dad said once."

"That's valuable advice, and it will serve you well."

"But we're running out of time. We've got to be cutting it close, right?" Brent told me there was a time limit, and while Brent's lie has caused me to doubt everything he's told me, Captain Wilson takes too long to answer, and that is an answer in and of itself. "I'll never remember in time to stop her."

I can try to help you remember, but you'll struggle if you don't let yourself try to remember. If you spend your energy worrying about what will happen if you do remember, you'll prevent yourself."

I shrug. "I guess so."

Captain Wilson gives my shoulders a squeeze. "Let's go for a walk, huh? We'll talk a little about the past. The fun stuff. It will relax you and help you remember."

I agree, and Captain Wilson and I head out the door.

~~~

"Your mother never forgave me for giving her that hideous orange sweater."
~~~

Tears stream down my face from laughter. Captain Wilson's birthday gift faux pa story has to be one of the funniest things I've ever heard. I can picture my mom's face when she saw it, and it makes me happy to realize that I can picture her face.

I've been able to ever since the day I remembered the starfish metaphor when I was with Daisy. Sometimes it's hazy, and sometimes it's clear, but I can always remember her face now. And I could clearly remember Captain Wilson's face because of the letter and picture. But my dad's face remains a mystery. I saw it once, when Captain Wilson was talking about him, but now it's like trying to remember a dream after you wake up: I know I knew it once, but it's just out reach now.

"Was he a good king? My father?" I ask. "I mean, I know he was beloved, but was he a good king?"

Captain Wilson smiles. "Your father was a great king. The best that anyone can remember. Better than his father and his father before him. He was kind but fair and protective. Everything a king should be."

"I hope I can be even as half as good as he was."

"I know you will be."

"How do you know?"

"Because I know you. You have his heart and your mother's wisdom. He trained you for this up until he died. And because you asked that question without worrying about your memory."

I stop walking when Captain Wilson says this. He's right. I didn't think about my memory. I just thought about being a ruler. I guess that's somewhat encouraging but also somewhat terrifying.

"You know," Captain Wilson says, "your dad loved taking you on those trips to Trilland's provinces. It was one of his favorite things to do. He was so proud of his little country, and so he loved showing it off. Plus, he thought you would be a better ruler for seeing it. You have to know your people to govern them, he'd say. He made me promise to continue taking you. I just wish the last trip hadn't ended so tragically."

I shrug my shoulders. "It's not so tragic. Nobody died."

Captain Wilson laughs a little. "No, maybe not, but to Trilland, you did."

I think about Captain Wilson's words, how we used to take these trips, how I took trips like that with my dad before him. Maybe that's the answer. I was so disheartened when my memory didn't immediately come back when I got to Gessend and reconnected with Captain Wilson, but that doesn't mean this was the wrong choice. I have regained more memories. Maybe continuing to travel would jog more.

"I have an idea," I say.

"Let's hear it."

"Let's retrace our journey," I say. "Instead of going straight for the Trilland mainland, let's go backwards through the provinces, starting with whatever province we were in last before the mutiny. Was it Anden?"

"It was."

I smile, glad that I remembered something without prompting. "Okay, so we go to Anden and we go backwards from there to Trilland. Not only does that give me more time and more opportunities to remember, but it also creates some buzz. Cassandra and the rest of Trilland will already know we're coming before we get there. What do you think?"

Captain Wilson considers it for a long time, which only makes me nervous. Maybe he thinks it's a bad idea. Maybe he thinks it's a stupid idea. Maybe it's too soon.

Captain Wilson draws circles in the sand with his foot while he strokes his chin. He looks so stereotypically deep in thought. He considers it for a long time. Or maybe it's a short time and it just feels long.

Finally, he says, "I love it."

"Yeah? Do you think we have time?"

Captain Wilson shifts back and forth a little. "If we don't waste too much time, yes. We couldn't spend more than a day anywhere."

"But is it a good idea?"

"Yeah. I think it's a great idea. You're right. You remember the mutiny, right?"

"Yes."

"So it would be like tracing backwards. Seems like it would work to me."

"Brent tried that back on the island, and it worked, but it only worked so much. I think maybe it will work better when we're actually in Trilland-owned land."

"I think so, too. And you're right, it'll have Cassandra shaking in her boots—er, high heels—before we even get there. When do you want to go?"

"Soon. The more I think about it, the more I'll hesitate and second-guess myself."

"I can probably secure a ship and crew by the day after tomorrow. Is that soon enough?"

"Yes," I force myself to say. The day after tomorrow seems too soon and not soon enough all at the same time.

"Now, I hate to bring it up because I don't know if you want to talk about it or not, but we need to be on the same page. Is Brent coming with us or not?"

I knew I would have to address this eventually, and yet I still don't have an answer. Part of me really wants him to come because he's gotten me this far, but another part, possibly the bigger part, is still really angry with him. Which one is more important? Which outweighs which?

"I honestly don't know. Let me think about it tonight."

"Fair enough. Come on, let's go get some dinner."

# Chapter 16

I wish there was a way to travel from province to province without stepping foot on a ship. I guess there's flying, but that seems like a tremendously bad idea for someone who gets sea sick. Air sickness seems worse. If I hurl, it's over the side of the boat; I'm not stuck on the boat with it. But where does it go on a plane? Besides, there are no planes going between these islands since they're so small and so close together.

"You're not still sick, are you?" Captain Wilson calls out from the wheel.

"I'm fine," I say, though I'm definitely not fine.

Captain Wilson says, "You never get seasick. What's up? Are you nervous?"

"I got seasick on the way to Gessend too. My theory is that it's because of the storm and the mutiny."

"Oh," Captain Wilson says as if I have said something he hadn't yet considered. "I guess that makes sense. Do you think that'll go away when you get your memory back?"

And what will I do if I don't get my memory back? "I don't know."

I sit down on the steps next to Captain Wilson and force myself to watch the sailors instead of the waves. Their movements are kind of wave-like, which makes them maybe not the best thing to focus on, but I find their work fascinating. It's like watching the fishermen back home or the fishermen in Gessend. They have a job to do, and they do it without pomp, without boasting. They just get the job done in the best way they can. I wish I could do that.

"Land!" one of the sailors shouts. We all look up and see the island from the distance. It's big. Really big. It has to be twice the size of Gessend, maybe three or four times the size of my little island. Clearly this was a bad idea. What will I do in the presence of all those people?

"Any bells?" Captain Wilson asks.

"Bells? What bells? There are bells?"

Captain Wilson laughs. "Does the island ring any bells for you?" I shake my head. "Maybe it will when we get closer."

The last leg of the journey to the island goes entirely too fast. There's actually a formal port here. The ports at Gessend and my island are really nothing more than just beaches. Gessend had a sign. Anden has a full dock, boating house, and multiple ships pulling in. Maybe I can get lost in the chaos of all those ships. That would be fantastic.

Captain Wilson smiles and starts spinning the wheel, and I try not to focus on the leaning of the ship. He looks so happy standing there. Even though he periodically stumbles because of the waves and his poor leg, and he's had to rely on the help of the first captain more than he clearly wants to, he still looks like there's nowhere else he'd rather be.

"Lorraine," he says, "we're going to pull into the dock all the way on the end there." He points all the way to the left, and I take a breath of relief. "We're going to take our time, okay? It's late in the day, so if you don't want to go on shore today, we don't have to if you'd rather wait for the morning. Okay? We'll just pull in, and then you can decide."

I stop watching the sailors because now they're prepping for arrival, and I don't want to think about arrival. I admire the coastline as if

I'm looking at a picture or a postcard, something distant and not immediate. It's pretty if I think of it that way. The houses along the coast are pretty big and all painted sea foam green. Everything is very uniform on this island, unlike mine or Gessend. It's kind of weird. How do people keep from getting lost if everything looks the same?

Captain Wilson barks out orders to the sailors and then turns to me and says, "Would you come with me and help me find my journal?"

I follow Captain Wilson into the cabin. He likes to record his arrival and departure times in a journal. He says he's been doing it ever since he started sailing. It's kind of interesting, but I don't know why he does it.

Once in the cabin, he immediately sits down and starts jotting figures in his journal. I flip through one of the books in the cabin, not really reading. I think it's an almanac, but I don't really want to read it. I just need a distraction from my thoughts while Captain Wilson is unable to fill that role.

"Okay." Captain Wilson very suddenly slams his book closed. "So, what would you like to do?"

"Hey, why did we stop? Are we—" Brent pauses when he spots me, "there?"

We briefly make eye contact, but I look away. We still haven't spoken since we had our altercation on the beach of Gessend. I don't really want to talk to him. Sometimes I wonder why I told Captain Wilson that I wanted him to come along. Sometimes I fear that it was some form of debt to repay because he found me and offered me my first memory. Sometimes I fear even more that it's because I have feelings for him, and I don't want to have feelings for him because I worry that will endanger my feelings for Zane and thus endanger his for me. But in the end, I knew I couldn't leave him behind. Like it or not, he has become a part of this journey, and right now, I definitely like it not.

"We just pulled in," Captain Wilson says. "We're trying to decide whether to go on shore today or wait until tomorrow. Lorraine?"

Captain Wilson looks at me, but Brent does not. He stares at the floor, scuffing his foot on the wood. I won't let him think I'm afraid.

"Why don't we go get dinner?" That's something quick and relatively painless.

Captain Wilson shrugs. "Sounds good to me. Brent, are you coming?"

Brent mimics the captain's shrug. "I guess so. Gotta eat sometime."

Captain Wilson walks with certainty back onto the deck, and I follow, strangely aware of Brent's presence behind me. Captain Wilson grabs a few sailors, some of the older men who seem to be some kind of leaders, and heads for the ramp. Everything in my body is screaming at me not to step foot on that ramp and leave the safety of the ship, but Brent is right behind me, and I won't show weakness in front of him. Not anymore.

"There's a restaurant just to the right here," Captain Wilson says. "I always used to stop there whenever I brought your father to Anden. They've got the best clams around."

"Have I ever been there?"

"We went here before the mutiny, yes. And I think you used to come with your father when you were little, but I doubt you'd remember that."

I don't really see the distinction between not remembering based on age or based on amnesia at this point, but whatever. I follow Captain Wilson to the restaurant. It's a short walk, and I find myself undecided about whether or not that's a good thing. On one hand, it means less time to be noticed and less time to second guess my decision. On the other, it means we arrive at the door far too quickly.

There is something vaguely familiar about the place though. The smell is very familiar—that classic seafood smell of the fish and the saltwater and too many people who've all been sweating on the beach all day crammed into one place. It's not exactly the most pleasant smell, but right now, I'll take any memory I can get. I do remember being here, but as a kid, oddly enough. I can see my dad's face—actually see it. It has a weird haze about it, kind of like I'm looking at him in direct sunlight and there's a glare, but it's his face nonetheless. I think he was introducing me to someone. Can't see his face though.

"Right here," Captain Wilson says, gesturing to a table and sitting down. "This is my table. The owner always reserves it just for me."

"Really?"

"Well, technically it's reserved for your father, but he always lets me sit here."

I smile a little sadly. Now, I can see a blurry version of his face and remember his voice, and it hurts a little to realize that that's all there is now. These hazy memories are my only chance to see him again and hear his voice again. I wonder if there are recordings of his speeches in Trilland.

An older gentleman approaches the table and starts cackling loudly with Captain Wilson, and he looks so familiar. His name is right on the tip of my tongue, but I just can't get a hold of it. Every time he smiles, I feel like I can almost grab the name right out of the air.

"Where've you been, old man?" the man says to Captain Wilson. "You haven't been around for years."

"Ran into a little trouble, but I finally made it back for the best clams in town."

"And you've brought friends," he says with a smile. "I always like when you bring more customers for me to—" he stops suddenly when he makes eye contact with me. "Lorrie-bell?"

"Mr. Yates!"

He throws his arms around me, and he smells kind of gross, but I don't care because that's how Mr. Yates always smells—like seafood and sweat and grease—and I can remember that. I can barely get my arms around him because his belly sticks out so far, but I think he's actually lost weight since I was a kid. Or maybe I just got bigger. I can feel both Brent and Captain Wilson staring at me, but I don't want to look because Mr. Yates will notice.

"But—I thought—we thought—"

"I know."

"Where have you been?" Mr. Yates says, pulling up a chair next to Brent.

"On a little island south of here."

"What happened?"

"Cassandra tried to have her killed," says Captain Wilson, "so she could take over."

Mr. Yates starts to tear up again. "You've been out there this whole time?" I nod. "Why didn't you contact me? I would have come to get you if I had known."

My face burns red, and I don't know how to answer, but thankfully, Captain Wilson jumps in.

"She couldn't contact anyone. She was injured for a while and then had no way to get in touch. That's why I sent Brent here to find her."

"Well thanks, son." Mr. Yates shakes Brent's hand.

"Just glad I could help," says Brent. If only Mr. Yates knew how much Brent didn't help and did help at the same time.

"So, what are you doing here?"

"Didn't I say we were here for clams?" Captain Wilson says.

"You and I both know you didn't come here just for clams." Mr. Yates's mouth twists into a smirk.

"We're on our way back to Trilland," I blurt out. "Captain Wilson and I are just making a few stops along the way. We wanted to see you."

Mr. Yates raises an eyebrow. The left one, because he has a scar on the right one from a fight when he was twenty, and it doesn't move anymore. "Back to Trilland?" We all nod. "Go get her, Lorrie-bell."

"I'll try."

"Hang on, I've got something to show you."

Mr. Yates races upstairs to the balcony above the restaurant and ducks through a little door in the corner. I exhale fully for the first time since the ship docked and finally allow myself to look at Captain Wilson.

"You remember him?"

I nod. "I kind of remembered his face, but when he called me Lorrie-bell, it came back. But I don't remember being here before the mutiny. I remember him from when I was a kid."

"We hadn't been here in years before that."

"My dad brought me here when I was maybe twelve. I think that was the last time."

"And you remember that?"

"That's how it usually works," Brent says suddenly but without looking up. "Long-term memories, usually childhood memories, come back first."

"Well, you did great," Captain Wilson says. "He doesn't suspect a thing."

"Because there's nothing to suspect with him. I remember him. What if I don't remember by the time we get to Trilland?"

"You will," Brent says, but I refuse to look at him.

"You won't be alone," Captain Wilson says. "You're doing great."

"Here we are," Mr. Yates says when he returns. He takes his seat next to Brent again and holds out his hand for mine. I reach out to hold his hand, but he flips my hand over so my palm is facing up and places a little box delicately on top. "This was your father's. He gave it to me many years ago."

I open the box and inside is a little golden key. It doesn't really look like it'll actually open anything, but it's beautifully crafted. Underneath the key is a gold-trimmed card that reads: *This key hereby grants Mr. August Yates honorary mayorship of Anden in honor of his entrepreneurial work and his charitable work. Signed, His Royal Majesty the King Andrew Everhart and Her Royal Highness Princess Lorraine Everhart.*

"Oh my goodness, I remember this," I say with a laugh.

"What?" Captain Wilson asks, so I read the card aloud, and he laughs heartily. "I didn't know about that."

"You're the mayor?" Brent asks.

Mr. Yates chuckles. "No, no. When Lorraine was little, the mayor of Anden passed away, and everyone was trying to figure out who the new mayor would be. Lorraine insisted it had to be me."

"I still stand by that," I say.

"There was no convincing her that that wasn't how elections worked and that I didn't want to run anyway. She demanded that I be mayor even after another mayor was chosen. Mr. Gibbons. Good man."

"Not as good as you."

"Anyway, to appease her, her dad presented me with this. At the time, she really thought this made me the mayor."

Captain Wilson explodes with laughter. "That sounds like you. How old were you?"

"I must have been six or seven," I say. "I felt like the most powerful person in the world that day, like I had actually swayed the political process by throwing a tantrum."

"That's really cute," Brent says smiling, looking directly at me for the first time in days. For a moment, just a brief moment, I'm happy that Brent is smiling at me. There's a small part of me that flutters at the thought that Brent's distance from me has closed just a little bit. But then I see Captain Wilson's face again, that face that took over his beautiful smile the moment I told him that I didn't remember, that I have amnesia, and suddenly the flutters turn to lead in my stomach. I wonder if I'll ever be able to look at Brent again without seeing that face and feeling that lead.

I run my fingers along the carvings on the key a few times, repeating the pattern, before I realize that no one is talking. I glance up and notice a waiter talking to Mr. Yates, and Mr. Yates looks somewhat concerned. He waves the waiter away and leans across the table to speak quietly to Captain Wilson and me, so close that Brent struggles to hear him even though he is next to him.

"I don't want to worry you, but some of the other diners are starting to notice you."

"Notice how?" Captain Wilson says.

"They recognize Lorraine. Some people think that you are a look-a-like, others think it's really you. Either way, they're noticing. Unless you're looking to make a scene right now, you might want to duck out. I can box your food up for you."

"Well—"

"Let's go," I cut off Captain Wilson. "It seems like the best option right now."

"Why do you say that?" Captain Wilson asks.

Because knowing that all these people are watching me is making me sick to my stomach. "Because if we're going to make contact with the people here, it should happen differently than this. I don't want to look like I'm hiding."

He shrugs. "Fair enough."

Mr. Yates gets up. "I'll grab your food, and you'll be on your way. Please say goodbye before you continue on to Trilland."

Mr. Yates ducks into the kitchen, and I now notice the eyes on me and wonder how I didn't feel the tremendous weight of their stares earlier. People all around us are whispering to each other, pointing not-so-subtly at me, eyes enlarged and legs fidgeting. The individually quiet whispers are building into a din together, and I feel sweat forming on the back of my neck. I'm about to bolt from the table when Captain Wilson grabs my hand.

"Don't do that. It'll look bad. As soon as August brings the food, we're going to smile, shake his hand, give him a hug, whatever, and then walk out of here calmly. Got it?" Captain Wilson says it to me but looks at Brent sternly.

"Got it," we say in unison.

Mr. Yates brings the food after about five minutes that feel like an hour each, and we follow the script: Captain Wilson and Brent both shake his hand, I let him give me a bear hug, and we all walk toward the door looking calm even though we are anything but. At least, I'm not calm.

A few people actually follow us out of the restaurant which gives me the feeling of being stalked. I can hear their whisperings behind me, real or perceived, and it's like the whispers are catching up to us faster than their owners. The murmurs become vapors which become hands that begin to wrap around my throat, and I'm not sure if they will make me vomit, pass out, choke, or induce a delightful combination of any of the three.

Brent starts to turn backward, obviously just as plagued by the bodiless voices as I am, but Captain Wilson pushes his head forward.

"No. Don't do that. Just keep walking. People are just curious."

Captain Wilson's words are calm and reassuring, but the shaking of his voice and the largeness of his eyes negates any comfort he attempted to offer. I think I hear my name—my real name, that is—but I was just warned about looking back, so I train my eyes on the horizon, waiting for Captain Wilson to guide me to the right to the docks. But then I hear it again—a distant "Lorraine" echoing through the cloud of monotone voices.

"Do you hear that?" Brent asks.

I nod, but I'm either too afraid or too angry to answer him verbally.

I hear the ghostly "Lorraine" again, but this time it doesn't sound so distant. The speaker is gaining ground. Before I know it, he's standing before us.

"Lorraine! It is you. I knew it had to be." The speaker corrects his wind-mussed hair and smiles a friendly smile. "And Lawrence, is that you?" He juts out his hand and Captain Wilson shakes it. "It's good to see you again."

"You as well. This is our travel companion, Brent. Brent, this is Dean Winston. He oversees all the shipping in Anden." I silently say a prayer of thanks for Captain Wilson for secretly introducing Dean Winston to me as well as to Brent.

The problem is that I still don't have any idea who he is. He doesn't look familiar, and nothing about him is ringing a bell. I don't even know if I know him personally or if he just knows of me. Either way, he will expect me to know who he is, and I've got nothing.

"Where on earth have you been?" Dean says to me.

"I—uh—had a little complication on my last voyage."

"I should say so. Was it Cassandra?"

"Yes."

Dean snaps his fingers. "I knew it. I always knew she was after your throne. And now she's got it."

"Not for long," Captain Wilson says with a big grin.

"You're on your way back to Trilland?" Dean looks at me expectantly.

"We are," I say. "We've just been stopping in a few provinces on the way."

"I'm glad you stopped by, but the people around here weren't really expecting to see you. You've drawn quite a crowd."

"I know. I didn't mean to cause such a stir."

"It's hard for you to do anything but." Dean smiles, but his words still make me uneasy. They feel like a warning. We're still walking toward the ship, but it feels like we can't walk fast enough. "So what's the plan when you get back?"

"Expel Cassandra."

"Well, of course, but do you even have time? And what about after that? Are you going to become queen? Or abdicate and create a new government? Or let Parliament run things until you get your feet under you?"

I haven't considered any of this. Absolutely none of this. I've been so consumed with trying to get my memory back and focusing on dealing with Cassandra, I haven't thought five minutes past Cassandra's hypothetical arrest. What *am* I going to do? What would be best for Trilland? What if what's best isn't me?

"Well?" Dean asks with a smile, but his face is littered with concern. I realize it's been some time since he asked my plans, and I've been staring off into space.

"I'm not sure," I say, and immediately regret it. "Right now, I'm focused on Cassandra. She needs to be removed before anything else happens."

"Definitely, but your return is going to cause chaos. A good kind of chaos, but chaos nonetheless. What are you going to do?"

Captain Wilson says, "We're taking this one step at a time."

"People've been waiting for this for a long time." Dean's mouth is thin with gravitas. "Even people who really believed you were dead have quietly hoped for this. You can't disappoint them."

"She won't. Everything will be fine."

I turn around and see a large crowd following us to the docks. Now that we've reached the docks, they stop, but they all look at me with mixed emotions: some happy, some crying, some slightly angry.

"Are you going to help us?" a middle-aged woman calls out. I feel for her. She's holding a baby in one hand and holds the hand of a young child with her other. She must have been through so much.

"I'm going to try."

"Where have you been all this time?" an older man calls out. "Why didn't you come back?" His eyebrows furrow in anger, and several other people call out in agreement. "Why did you desert us?"

"I didn't, I—"

"She's coming back to help," Brent calls out.

"You left us." People start calling out all kinds of derivatives of the same sentiment: they are all furious that I haven't been there for a year. I can only imagine what Cassandra has put them through. I want to help, I do. But how can I? How can I help when they're already so angry at me? How can I help when I don't even know what to do? How can I help when I don't even know who I am?

"I want to help," I call out, but Captain Wilson gently grips my shoulder and turns me toward the ship ramp. He pushes me up onto the ship while I'm still half-uttering phrases of concern and wanting to help. We get up onto the ship, and I see Dean still standing at the bottom of the ramp. He waves a friendly wave, and I see several unfriendly waves from the crowd behind him that's quickly becoming a mob.

"Well, I'm rooting for you, Lorraine," Dean calls out. "I know you can do this." His face says otherwise.

Captain Wilson starts urging people to prepare for sail, and Brent says something about sailing at night.

"It'll be fine," Captain Wilson says. "We won't go far, just off the coast, let people cool off."

He continues to bark orders, and Brent turns to look at me, and it's only then that I become aware that tears are streaming down my face. I hope I didn't start crying until now. I hope I didn't cry in front of those angry people, in front of Dean.

"Come on," Brent says, pushing me toward the captain's cabin.

He closes the door behind us and drops the bag of food from Mr. Yates on the table. I had completely forgotten about it.

"Brent, I—" my voice hiccups, and I start sobbing.

"I know." Brent holds out his arms, and for the first time since we met up with Captain Wilson, I don't push Brent away. I run straight into his arms and sob violently into his shoulder. I'm incredibly embarrassed at how awful I sound, all snotty and hiccuping, but Brent, for once, doesn't say anything. He just holds me and rubs my back. After I calm down a little, he brushes my hair back.

"Do you want to try to eat something?"

"No."

Somehow, I don't think I can eat clams tonight.

# Chapter 17

I'm not as seasick this time around, probably because the waters have been pretty calm, but I feel just as nauseous. I was feeling so good back at Gessend about how much I remember now, but it still doesn't feel like enough to do what everyone wants me to do. That catastrophe at Anden has me more rattled than my stomach on this ship. I'm not prepared for this. Not at all. I have no idea what I'm doing. Is this even the right decision for Trilland, my return? Am I really the best thing for it? I'm such a train wreck right now. Captain Wilson will help me, of course, but when it comes down to it, what will matter is what's in my head, not what's in his. Brent keeps coming by to try to help, but I don't want his help right now.

"How far out are we, Captain?" I ask Captain Wilson, stumbling over to him. Clearly amnesia causes you to lose your sea legs, too.

"Not too far," Captain Wilson calls out over the roar of the waves. "And, uh, Lorraine?"

"Yes?"

"Could you try to get used to calling me Uncle Lawrence?"

"*Uncle?*"

Captain Wilson smiles sadly. "It's what you used to call me. I know you're not used to it anymore, but if you call me 'Captain' around Cassandra, she'll know something is up. I think August Yates noticed, and others will, too. I'm sorry, I know that might be weird for you, but could you try? Or at least just not call me 'Captain' around her?"

I shrug uneasily. "I'll try, I guess. What if it doesn't sound natural?"

"It'll be fine. Thank you."

I feel bad because I can tell how much it hurts him to have to tell me to call him that, but I have no memory of that whatsoever. I'm sure he's telling the truth, but that feels so weird. I'll have to make a conscious effort to remember that.

"Hey, are you okay? I know Anden was kind of rough."

"I'm fine."

"Are you sure? Because if you're not, it's okay—"

"I'm fine." I turn around to get away from him and nearly run straight into Brent.

"Hey, I was just looking for you." Brent presses his lips together into a slight smile. "You okay today?"

"I wish everyone would stop asking me that. I'm fine." I push past Brent and start heading for the captain's cabin.

"Please don't take off again," Brent pleads. "We have to talk."

"I don't want to talk." I start to walk away, but a wave throws off my balance, and Brent has to catch me.

"I know, but hear me out. If we show up at Trilland and we're not speaking, people will ask why. Do you really want to tell them it's because I lied about your having amnesia? The last thing you want to do is give away exactly what you're trying to conceal. You don't have to like me right now, but can we at least be civil and cooperate for the sake of the show?"

I want to tell Brent he's wrong, but he isn't. We'll have to work together to pull this off. "Fine. You're right. We'll talk as much as we have to. No more."

"Fine." Brent puts his hands up in surrender. "Are you ready? We're almost there."

"Yes. I just have to get my stuff together."

"I really am sorry, Lorraine. I wish it wasn't like this."

I shake my head. "We'll talk as much as we have to. No more," I remind him and walk back to my cabin.

~~~

When I hear Captain Wilson shouting that we're about to dock, I emerge from my cabin for the first time since I spoke to Brent. I didn't want to talk to anyone else anymore. I needed to be by myself until the absolute last possible second. I stupidly hoped that my memory would miraculously come back to me before we made landfall in Trilland, but, of course, that didn't happen. I put on the sun dress that Elise let me borrow and let my hair wrap around my neck. It looks kind of pretty today, so I might as well take advantage of it.

I fling the door open and walk right past Brent without looking at him, only answering yes when he asks if I'm ready. I march straight toward Captain Wilson and put on my best smile of confidence and self-assurance even though it probably looks as fake as it feels.

"Are you ready?" he asks.

I smile and nod for the crew to see, but through my teeth I say no.

Captain Wilson gives my arm a squeeze. "Everything'll be fine."

"I hope you're right—Uncle—Lawrence." It's hard to say, and I'm glad I made the decision to say it for the first time away from anyone else, especially Cassandra. It doesn't sound natural at all, and anyone could see straight through it. If that's as good of an actress I am, then I'm in big trouble.

But Captain Wilson doesn't react like I've just told the most unconvincing lie of my life because I probably have. He smiles, his cheeks lighting up cherry red, his eyes studded with tears he's trying des-
~~~

perately to pretend aren't there. He pulls me into a hug, completely ignoring the fact that he's supposed to be steering the ship into the dock.

"Thank you," he mumbles into my shoulder.

"It sounded so fake."

He pulls back and wipes away a tear that dared to escape and chuckles. "I know. But you said it. It'll sound better next time. I just missed hearing that." Captain Wilson takes a deep breath and composes himself. "Okay, time to go. Welcome back to Trilland."

With that, Captain Wilson pulls the ship into the dock with a kind of savvy that only comes from years of experience. The shore is beautiful. The seaside houses cluster together, clinging to the edge of the cliffs. It looks like several people built their houses on little private cliffs like the one I have back on the island. The buildings are all white-washed though, destroying the illusion of personal decision.

It's certainly a busy city. There are people everywhere, all hustling to get where they're going. No one even seems to notice that we've arrived. I guess that's good. I kind of need to be inconspicuous until after I confront Cassandra. With any luck, I'll get at least some more of my memory back before I have to interact with the people of Trilland at all. I'm terrified of saying the wrong thing around them, especially after what happened in Anden. If that was just a province, how much worse could things be in Trilland? What if people are so much angrier on the mainland? People don't seem to notice us right now, but that all might change when they see me. Still, it's weird that everyone seems oblivious to the giant ship that has just pulled in to dock. I guess ships coming in here isn't so uncommon as it is back home.

I squeeze Captain Wilson's arm. "What are we going to do? Just walk through town? Surely someone will recognize me."

Captain Wilson shouts out some orders to the crew before turning to me. "It'll be okay. Brent and I are going to go with you, and we're going to go in front of you. If you keep your head down, no one will know. It's not like anyone's expecting to see you."

"I guess so."

Captain Wilson calls Brent over, and we huddle together over by the wheel so the crew won't overhear us. "Okay, here's the plan. We've got to make a beeline for the palace. No looking around, no drawing attention to ourselves. We don't want to look suspicious. As long as we blend in, no one will think anything is unusual about us. Okay?" Brent and I both nod. "Good. Lorraine, here are some sunglasses. Put them on. No sense taking any risks of someone seeing you, right?"

I push the dark sunglasses up my nose and try to look inconspicuous. Okay, deep breaths. Now is not a good time to throw up. That would definitely draw attention.

"Okay kids, let's go." Captain Wilson gestures for me and Brent to follow.

We step onto the dock and push our way into the crowded streets, following the natural flow of people so we don't stand out. I don't know what people think we are doing here, but clearly no one cares because no one takes so much as a second glance at us. This city looks like a much more stressful and populated version of my little village. I have to say, I prefer my village the way it is.

Luckily for us, the palace is near the water, so we don't have to walk far. Surprisingly, there's very little security. When I ask Captain Wilson why, he tells me it's because it was never really necessary. No one ever wanted to bother the royal family until Cassandra came along. A few guards were always more than enough.

When you try to picture the house you grew up in, I think most people generally picture a modest little house, maybe a cottage style or a bungalow, with a white picket fence and silly lawn ornaments. When trying to picture a palace or a mansion, most people probably picture an excessively large house that screams pretentious and ornate, with lavish decorations and more rooms than could possibly be necessary. My childhood home is neither of the two. It's certainly the most extravagant house of the city, but it doesn't look like a monument to human vanity like I thought it would. Even though this city feels far more industrious to me than the little village, it's still very much a beach town, so the palace looks more like the beach house of a wealthy family. It's painted a lovely cream color with white trim and a white roof. There's a beautiful little garden to the side, and even from a distance, you can tell it overlooks the water. It's not very big in surface area, but it is three stories high. The gravel path leading to the front door has clearly been paved in the past but not very recently.

The closer we get to the front door, the more I'm panicking. What, are we just going to waltz inside? The guards open the gate for us with no hesitation. Is that because they recognize Captain Wilson, or is that just how it is here? Are they just going to swing the door open, too?

"Captain?" I say hesitantly. Captain Wilson spins around and looks me straight in the eye.

"Cassandra doesn't know anything," he says. "Use it to your advantage. Just fake it, and she'll believe you."

I nod, and we walk toward the door, but I don't feel any better. I don't know if she will believe it. Cassandra is one person who, despite the number of memories that have returned, appears in none of them. I don't remember a thing about her. I have no idea how to approach her, and I don't know how to avoid saying the wrong thing. Based on what I've heard, she isn't going down without a fight, and I can't help but feel hopelessly unarmed.

"May I help you?" one of the guards by the door asks us. I guess the answer is no, they won't just swing the door open.

"We're here to speak to Cassandra Wellington," Captain Wilson says.

"And you are?"

"A captain in the royal navy. Wilson."

The guard who spoke looks stern and like he's about to say no, but the guard on the right elbows him and nods. They start whispering to each other, and the guard on the right keeps eying me and Captain Wilson. He looks kind of familiar, but I'm not really sure why. I can't imagine any of these guards are the same from a year ago. Surely Cassandra would have replaced them all.

"Cassandra will have our heads," the first guard hisses.

"Do you want to tell her we let someone who looks just like the princess walk away? That would be worse."

"There's no way that's really her."

"You really want to make that call?"

The first guard huffs and turns back to us. "All right. Wait inside the entryway. Miss Cassandra will be right with you."

The three of us step into the entryway, and I almost gasp at how beautiful it is. There is a gorgeous spiral staircase ahead of us, and the tile floors almost look like ice. I feel funny when I look at it, like I'm looking at it with watery eyes, so that it is a little blurry, but I blink a few times, and the weird feeling doesn't really go away. The guards wander about, occasionally giving me a weird glance, but mostly we're left to ourselves. The guards who let us in stand a little ways behind us. After a few minutes, we hear heels clicking upstairs.

"Who on earth is walking around my house so early—" the voice echoing down from the staircase stops suddenly. "Lorraine? How is that possible?"

Cassandra stays up a few steps, probably to feel like she is more powerful than us. She's beautiful, if not a little severe, her brown locks falling into perfect waves over her shoulder, hitting the red gown she wears that is much too formal for midday on a weekday. She tries to force a fake smile, but she can't overcome the shock that has taken over her face.

"Who let you into my house?" Cassandra searches the room, and spotting the guards, growls, "How dare you?"

"It was his idea, Miss," the first guard says. The second guard whips his head around and glares at his traitor. "He said you'd want to see her."

"Why would I want to see this impostor?"

"She's not an impostor," Captain Wilson says, recognizing that I haven't quite worked up the nerve to speak yet. "Your plan didn't work. Lorraine survived that mutiny."

"Mutiny?" Cassandra feigns surprise and offense. "I don't know what you are talking about, Captain Wilson. And where have you been all this time? Hiding on some desolate island somewhere because you couldn't manage to keep the princess safe? And who are you?" Cassandra points at Brent.

"Someone who knows the truth about you. Now that Lorraine is back, you'll be forced to surrender the throne," Brent says.

"So I'm just supposed to believe you all that this is Lorraine?" she points at me skeptically, trying to hide her own panic.

"You recognized her yourself," Brent snaps.

"She bears a resemblance."

"I *am* Lorraine, Cassandra. Anyone can see it," The line was good, but my voice is weak, and it wavers. Cassandra picks up on my insecurities immediately.

"Really?" Cassandra cackles. "I'm supposed to believe that this timid thing is the lost princess Lorraine Everhart?" Cassandra points to a family portrait to her right, and I'm panicking because I don't know how to respond, but I glance up at the painting, and it's like some dark cloud clears in my brain when I see my parents' smiling faces, not the image in this painting, but my real parents as I remember them, flash before my eyes. I remember posing for that painting. The artist got mad at my dad because he couldn't keep his hands off my mom. He also got mad at me because I kept fidgeting with the collar of my baby blue dress. Memories start flooding back, almost too quickly for me to grasp each one of them, but also not quickly enough. I want to remember everything now. I remember my father teaching me to walk on that slippery tile floor, his mustache furrowing with gentle laughter every time I slipped and clutched his leg. I remember my mother singing me to sleep at night, her pretty inky black hair curling around her ears. I remember staying up past my bedtime to sneak downstairs to eat ice cream and catching my parents dancing and giggling in the dining room together. I remember smiling wide and eating my contraband ice cream while I watched the show. I remember hoping I could one day find a love like that. I remember when I saw Prince Alex from Eterand kiss the trampy princess from Riagala and being heartbroken because, as a thirteen-year-old, I thought we would end up together. My best friend Jane and I competing to see who could braid the better braid in each other's hair. How beautiful my mother looked in her favorite dress, the purple one with the sweetheart neckline, the one that was only her favorite because it was my dad's favorite. I can remember my parents and how they died, and I'm sad, but I've never been so glad to be sad. How my Uncle Lawrence held me when I cried over their deaths and reassured me that everything would be all right. How Cassandra's rebellion started slowly and steadily, like a rumbling of thunder. When Uncle Lawrence suggested taking the trip to the provinces because he thought it would calm the unrest, and I remember the unrest in Trilland leading up to Cassandra's rebellion taking over, and my memory of the mutiny no longer feels fuzzy and distant. I can remember everything except how I could have possibly forgotten it all.

Unless, perhaps, I don't remember it all. There could still be blurry spots. I guess I won't know for a while, which is scary. But right now, I know what I need to do.

And most of all, I remember myself. I remember how to be me.

"You've had your fun here, Cassandra, but it's over. You've been trying to get at my throne for years, and I'm not standing for it anymore. This little childish rebellion of yours is done." I remember Cassandra's evil smile now and how I never used to fear it because it's nothing but a bluff. She is nothing more than a wannabe and a fake. I can remember being friends with her once, when we were small children and our parents wanted us to be close cousins, until her jealousy of my crown and my crayons became too much for me. I remember all her plans to centralize the economy so that she could waste away all of Trilland's reserves. She wanted to get rid of Parliament so that there would be no one to tell her when she was wrong. She always argued that a monarchy was dangerous because they are unelected, apparently completely oblivious to the irony of her making that statement. "You will be tried for treason and attempted murder of the royal family and will most likely be banished from Trilland, you and all of your rebels. You've gotten away with this for too long, and I'm putting a stop to it now."

Brent stares at me in shock, Uncle Lawrence smiles, and Cassandra takes a physical step backward from me in horror.

"Who do you think you are?" Cassandra tries to regain some kind of control over the situation, over me, but her voice betrays her own doubt and uncertainty, so I seize it.

"I *think* I'm the rightful ruler of Trilland and that you're just an out of control anarchist trying to pretend she's a princess. I won't stand for your little games any longer."

Cassandra laughs. She actually laughs. She descends a few more steps, laughs some more, and descends further until we're standing face to face. She keeps one hand on the stair railing and leans back with an ease that makes me uncomfortable. She has actually drawn a crowd at this point. Several guards have come in, a few maids, and even a few people have gathered in the garden behind us.

"And just what were you planning on doing about it?" Cassandra says trying to sound calm but gritting her teeth the entire time.

Briefly, I find myself unable to speak. What was I thinking? What was my plan here? Did we not have a thorough plan, or can I not remember it? I didn't think through what I would do if Cassandra didn't back down upon seeing me, which was stupid. Someone willing to murder me isn't going to give up easily.

"At a loss for words?" Cassandra says. "Don't worry, I'll fill in the blanks for you. What I see before me is a captain in the royal navy who has been accused of treason, some scruffy guy who clearly doesn't belong here, and a girl desperately trying to pretend that she's the princess. Funny, since that's what you accused me of. It's cute that you think you can stand in my way."

"I did not commit treason," Uncle Lawrence growls. "Lorraine is standing right here. You have no claim anymore."

"Well, see, it's funny that you should mention that," Cassandra says as she saunters toward Uncle Lawrence, "because I'm currently the only person left with any relation to the Everhart family. I'm the only one with any claim. And before you start whining about being an Everhart, let me be clear: you missed your chance."

"I haven't missed anything," I say, but I suddenly feel cold at Cassandra's words.

"Oh, but you have. You might not be aware since you're obviously a fake, but Trilland law has a safeguard in place just in case something ever happens to the heir. I'm sure they never thought it would apply because of a navy captain, but nonetheless, here we are."

Uncle Lawrence huffs. "Cassandra, I—"

"Hush. As the only person left with even the most remote connection to the Everhart family, I am the obvious choice. And since that particular law went into place earlier this week, even if the real Lorraine showed up, she would simply be too late. She is officially considered a deserter who abdicated. I now have legal claim to the throne, and I will be officially sworn in later this week."

"You monster!" Uncle Lawrence lunges at Cassandra and manages to get a pretty decent scratch on her face and arm before the guards pull him off. "You'll pay for this. You'll pay for what you've done," he screams as they drag him away.

Cassandra looks startled by the attack but retains that irritating calm. She gingerly touches the scratch on her face and says, "Take him to prison. I'm tired of his antics."

I hear Brent talking, but I can't seem to find his words. I'm too late. She's right. I remember that law. It exists. She's the ruler of Trilland now. I came all this way.

"The fact of the matter is that there is nothing you can do about it now, not that you could have done anything anyway," Cassandra says to Brent.

"When Trilland finds out about Lorraine—"

"When Trilland finds out what? That I arrested an impersonator? That someone dared to come into Trilland pretending to be our beloved and late princess? That I had to look at someone who bears a remarkable resemblance to my dear cousin and turn her away, knowing she was a fake?" Cassandra actually forces a tear out of her eye. "Why would I put Trilland through the pain of seeing an impostor? Oh, I'll tell Trilland what happened, rest assured. I'll tell them everything while you sit in prison."

"You can't," I say, but I've lost the fire I had before.

"Watch me." Cassandra points at the guard who let us in—I remember Timothy now—and snaps her fingers. "You. Try to redeem yourself for letting these traitors in by taking them to prison. See if you can do that simple task without messing up."

Timothy nods, and he and another guard come toward us. Brent fights back, and I'm aware that he's yelling, but I find myself walking even though my legs feel like lead. Timothy handcuffs me and keeps a firm but oddly not aggressive hold on my arm while the other guard has to restrain Brent to get him out of the palace and into the car. My body feels detached from me, and I feel like I see it moving, walking, getting into the car, but I don't feel like I'm the one controlling it. Maybe Cassandra is controlling it just like she's controlling everything else.

When Timothy starts driving, I find myself incredibly nauseated, though I don't think it's a form of motion sickness this time. Brent is still muttering and fidgeting in his handcuffs, but both guards are mostly ignoring us now. I start to feel the clams I never ate coming up at me when Brent elbows me hard.

"We have to do something," he whispers.

"Do what?"

"I don't know. Something. We can't let them take us to prison."

"Why?"

"Lorraine, what's wrong with you? Snap out of it. If Cassandra locks us up, we'll never get out."

I shrug. "There's nothing we can do anyway."

"Uh-uh, no, you are not starting down that road of surrender. We've got to—"

The car lurches forward so suddenly that Brent and I both hit our heads on the headrests in front of us. For a moment, I have a paralyzing fear that hitting my head like that will cause me to lose my memory again, but when I find that that doesn't happen, I almost laugh at how stupid of me it is to think that, especially since it would almost be better to lose it again at this point.

"What the—what just happened?" the second guard says, rubbing his neck.

"I don't know," Timothy says. "The car just seized up on me."

"Try it again."

He starts driving again, but we all get jerked around again, though not as severely since he was going slower.

The guard curses under his breath. "We don't have time for this."

"Come on, just help me look."

They both get out of the car and pop the hood and start looking. I can hear them talking, but I can't make out what they're saying, and with the hood up, I can't even see their expressions.

"You okay?" Brent asks.

"Yeah. You?"

He nods. "Come on, now's our chance. Let's go."

But when I pull the handle, I find that the doors are locked. Of course, they're not stupid.

Brent twists his mouth and starts rummaging around in the console. I'm not sure what he's looking for, but whatever it is, I don't think he's finding it. He starts to head for the glove compartment when we hear Timothy's voice getting closer, so Brent slams back into his seat.

"Let me see if I have anything to clean that off," he says as he opens the driver's side door. He grabs an old towel from the cup holder, makes eye contact with us, then grabs the keys to our handcuffs from the glove compartment. He tosses a key in each of our laps and smiles.

He whispers, "I'm leaving the doors unlocked. Go quickly before he realizes you're gone."

"What?" I say.

"Get somewhere safe and come back for Trilland."

He smiles one more time and slams the door. For a split-second, Brent and I just stare at each other, but he quickly adjusts and nudges my knee with his.

"Come on, that way," he says. "We can duck past those buildings."

Brent and I both palm our keys, too anxious to try to deal with that now, and I open my car door as quietly as I can. When I first get it open, I don't push it out, just in case the guard heard it, but after a few seconds of conversation about the car, Brent urges me to move. I push the door open, we both slide out pretty noiselessly, and bolt as quickly as we can. I keep expecting to hear them coming after us, but all I hear is the sound of Brent and I running. When we're both out of breath, we stop. We end up leaning against a building panting and struggling to undo our handcuffs.

"Hand them to me," Brent says, so I do, and Brent stashes them in a trashcan from a nearby house. He puts his hands on his knees and takes a deep breath. "So what do we do now?"

"What do you mean? We go back to the ship." I start walking toward the docks. Luckily, we're pretty close. We're on the southern side of the island right behind the neighborhood on third street, so it's not a long walk. Five, ten minutes tops. The other good news is we'll be mostly obscured by the houses for almost the whole walk, so there's little chance of getting caught again. As long as we're smart, it'll be okay.

"Go back to the ship?" Brent, for some reason, sounds surprised. What did he think we were going to do? "Aren't we going to do something?"

"Do what, Brent? It's over. We lost. Let's just go back to Gessend or the little island or wherever. It doesn't matter anymore."

"Of course it matters. You're not going to let Cassandra win, are you? We have to do something, try something, anything."

"You heard her. It's the law. There's nothing we can do. We're too late."

"We can't be too late. You're the rightful heir, and she's a tyrant. People will want you over her."

I stop in my tracks and spin around to face Brent. "It doesn't matter what people want. She legally has control of the throne. There's nothing we can do. Technically, now I'm trespassing by showing up there because I'm nobody now. Nobody cares that my last name is Everhart anymore. I'm a deserter legally, and Cassandra can continue her reign of terror." I'm aware that I'm yelling, and I probably shouldn't be because we're fugitives, so I consciously make an effort to lower my voice. "We had our chance, and we missed it by a few days. And after everything that happened, after everything we did to get my memory back, I get it back just in time to lose to Cassandra, so now I get to remember Trilland and live with the pain of knowing that she's ruining my country, so I'd rather just go back to the little island and never again have to see the damage I've caused."

"You—you what?"

Before Brent can continue, and before I can answer him, an older woman comes out of one of the houses behind us. She must have heard me screaming and come out to see what was happening, but based on the look on her face, she definitely didn't expect to see Lorraine Everhart in a dirty sundress with frizzy hair screaming at some random guy. When she comes a little closer and holds out her hand, I take it and realize, the moment she smiles, that I know her.

"Ms. Margaret," I say. "Is that really you?"

"I should be saying that to you," she says, gripping my hand. "I had to touch your hand to make sure I wasn't seeing a ghost. How are you here? Where have you been?"

"I—I was shipwrecked and couldn't make it back here until now." Not exactly a lie but it's far enough from the truth.

"Oh sweetie," Ms. Margaret touches my cheek, "I'm so glad to see you. But what are you doing all the way out here? You should be at the palace."

"I was. Cassandra threw me out and tried to have me arrested."

"Lorraine," Brent hisses, so I turn around, still gripping Ms. Margaret's hand.

"I've known her all my life. I trust her."

Ms Margaret cackles. "And who is this paranoid young man?"

"This is Brent. He helped me get back."

She smiles. "Well, don't let Cassandra stop you. She's just afraid of you."

"I guess so."

She lifts my chin even though she is shorter than me. "Have faith, dear. I know you can beat her. Don't let a silly thing like getting arrested stop you."

I can't help but smile. She makes it sound so easy, so simple. "It's so good to see you again."

"You too, dear. Now go. Don't let me interrupt you. If I could help, I would."

Brent and I wait until Ms. Margaret gets back inside her house before talking. When I see Brent about to speak, I turn away from him and start walking again.

"Wait," he says, but follows me anyway. "You got your memory back? All of it?"

"I think so. As far as I can tell, it's all there."

"When did it come back?"

"At the palace. When I looked up at the family portrait that Cassandra pointed to, something clicked."

"You don't seem excited."

"Why would I be?"

"The answer to that seems obvious."

I shrug. "I don't know, I guess I don't have anything to miss anymore now that it's back. Besides, it's useless to me now."

"What? That's not true. Now you can—"

"Now I can what, Brent? I already got thrown out and arrested. Trilland law prevents my return at this point. I lost. Get over it."

"We didn't lose, we just—"

"There is no 'we' here, do you understand that? This is your fault."

"My fault? How is this my fault? I'm the one that got you here."

"You're the one who got us here *late*. If you hadn't wasted so much time back on the island or back at Gessend, we might've made it."

"I didn't waste time. I wanted you to get your memory before we returned so you wouldn't be in over your head."

I stop because I see the docks in the distance, and we need to be quiet if we're going to walk out in the open to the ship. "I told you I needed Uncle Lawrence, and you wouldn't take me to him. You didn't even tell him what happened. And you kept information from me every step of the way. If it weren't for you, we could have gotten here sooner, I would have seen the picture sooner, and we could have gotten to Cassandra before a law expired on me."

"You cannot blame that on me. Yes, I delayed meeting up with Captain Wilson, but that was, like, a day. We're several days late. Maybe if you hadn't wasted so much time on the island being mopey and refusing to work with me, we would have left sooner."

"Mopey? I didn't know who I was, I didn't know if I could trust you, and clearly I couldn't. How dare you try to blame this whole thing on my psychological state?"

"How dare I?" Brent scoffs. "Well, you certainly sound like royalty now. You should have tried some of that language with Cassandra, and maybe we wouldn't be arguing behind a palm tree right now."

"You don't get it. *I* know the law. I know what it says. There is no way out. And you are to blame, whether you're willing to admit it or not."

Brent says my name a few times, but I ignore him, walking straight for the docks. When it looks like everyone is distracted, I slip past and onto our ship. None of the sailors are here which is a little concerning. I wonder where they went. Did they abandon, or were they arrested? I might have to hitch a ride with someone to get back to the little island. I wonder if Zane will even speak to me when I get back.

I go into the cabin and close the door. I do not want to see Brent or hear his voice right now. I'm so livid that I will probably start screaming at him again, and we can't afford to draw attention to ourselves.

Uncle Lawrence's books are still open all over the table. When I see them, I remember that Uncle Lawrence is in prison right now. Can I really leave him behind and just go back? Can I leave Trilland behind? Do I even have a choice?

I sit down on the cot in the corner to think, but I find my eyelids forcibly closing with exhaustion and despair. I slump down onto the floor, leaning against the cabin wall. It's obvious I can't think clearly like this. But will I be able to think more clearly after taking a nap? Is it even safe to take a nap now that Brent and I are on the run? A million possibilities run through my head about Cassandra, Trilland, Uncle Lawrence, Brent, and Zane, but I find that I can't hold on to any of them, and my mind drifts to sleep.

## Chapter 18

I'm woken up by the sun attempting to penetrate into my brain through my eyelids, and I bolt upright. I must have only fallen asleep for a few minutes, and I almost feel worse than I did before. The sun is setting, and it's in the perfect position to come through the window and try to blind me. I try to cover my eyes, but it's futile, so I get up and change out of the dress that's ruined and think about how Elise will kill me when she sees its condition. I sit on the edge of the bed and think back to earlier in the day, recalling every event, making sure it wasn't a dream. Then I recall every memory I can think of and make sure that *that* wasn't a dream, and I'm simultaneously happy and sad to find that in both cases it was not a dream. I walk over to the table and start flipping through Uncle Lawrence's captain's log. I was hoping that I would wake up knowing what to do about him, but I'm disappointed to find that I still don't. Maybe the best option is to break him out of jail and then bring him back to Gessend or the island or something. There's no place for him here anymore. There's no place for me anymore.

I flip to the last page he wrote when we docked here and read his short summary of the time, weather, and events. I flip back a few pages to when we left Gessend. It's all pretty ordinary, but one page catches my eye because there's an extra sentence at the bottom. It's the page from when we left Gessend. His normal notes are all jotted down, but at the bottom, in his perfect handwriting, I see the sentence, "She's here with me again."

I smile a little and flip to the next page where I find another sentence that reads: "She's back and she's going to fix everything."

He never told me that he wrote these things or even thought these things. I know he was happy to see me again, but I didn't know that he was so convinced that I would be able to fix everything in Trilland. I wonder if he remembered that law. He must not have. He seemed surprised when Cassandra brought it up. I actually do remember that law. It was designed to prevent the country from falling into anarchy due to a defective or dysfunctional ruler. How ironic that it should now stand in my way of removing Cassandra from power.

But then something occurs to me, some distant memory from when that law was passed. There just might be a loophole. But if I'm going to go through that loophole, I'm going to need help. First on the list is Uncle Lawrence, but I'll need help getting to him. I wish Zane were here. I feel like he would know what to do. But I can't sit around waiting for Zane when he's not here. I have to do this myself. Unfortunately, that means I'm going to need Brent's help whether I want it or not. I'm also going to need some food because I'm starving. I haven't eaten since yesterday because I was too nervous to eat this morning.

I open the door to the cabin hesitantly and scan the boat for Brent. For a split second, when I don't see him, I panic and think that maybe Cassandra's guards came back for us and they've already arrested Brent, but then I spot him on the far end of the ship. I walk all the way over to him before speaking, and when I do, he jumps.

"Sorry, I didn't mean to startle you."

"It's fine," Brent says, but he sounds exhausted. Looks like we both could use some sleep. "What were you doing?"

"I was flipping through Uncle Lawrence's books and dozed off for a minute. I didn't mean to, but I kind of just passed out."

"I don't blame you."

"Has anyone come back? Any of the other sailors?"

"Some guards went by earlier. Got a little nervous that they were going to come onto the ship." Brent shrugs. "I guess they haven't figured out which one we're on yet or maybe someone saw you and tipped them off. They were circling that neighborhood over there for a while." He points to Ms. Margaret's street.

Neither of us speaks for a while, but I can't stand the silence, so I say, "Are you hungry?"

Brent smiles just slightly before returning his mouth to a tight, thin line. "Starving. I tried eating some of the stuff we had on board, but it's not great. Do you know of anywhere nearby we could get some food?"

I nod and point at a little white building with a blue roof. "That restaurant right there is owned by an old family friend, and it doesn't get busy at night. It's more of a lunch place."

"What are you going to do? Walk in and catch up on old times?"

I roll my eyes. "I'm not going in there to chat. I'm just saying that I know the environment there, and we should be able to slip in and out relatively unnoticed."

Brent nods. "We should probably wait until it gets a little darker. It'll be easier to avoid getting seen."

I nod again. I guess this is what our conversation has been reduced to. Just nodding and saying nothing of any substance. At least we're speaking. I guess that's something.

"I want to talk to you about something," I say, and when Brent raises his eyebrows, I continue. "I think there might still be a way to get past this law."

Brent leans against the railing, folds his arms, and smiles. "Yeah?"

"I actually remember the law she's talking about. My father is the one who signed it. It's designed to prevent the country from being without a ruler for too long. If a ruler is absent from the throne for a year, then it goes to the next of kin."

"Right, which is how Cassandra took over. So what's the catch?"

"The law is very specific about the circumstances behind the ruler's absence. The ruler has to desert the throne."

"Really? I thought it was any absence."

"That's what Cassandra wants everyone to think, but no. The ruler basically has to abandon the country."

"But you didn't do that."

"Exactly. I was stranded. She tried to have me killed. That's not desertion. If I can prove that, then I still have legal claim to the throne, especially if I can prove that it was Cassandra's fault."

"But how do we prove that?"

I lean against the railing next to Brent and sigh. "Well, that's the hard part. I'm not sure how to prove it. If we could get someone to confess, then it would be easy, but I don't know if that's possible."

Brent nods, but then he points at the ship pulling into the docks. It's a merchant ship, probably returning from carrying supplies to the provinces. Its flags are Trilland flags. I don't know why he's pointing it out. These ships come pretty frequently. It isn't unusual.

"Look, a bunch of people are getting off that ship right now. Let's go." Brent jumps up and starts grabbing some of his stuff.

"Go where?"

"To the restaurant. With all those people getting off the ship, it's the perfect opportunity. We'll be able to blend in with them, and we won't have to wait until dark. It's a win-win."

I want to argue, but it's as good a plan as any other. I run back into the cabin, throw on a jacket and some sunglasses, let my hair down, and head back out to Brent. It's not exactly a foolproof disguise, but it's better than nothing. At the last minute, I grab some of the money Uncle Lawrence left behind.

"Ready?" Brent says, and I nod.

We wait for the flow of people to get going first before we get off the ship. The last thing we need is to be noticed, so we don't want to be the first ones on the dock. After a few people get off, we walk as quickly as we can while still looking casual and blend in with the crowd.

This is eerily reminiscent of when we got to Trilland earlier today and had to blend in with the crowd for a different reason. In the distance, you can see the palace from here, except this time, the guards are visible. Cassandra must be paranoid since she's surely gotten word by now that Brent and I escaped. I look over at Brent and realize that he's not wearing sunglasses or a hat or anything. I wonder how recognizable he is at this point and whether or not we should have considered hiding his face before coming out here.

The crowd gets a little dense in one spot, so Brent takes my hand, and I can only assume it's to prevent separation. Yet somehow, even though it's purely practical, holding Brent's hand feels wrong. He's not the one I wish were here, holding my hand. I still find myself wishing Zane were here. I feel stupid for thinking that because Zane chose not to say goodbye, and he chose to let me leave. I should be angry, and part of me is, but a bigger part of me feels the giant hole in my life he leaves by not being here.

Brent tugs on my hand as he moves to the right, in the direction of the restaurant, but I struggle to keep up with him because people are moving very quickly around me. Someone bumps my shoulder and keeps going, obviously in a hurry, but when I turn to see who bumped into me, I see someone who looks remarkably like Zane. I tell myself that this obviously isn't Zane because Zane is still back on the little island and this guy has facial hair, but I can't shake Zane's face out of my head. How pathetic that I want to see him so desperately that I'm actually hallucinating his face in the middle of a crowd.

But when Zane's doppelganger turns around, obviously looking for someone, his eyes lock on mine and at the exact same moment, Zane and I realize we are looking at each other.

"Maris," Zane calls out, and I drop Brent's hand and run through the crowd as quickly as I can manage without bumping into people or causing too much of a scene.

As soon as I reach Zane, he throws his arms out, and I run into them, never happier to see him. He kisses my cheek and holds on tightly, and I hold on just as tightly. The scruff on his cheeks tickles my face, and it feels weird because he's never had that before, but I don't even care because Zane is here.

"What are you doing here?" I say.

"I came for you," he says with an eye roll. "What other reason do I have to come to Trilland?"

"But how—"

"I hitched a ride on one of the merchant ships. I promised to teach them some fishing tips in return."

"Zane, I'm so happy to see you. I really need to talk to you."

But before I can tell Zane everything, about how my memory is back, how Cassandra tried to have me arrested, how now I have to prove my innocence, Brent catches up to us.

"Hey, I know everyone's all excited here, but we have to keep moving. You and I are fugitives, remember?"

"What?" Zane says.

"I'll explain later," I say. "Come on, we're getting food and going back to the ship. Hungry?"

"Starving," he says.

Zane laces his fingers through mine, and this time, holding someone's hand feels right.

# Chapter 19

While Brent organizes our food back on the ship, I take Zane into the cabin and explain what happened with Cassandra. He interrupts a few times to express his exasperation, as per usual, but lets me get it all out before asking questions. The only thing I can't seem to put into words is the memory. I was so excited to tell him when I first saw him, but now I don't know how to say the words. What if it changes things between us? He's only ever known me as the amnesiac girl from the island. He's never known Lorraine Everhart, princess of Trilland. Will he still feel the same way?

"I can't believe she just arrested you," he says. "So, what are you going to do?"

"I'm not sure. Brent and I have been trying to figure out a plan."

Zane scoffs. "Yeah, because Brent is so helpful, right?"

"Don't do that. I needed to get to Trilland, and he was the way to get here. That's all."

"Was it really such a desperate mission to get here? Now Cassandra probably wants you dead."

Well, this is it. This is my chance to tell Zane. This is the moment when our friendship either changes forever or ends forever.

"Zane, listen to me. I needed to come to Trilland. There was something I needed that I couldn't get back on the island."

"What? What could you have possibly needed that we couldn't have done for you? What's wrong with our island? What don't we have that fancy Trilland—"

"My memory, Zane," I say. "Trilland had my memory."

"You mean—"

"Yes," I say, a smile too big for my face taking over. "I've been dying to tell you. My memory came back. This morning, it came back."

"That's fantastic." Zane picks me up and spins me around in a circle. "I'm so happy for you."

"Thank you," I say, still giggling from the spin.

"Oh man." Zane's face looks suddenly solemn. "I'm so sorry. You knew you needed to go to Trilland, and it turns out it was the answer, and I tried to stop you. I'm so sorry."

"You were angry, and rightfully so. It makes sense."

"But I was still wrong."

Before I can say anything, Brent knocks on the door and cracks it open. "Ready for dinner?"

I can tell Zane is seething at Brent's interruption, but we don't have time for their testosterone competition right now. I grab Zane's arm, and say, "It doesn't matter anymore. We're here now, and we have to deal with Cassandra."

"How?"

"Well, I think there might be a way to prove that I didn't desert Trilland, but it's tricky." Zane and I walk back out to the deck and sit down to eat with Brent. "We'd have to get someone to confess."

"Someone like who?" Zane asks.

Brent answers, "One of Cassandra's crew members that was a part of the mutiny. There has to be someone who, for whatever reason, has fallen out of favor with Cassandra and would be willing to confess."

"Seems unlikely," Zane says.

Ever since Zane got here, he and Brent have been kind of short with each other. They are clearly still at odds, but it hasn't exploded into a full-on fight yet. They mostly just keep contradicting each other over absolutely everything.

"It's our best chance," Brent says.

Zane says, "Is it?"

"The problem," I say, "is that we have no idea where to find someone like that."

"So, where do we start?" Zane says.

"We should start by getting off this ship," Brent says. "It's only a matter of time before they start searching every ship at the dock."

"And where do we go then?" Zane's voice has the slightest edge that he is making no effort to conceal.

"Anywhere that doesn't have a big target on it."

"Well, obviously, we have to go get Uncle Lawrence out of prison," I say.

"I don't think that's such a good idea," Brent says. "Going over there will only get us all arrested, you and me for the second time. You really think Cassandra will let us get away again?"

"Well, I need him here."

"He wouldn't want you to risk your own safety for him."

"You don't know anything about what he would want," I say.

"Brent has a point," Zane says, and even Brent looks surprised that Zane agreed with him. "Once we prove your innocence, you can just order him to be released."

"I can't just leave him there. We don't know how long this will take. Besides, I need him now. He always knows what to do."

"It's just not a good idea," Brent says. "I can't let you go. You're endangering yourself."

"What do you mean you can't 'let' me go? It's not really up to you."

"I'm just trying to protect you."

"Well, I don't need you to protect me. You've certainly done enough of that. Don't you think you've caused enough problems?"

"That's completely unfair."

"Is it?"

"What are you guys talking about?" Zane says.

"Oh, that's right, Zane," I say. "You don't know about how Brent has been lying to me this whole time. He never told Uncle Lawrence about my memory loss. He kept him in the dark, never told me, and then tried to delay our meeting because he knew his lie would come out."

"That is not what happened," Brent says. "You're making me sound like some kind of villain. That's not at all how it happened."

"Sure it is."

"How could you keep that from her?" Zane says. "That's way out of line."

"You've got a lot of nerve judging me. You're the one who told her not to trust me or the captain."

"Well obviously I was right about you."

"And Captain Wilson?"

"Why did I have any reason to believe you? You've been nothing but untrustworthy. All you've done is mess with her head. You're the one who convinced her to come here without any planning whatsoever."

"Nobody made me come here," I say. "I wanted to come here."

Zane shakes his head. "That's all just Brent in your head."

"No," Brent says, "her refusal to trust me is just you in her head."

I yell, "Both of you shut up. Both of you have let me down and caused me problems, and we're not going to get anywhere by screaming at each other. Now, listen. I'm the reason we're all here. I'm the rightful princess, and I'm the one who has to take Cassandra down, so I call the shots right now. And I say that the first thing we do is find Uncle Lawrence because he's the only one who hasn't let me down so far. He'll know what to do. Now, the sun is almost down, and we should go during the night when we won't be seen. Let's leave in about an hour or so. Until then, I'm going down to the beach, and don't either one of you try to stop me."

I get up, look around to make sure no one is watching us, and slip down the plank, down the docks, and down to the little beach next to the docks. I walk down so that I'm behind the ship and out of view of anyone who might be walking by, not that there are many people around this late at night. I don't expect for anyone to be here, so when I hear someone walking up behind me I get nervous, but then I realize that it's Zane.

Zane hesitates, then says, "I've never seen you talk to someone like that before."

I shrug. "I've never been in a situation like this before, I guess."

Zane kicks the sand a little, avoiding eye contact and rubbing the back of his neck nervously. "I should've been there."

"Where?"

"The day you left. I shouldn't have let you leave without saying goodbye. I've been kicking myself for it."

I nod. "And I shouldn't have kissed Brent."

Then, as if remembering that he was supposed to be angry with me, Zane folds his arms and looks askance at me. "So Brent lied to the captain?"

"Yeah. Found that out when he started talking to me like I remembered everything and knew who he was."

"I told you not to trust him," Zane says, irritation lacing his words. "Why didn't you believe me?"

"Because I needed to trust him. I needed to know if he was telling the truth. And he was, just not about that."

"Well, that's kind of significant."

"But I needed to know who I was. It wasn't really important to me how I found out."

"It's kind of important," Zane says, his voice starting to rise in anger. "You just took off on me, running around with some guy who's been around for two seconds and doesn't know anything about you. *I* know you. I always have."

I shake my head. "Zane, you are simultaneously the person who knows me the best and knows me the least. You are my best friend, and I care about you more than anyone, but you met someone that wasn't me. The girl you knew didn't even know herself."

"Just because you couldn't remember yourself doesn't mean you're not still the same person. I *do* know you. I know everything about you. How else could I have fallen in love—" Zane stops suddenly, flushing fiercely red and tightening his folded arms. His voice drops very low and he says, "I refuse to believe that I don't know you, especially not better than Brent knows you."

My eyes sting a little bit with happiness. Zane still cares. Even after everything that's happened, even knowing who I really am now, Zane cares far more than I ever hoped he did. "Zane, no one knows me better than you. Especially not Brent. You are the one I always come back to."

I take Zane's hand into mine and look into his eyes to make him believe what I've just said. Apparently it works because Zane pulls me into him and kisses me as passionately as if we had been apart for years. It feels so good to be kissed by Zane again, so good that I hold the back of his neck gently to make it last as long as I can. I didn't know how badly I had missed kissing Zane. It just feels so right being in his arms.

When we finally manage to separate, Zane keeps a firm hold on my back, keeping me close to him.

"Oh, Maris," Zane says softly into my ear, and I jolt involuntarily. "What? What's wrong?"

"It's just—it sounds so weird being called Maris now," I say.

Zane chuckles. "Why? Did you get too used to Trilland already? I've been calling you Maris for a year."

"It just means something different to me now, I guess."

"I'm sorry I tried to stop you from coming to Trilland."

I smile. "You already apologized for that."

"I know, but I shouldn't have let my anger stop you from doing what you needed to do. What can I do to make it up to you?"

"Never leave me again." I smile and pull him in for another kiss. "And help me get Uncle Lawrence back."

"You've got it," Zane says and kisses me again.

We lace our fingers together again and start walking back to the ship. It really is dangerous to be out here. Plus, we need to plan how we're going to get to the prison and get Uncle Lawrence out. But now that I have Zane again and I know that he still loves me, I feel like I can do anything.

"So, should I call you Lorraine now?" Zane says tentatively.

"No," I say, after very little hesitation. "It would be too weird for you to call me anything but the name you gave me."

"It won't be weirder for me not to call you by name?"

I shrug. "In many ways, both Maris and Lorraine are my name."

<center>~~~</center>

When I insisted that I had to get Uncle Lawrence out of prison, for some reason, I thought it would be easy. I'm not sure why I thought we would be able just to walk into the prison and walk back out with Uncle Lawrence. Now that Brent, Zane, and I are sneaking around through the palm trees, mosquitoes nipping at our legs, I'm questioning my plan. Obviously, going overnight was the right decision because we're less likely to be discovered, but what do we do once we get there? I imagine the prison is guarded. I imagine a man accused of treason is heavily guarded. I imagine a man accused of treason who showed up with potentially the lost princess of Trilland who is a major threat to the egotistical ruler is especially heavily guarded. My logic was that since Brent and I are public enemies #1 and #2, Cassandra isn't really interested in having guards at the prison right now. Plus, we saw a ton of guards going the opposite direction—probably looking for me—so whatever guards were there probably aren't now. But what if I'm wrong? How on earth do we do this?

The one thing I know for sure is that I'm not going to admit any of this to either Brent or Zane. After my explosion about how they need to respect me, I'm not going to admit weakness. And yet, even though I don't want to admit it—I certainly won't admit it if I can help it—I still find it comforting to have Zane—and even Brent—here. I wonder if I could do this alone.

Most of our communication thus far has been nonverbal—partially because we're all afraid of getting caught and partially because Zane and Brent are not speaking—but when I see the prison up ahead, I utter one word: "Stop."

Brent and Zane stop almost simultaneously and both turn to look at me. Zane raises his arms into a gesture that says, "Why on earth are we stopping?"

I whisper, "There's a back door on the right side. We should go in there."

"Is it open?" Brent asks.

I nod. "The guards like to take breaks during the night, so they leave that door open. It'll be easier to slip through instead of trying to walk through the front door."

Zane shrugs. "Seems like a good idea to me."

"Okay, follow me," I say. "At a certain point, the guards will step outside for at least fifteen minutes or so. We can slip in then. But we'll have to move quickly. Once they realize Uncle Lawrence is gone, they're sure to send out a search party."

Brent and Zane both nod, so I nod, too, and we start walking again. We stop just short of the building where we're still under the cover of the palm trees and wait. It doesn't take long for two guards to step outside, each with a cigarette, and start chatting and joking around with each other. They're so distracted, I think we could just walk right in, but we still sneak in as quietly as possible.

Once inside the jail, I'm surprised by how small it is. I visited it as a child, but I remember it much bigger. I guess that's the way it is when you get older—when you're small, everything seems big; it isn't until you get older that you realized it never was big. The entire place is one room with about ten cells. Only three of them are filled: Uncle Lawrence, some random guy who is muttering something about being framed, and Timothy. I run straight for Uncle Lawrence, and Zane follows me, but Brent grabs the keys and heads for Timothy.

"What are you doing here?" Uncle Lawrence says. "You should leave. This isn't safe."

"I had to come get you. I need your help."

"It isn't safe," he says again. "I heard something about you getting arrested. How'd you escape?"

"We'll explain later," Zane says. "We need to hurry."

Uncle Lawrence looks at Zane quizzically. "Who are you?"

"Friend from the island," I say. "I'll explain everything. Brent, where are the keys to Uncle Lawrence's cell?"

Brent unlocks Timothy's cell and passes the keys to Zane who starts unlocking Uncle Lawrence's cell, but he doesn't leave Timothy. When Brent sees me staring at them, I raise one eyebrow, and Brent waves us all over.

"You're going to want to hear this."

"What?" I say.

"Timothy knows where we can find one of the sailors from the mutiny."

I spin around to face Timothy. "Really?"

He nods. "His name is Derek Ingraham. I'm not sure where he lives exactly, but I know it's near the docks. He works down there maintaining the ships."

"And he'd be willing to help us?"

He nods again. "A lot of those guys came back kind of shaken over the idea that they had killed you. A few of them just decided to collect their payment and bolt. He was one of them. I think he'd be willing to help, especially if you promise him something in return. Money or something."

"That's fantastic," says Uncle Lawrence. "We'll go find him right now."

"Are you coming with us?" I say to Timothy, but he shakes his head.

"I'm going to stay with a friend until you take the throne back and I can return home. Good luck. I know you can do it."

"Thank you, Tim. Your help will not be forgotten."

"Anything for you." Timothy smirks. "But you know better than to call me 'Tim.'"

I shrug. "You know I had to get one in."

"Uh, we really need to get going," Zane says while peeking out the door. "I think these guys are nearing the end of their break, and we want to be far away when they realize two prisoners are gone."

Timothy smiles one last time and then sneaks out the door. When we're sure he's gotten past unnoticed, the four of us slip out, too. Zane first, then me, then Uncle Lawrence, then Brent. It doesn't take us long to get back to the palm trees, but we don't slow our pace there. As soon as they realize Uncle Lawrence and Timothy are gone, they're going to come after us.

We get going as quickly as we can, and it's a good thing, because we hear the guards shouting in the distance. I guess they just noticed they lost two prisoners. Since Timothy ran the opposite direction, we cause enough confusion that it doesn't seem like the guards know which direction to run. We use that to our advantage and hurry toward the docks.

Luckily, we're not far from the docks, and even with Uncle Lawrence limping, it doesn't take us long to get back. We never communicated this, but we all seem to understand that the plan is to go back to the ship, regroup, and then go looking for Derek Ingraham. Our best chance of finding him is now while we still have the cover of night and there isn't a country-wide search party for us. But when we get within a short distance of the docks, we all stop at the same moment because we all see the same thing: the ship is being raided.

# Chapter 20

The ship is swarming with soldiers who are overturning crates, checking behind every door, and flashing lights into every corner. They're already looking for us. Every time I try to count how many of them there are, I lose count around twenty-something. It's way too many, and they don't look like they're leaving any time soon.

"What do we do?" Brent whispers.

"We have to keep moving," Zane says. "We're too vulnerable here."

"But where are we going to go?" Brent says. "You see what's happening."

Zane says something in response, but Ms. Margaret's words from earlier come back to me: *If I could help, I would.*

"I have an idea," I say. "Brent, do you remember where Ms. Margaret's house is?"

"Margaret Simmons?" Uncle Lawrence says, so I nod. "You saw her?"

"Yes."

"And you *remember* her?"

"Yes."

"Lorraine, that's fantastic." Uncle Lawrence throws his arms around me, but he's making a little too much noise, so I shush him.

"Brent, do you remember?"

"Yeah," Brent says.

"That's where we're going. Come on."

Luckily, the soldiers are so busy scouring the ship that they don't seem to be looking around. It's fairly easy for us to slip past the docks into the neighborhood on the other side. Once we're hidden behind the houses and the palm trees, we slow our pace only slightly to accommodate Uncle Lawrence. He seems pretty winded, and even though he won't admit it, I can tell he's in pain. There's a tension around us that's palpable, but none of us have the strength to address it. At least Ms. Margaret's house isn't far.

When we reach the little pink house, I knock very gingerly, then a little harder, until she opens the door.

"Your group is multiplying," she says.

"Mind if we come in for a little while?" I say, and she doesn't hesitate to usher us all in.

Her air conditioning hits strongly as soon as we get in, and it seems like it dissipates the tension at least a little bit. It feels almost too cold but still delightfully fresh after so many days on the ship. She immediately insists that we all sit down and brings us water, and it isn't until I start drinking that I realize how dehydrated I must be. I haven't had any water since dinner which was hours ago.

Her home hasn't changed at all in years. It's like the very house has a pink glow. The pink wallpaper, soft lights, and sweet baking smell mixed with musky perfume is exactly how I remember it. After several introductions of who everybody is and Uncle Lawrence and Ms. Margaret greeting each other, we explain our sudden arrival to Ms. Margaret.

"I'm glad you came, sweetie," she says. "Please, stay as long as you like. You're welcome to anything I have."

"Thank you," I say. "I don't know what we'd do without you."

"Well, you certainly wouldn't get a shower without me."

Uncle Lawrence laughs. "Is it bad?"

"Oh no." Ms. Margaret cackles. "Just unusual, that's all."

"I'll go first," Brent says. He pushes himself up off the couch and heads for the bathroom.

As soon as Ms. Margaret leaves the room to get towels for Brent, Uncle Lawrence throws his arm around my shoulders.

"You remember."

"Yes, I do."

Uncle Lawrence abandons all sense of decorum and wraps me in a big bear hug just like he used to when I was a kid. He hasn't done that in a long time except for when he first saw me in Gessend, but I didn't appreciate it then. I couldn't remember him. Now, it means so much more. He's shaking a little bit, and I can't figure out why until I feel a teardrop hit my shoulder.

"Uncle Lawrence, please don't cry," I say, rubbing his back and trying to get him to stop crushing my ribs with happiness.

"I'm sorry, I'm sorry." Uncle Lawrence releases and rubs his eyes. "I'm just so happy that you got your memory back. And I'm thrilled to know that the last few times you've called me 'Uncle Lawrence' have been genuine and not forced. You don't know how much I've missed that."

"I can't imagine calling you anything else."

He looks like he's about to say something, but Ms. Margaret walks back in right then and sits down. Uncle Lawrence and I decide to explain about the mutiny, and she listens intently, all while stirring her tea.

"So, what's the next step?"

"Cassandra is trying to enforce the royal abandonment clause as cause for her legal claim to the throne," I say. "She's claiming that since it's already past the year deadline, we can't do anything."

"Well, that just doesn't seem right," she says.

"It's not since I didn't voluntarily abandon Trilland. Now, we have to prove that. We think we might know of someone who was there for the mutiny and who would be willing to testify. That's who we were trying to find when we ended up here."

"What is his name?"

"Derek Ingraham."

Ms. Margaret nods. "He lives down by the docks."

"Do you know the address?" Zane asks.

Ms. Margaret gets up and shuffles over to a table behind her sofa. She starts flipping through an address book, writes down one of them, and sits back down and hands the note to Uncle Lawrence.

"That's his address, I believe. It isn't far from here."

"Yeah, but we can't go now," Zane says. "The docks are swarming with soldiers."

"Just wait until morning," she says. "You'll all feel better after a few hours of sleep."

Zane, Uncle Lawrence, and I all look at each other and shrug. It seems like the best idea. We're all exhausted, and maybe by the time that we get a little sleep, the soldiers will have moved on. We agree to stay, and Ms. Margaret finds herself all too eager to make tea for everyone even though Zane and Uncle Lawrence both hate tea. Uncle Lawrence goes to the kitchen with her to help, leaving me and Zane alone together for the first time since our fight and kiss on the beach. He looks at me and smiles this adorable sleepy smile, and I can't help but grin widely. Zane slumps back into the couch, and I nestle into the space between his chest and arm, resting my head on his upper arm. Zane kisses my head gently, and even though we're on the run, I've never been so happy.

"So, how did you get here?" I say. "To Trilland, I mean."

"I told you. I hitched a ride with the merchants."

"But when I left—"

"I know. After the ship sailed away, my mom came and told me what an idiot I was, and then Elise, and then my sister. And I don't know, something about Daisy screaming at me about how I was the stupidest boy she's ever known really hit me," he says, and I can't help but laugh. Daisy's the best friend a girl could ask for. "But I didn't need all of them to tell me I was an idiot. I regretted letting you go the second I saw the ship start sailing. I waited for the next merchant ship to come by and begged them to bring me along. They agreed in exchange for fishing tips because they saw the haul we were bringing in. Now that you know, tell me, what is it about Trilland? Do they not know how to fish?"

I laugh again. "Fishing is a major industry in Trilland."

"Then why does it seem like no one around here can fish?"

"Maybe you need to show them how it's done."

"I just may do that," Zane gloats. "Anyway, I got off at Gessend because Elise told me you were stopping there first to get Captain Wilson, but when I got there, they told me you had already left for Trilland. But those darn merchants stop *everywhere,* so it took forever to get here. Somehow though, I still got here relatively close to the time you did."

"We made a couple of stops on the way." I fill Zane in on our stops at Gessend and Anden, the good and the bad, and explain everything up until we got to Trilland, which he already knows.

"I know it was kind of crazy to chase you down all over the sea, but I just couldn't live with myself knowing I had pushed you away. Besides, Daisy didn't speak to me until I told her I was going to come to Trilland."

"Gotta love that girl."

"I'm just glad I made it." Zane tilts my chin toward his and kisses me softly. "I couldn't have lived with myself—or with Daisy—if I hadn't at least tried."

"I'm glad you did. I feel a lot better knowing you're here. I missed you."

"I missed you, too."

For a moment, we just stare at each other. I can hardly believe that I'm sitting here in Ms. Margaret's house in Trilland with Zane, and when I think about all of the events that led to this moment, it all feels so surreal. Still, I'm glad for this moment, and I'm enjoying the way Zane is gazing at me, the softest smile on his lips.

"Shower's free," Brent says, walking out of the bathroom shaking his wet hair. He sure knows how to ruin a moment.

Zane sighs. "I guess I'll go next."

"Wait," Uncle Lawrence says as he comes into the room with Ms. Margaret. "We need to talk." He nods to Ms. Margaret, and she starts talking.

"Cassandra is scheduled to give some kind of speech tomorrow. She announced it late today. I assume it has to do with your appearance."

"She's sure to make me out to be some kind of villain."

"We have to find Derek before then," Brent says.

"We should leave early in the morning," I say. "Around sunrise. We still need to avoid getting spotted until Cassandra's speech. Hopefully we can get Derek on board before then."

"And then what?" Brent says.

"We crash the party," Uncle Lawrence says. "If Derek agrees, then we show up at the speech, interrupt, and prove not only that Lorraine is alive but that she didn't willfully abandon the country. Cassandra won't have a chance."

"Perfect," I say, before either Brent or Zane can object. "It's fool-proof."

"As long as Derek agrees," Brent says.

"Well, we'll have to make him agree."

~~~

Ms. Margaret wakes us all up early in the morning, just before sunrise. We get ready to quickly and quietly—I don't think anyone really knows what to say—and Ms. Margaret brings us a breakfast of scones and coconut milk. The scones are hot and delicious, and we all eat at least three each. After we eat, Ms. Margaret pulls me aside and leads me to the guest room where she let me sleep last night.

"I don't know if you'll be able to get back to your ship, but I can't let you show up at that speech dressed like that."

Ms. Margaret points at me, and when I look down, I realize just how right she is. I'm still wearing the shorts and halter tank that I threw on when Brent and I got back to the ship after being arrested. The shorts, once green, are now dingy and wrinkled, and the gray shirt is starting to look more black than gray. But she's right. We don't know if the ship is clear or not. Something tells me Cassandra wouldn't want to leave the ship unattended just in case we tried to go back there to leave.

Ms. Margaret pulls out a couple of different outfit options from the closet. She tells me that they're her daughter's clothes that she left behind when she got married. A few of the options are really not my style—her daughter wore a lot of floral—but the last two seem appropriate, so I try on both and end up wearing the one that fits the best. I choose a three-quarter length sleeved cobalt blue shirt with a scoop neckline and a high-waisted black skirt that hits me just above the knee. It's still casual enough that I'll be comfortable, but nice enough that I won't look like a total trainwreck when I interrupt Cassandra's speech in front of all of Trilland. I undo my hair that I
~~~

braided last night after showering and let the crinkled hair fall around my shoulders. Ms. Margaret does my makeup, and by the end of it, I actually look pretty enough to feel at least a little comfortable being seen.

I reunite with the guys in the living room, and we quickly nail down the specifics. We're going directly for Derek's house. Assuming he agrees and depending on how long it takes, we may try to go to the ship. Otherwise, we'll head straight for Cassandra's speech, which should be beginning by then. It's a simple plan, but it's all predicated on Derek's agreeing to help. What if he doesn't? Or what if he alerts Cassandra of what we're doing and where we are? Everything surrounding Derek is risky, but there's nothing to do but take a risk now.

It's a short walk to Derek's house, but when we approach, none of us are really sure what to do. He isn't expecting us, and how will it look for two people whom he thought he killed to show up at his door? We decide it's best if Zane and Brent knock first since he has no knowledge of them, and Uncle Lawrence and I stand off to the side. It takes a few knocks to get Derek to answer, and when he does, it's clear that he was asleep.

"Can I help you?" he says with irritation lacing his words. "It's, like, seven in the morning."

"Are you Derek Ingraham?" Zane asks.

"Yeah. What do you want?"

"We need to talk to you about something very important," Brent says. "It's about your previous service to Cassandra Wellington."

Derek flinches visibly when Brent says Cassandra's name. "What about it? I don't work for her anymore, if that's what you're asking."

"Oh, we know," Brent says. "We need to talk to you about Princess Lorraine's death."

"What?"

Brent looks at me and nods, so Uncle Lawrence and I both step in front of the open door, and while Derek's face betrays his surprise, but it doesn't last long.

"I knew it," he says, almost whispers. "I knew it."

"Could we talk inside?" Uncle Lawrence says. "This isn't a conversation we can have out in the open like this."

Derek nods and steps aside for all of us to enter. His house is small and simple. There is minimal furniture and no decoration. It reminds me a little of Uncle Lawrence's house at Gessend. I wonder if that's something to do with sailors—maybe they all like simple living spaces.

All four us manage to squish onto the one couch Derek has in the living room, and he pulls up a chair from his dining table. I can remember his face but only vaguely. It's like seeing him triggers memories of the mutiny, but I can't really picture any of the sailors' faces. Distantly, I wonder if that will always be the case. When I first woke up on the island and realized I had amnesia, I did a lot of research. Sometimes, the brain tries to protect itself from trauma by blocking everything out. I wonder if my memories of the mutiny will always be hazy like this. Maybe my brain will never be ready to acknowledge what happened that day.

He seems hesitant to talk and keeps nervously glancing back and forth between me and Uncle Lawrence, so Brent volunteers to go first.

"Your name was given to us as someone who may be able to help us," he says. "Could you tell us why you no longer work for Cassandra?"

Derek shrugs and avoids eye contact. "I just couldn't do it anymore. I didn't want to be the person she wanted me to be."

"What do you mean?" Brent says.

"I'm just a sailor. I've always been a sailor. Both my dad and my granddad were sailors. It's a simple job, and I like it. But she wanted us to be her soldiers and servants and lackeys and henchmen. It's just not the life I wanted. But I haven't sailed a day since that trip."

"What do you mean?" Uncle Lawrence asks.

"We were promised money if we—if we made you disappear." Derek makes eye contact with me then quickly looks back down to the ground. "When we got back to Trilland and told Cassandra that you and Captain Wilson were both gone, she followed through and paid us all. It wasn't a lot, but it was something, and sailors don't make a lot. She promised all of us more money if we would continue sailing for her, but I was afraid of what that might entail. When one of the other men—an older gentleman who wanted to retire anyway—took the money and quit, I decided to do the same. I've been out here working at the docks ever since."

"Why did you quit if you could have kept sailing?" Uncle Lawrence says. "Because I remember you. You were one of the best."

Derek allows himself to smile just a little. "I regretted my role in the mutiny the moment it was over, the moment I saw you in the lifeboat, drifting away. But there was nothing I could do. It was too late. But I always suspected that maybe you had survived."

"Why?" I say.

"I've sailed with Captain Wilson before, and I know him pretty well. If you were really dead, I didn't think he would want to separate from you. I figured he would try to talk the crew into bringing the body back to Trilland to be buried properly. I had a feeling that he was trying to get you safely off the ship before things got worse."

"So you knew I was bluffing, and you didn't say anything?" Uncle Lawrence says.

Derek nods. "I was already feeling bad about what was happening, so I decided not to call attention to it. I want you both to know that

I am truly sorry for what I did, and I'm very glad to see that you are both still alive."

"Well, thank you for not giving me away back then," Uncle Lawrence says. "I couldn't have saved Lorraine if you had said something."

"It was the absolute least I could do. So, you said something about me being able to help you?"

Brent nods. "Cassandra is claiming that Lorraine can't take the throne back because she abandoned it and legally can no longer claim it. We need to be able to prove that Lorraine didn't intentionally abandon Trilland, and to do that, we need to prove that the mutiny happened."

"You want me to testify."

"Yes," I say. "If the people of Trilland see me, they won't believe Cassandra that I'm a fake. They won't want Cassandra anymore, and they'll want me. But if you show up as well, then Cassandra won't be able to try to stop me with some law that doesn't apply in this situation. We know it's a lot to ask, but we don't know how else to prove that she tried to have me killed."

Derek rubs the back of his neck and grimaces. "Cassandra's already not happy with me for refusing further service. She basically tolerates me out here as long as I keep quiet. Speaking against her is not going to win me any favors. Are you absolutely sure this will work?"

"Yes," I say, even though I'm not positive.

"Because if it fails, she will arrest me, maybe even kill me. I can't take that risk without being sure."

"We're sure," Uncle Lawrence says. "We've got a plan."

Derek takes a deep breath, closes his eyes, then exhales and looks at us again. He doesn't look happy, and he seems to fidget uneasily, but he says, "Okay. Tell me what I need to do."

# Chapter 21

By the time we get to the town square, Cassandra's speech has already started. It doesn't sound like she's gotten very far past the normal introductory stuff, but she's already vilifying me. What really stands out to me is the faces of the people in the crowd. There is a visible disappointment. Rumors of my appearance in the other provinces must have reached here by now, and people look distraught to hear Cassandra saying I'm a fake. We need to wait for the right opportunity to interrupt, but we can't wait long. I can't bear to see the people of Trilland look so sad.

"And what really hurts the most," Cassandra continues, forcing herself to appear on the verge of tears, "is that someone had so little concern for Trilland and for me that she gave all of us hope that our departed princess might still be out there. It was painful to look her in the eye and have her arrested. I'm so disappointed that someone would try such a stunt."

Cassandra's pouring it on pretty thick, and I'm happy to see that, based on the looks from the people in the crowd, they're not buying it. I smile to myself. At least Trilland never fell for her act.

Uncle Lawrence taps me on the shoulder, so I duck back behind the building we're currently using as cover.

"We have to go now," he says.

Suddenly, I have the feeling that we haven't really thought this through. "What am I going to do, just walk on stage, grab the microphone, and call Cassandra a liar?"

Uncle Lawrence shrugs and nods. "Something like that, yeah."

"What?"

"It won't take much. The second you're visible, there's going to be chaos. The hard part will be getting to the mic and talking before Cassandra can have you arrested. We'll go with you, but it'll be up to you to do the talking. Then call up Derek."

"I can't do that."

"Yes you can." Uncle Lawrence puts a hand on each of my shoulders and gives them a squeeze. "You have to. This is why we came here."

He turns around to talk to Derek, and Zane takes my hands in his. "It'll be fine. Just say exactly what you practiced with me earlier." Zane let me practice my speech on him, and every word of it sounded clunky, but he insisted it was perfect. He gives me a quick kiss and smiles. "I'm so excited to see my girlfriend take her country back."

I take several deep breaths, though it seems difficult to breathe out, and step up behind Brent. I risk a look back at Derek and immediately regret it because he's pale and looks as nervous as I feel. As Cassandra's talking about how I escaped before getting to prison and how she has search parties out for me, we start weaving through the crowd, me with my head down. We weren't able to get back to the ship because there were still soldiers swarming the docks, so I never had a chance to get sunglasses or a jacket or anything to hide my identity. A few people in the crowd do notice me and start shouting, and though Cassandra notices the uproar, she ignores it.

When we reach the stage, it's as if Uncle Lawrence senses my hesitation because he grabs my hand and prevents me from backing down. The four of us walk right onto the stage, and the look on Cassandra's face alone is enough to motivate me. I don't even need to hear the shouts from the crowd and the utter chaos happening in front of me. The look of fear in Cassandra's eyes is enough for me.

I rip the microphone off of the stand, and the words flow surprisingly easily. "Cassandra Wellington wants you to believe that I am dead and that I didn't show up yesterday, but I did. My name is Lorraine Alice Everhart, and I am the rightful ruler of Trilland."

The crowd erupts into a cacophony of cheering, shouting, and screaming. A few guards try to seize us, but Brent and Zane work to fend them off. Cassandra staggers back, and a few guards surround her. What a coward.

"A year ago, when I left to visit the outer provinces, Cassandra had organized a mutiny against Captain Wilson with the goal to have me killed. She thought she had succeeded, but she was wrong. I survived, and I'm here to reclaim my rightful position as princess."

Cassandra points in my direction, and the guards surrounding her shift toward me, one of whom grabs my arm and tries to pull me back. I yank my arm forward, and while I don't manage to wrench my arm free of his grip, it does surprise him. One of the other guards looks me in the eyes, and even when Cassandra directs him toward me, he doesn't move, and I know he believes me.

The first guard still hasn't let go of my arm, and Zane and Brent seem to have lost against the guards who now have them detained. Cassandra takes two delicate but deliberate steps toward me and shouts, "You are a liar and a fake. How dare you pretend to be the lost princess?"

"I'm not a fake."

"Prove it," Cassandra says, and the crowd falls eerily silent. "Prove it."

I look around the crowd, desperately trying to think of something convincing. What can I say? What will be enough? I decide to say many things instead.

"My father died two weeks after my thirteenth birthday of pneumonia that he contracted from swimming late at night. Late night swimming was his way of relieving stress and refocusing himself. My mother didn't get out of bed for weeks after that. I knew she was going to die before she ever declined in health. I was supposed to have six more years to learn from my father, and I felt wildly ill-equipped to lead the country. I remember having a breakdown at a parliament meeting after that and bursting into tears. Senator Emerson and Senator Robinson were kind enough to end the meeting there and let me go home. They never mentioned it again, and probably you, the people of Trilland, didn't know that happened until now."

The people all gasp and shake their heads. I see a few glares directed at Cassandra. It's probably obvious at this point that I'm the real Lorraine Everhart, but I don't want to stop. I don't want there to be any question. Plus, I'm finding it exhilarating to say all these memories out loud—memories I thought were gone forever—and I feel an adrenaline rush from this moment in front of my beautiful Trilland.

I look over and see Secretary of State Johnson standing just off the stage, and he looks stunned. His mouth is hanging open just slightly, and he's gripping the side of his arm so hard that his knuckles are white. When I see him, I know what I will say next.

"And I can tell you the last conversation I had before I left Trilland one year ago was with Secretary of State Johnson who warned us about the impending storm and urged us to be cautious. Captain Wilson assured him he would be, but he had no idea what was awaiting us. Secretary Johnson, do you remember that conversation?"

He nods very slowly, and though his voice is quiet, it seems that it echoes when he says, "I do remember that. Very clearly."

"It doesn't matter." Cassandra practically spits venom when she speaks. She's showing her true colors now, and the people of Trilland shout when she does. "You're too late. The law says—"

"That law says," I say as I finally break the guard's grip on my arm, "that I abdicate if I voluntarily abandon Trilland, and I didn't do that. You tried to have me killed."

"You have no proof of that."

"Actually, I do." I risk a glance at the guard who held my arm before, and he's staring at me with confusion clouding his face. He looks back and forth between me and Cassandra, and he seems unsure who to believe. When it seems that he isn't going to try to stop me, I return to the microphone and face the people. "I have the testimony of someone who was there. One of the sailors who was on the ship when the mutiny occurred is here and willing to explain exactly what happened."

I look over to where we left Derek waiting, but I don't see him, and suddenly, my blood runs cold. Where did he go? I look around the area desperately trying to find him, but he's nowhere to be found. What do I do if he abandoned us? I scan the area around where we were hiding, and I still don't see him. I don't know what to do if we've lost Derek. Did he run? Did he get arrested? Is he hiding? No matter what, if Derek isn't here, I don't think I have any cards left to play.

Cassandra notices the delay and starts laughing. "You have nothing. You have no claim, no credibility, and no throne. I'm the leader of Trilland now."

The guards surround me again, and just as one lays his hands on my arm, a voice carries out across the square.

"Wait."

We all turn and see Derek Ingraham walking up the steps of the stage, and it feels like my heart is finally beating again. He didn't desert us. He came back.

A guard, directed by Cassandra, moves to stop him, but I see a different guard, the one who made eye contact me, stop him from getting to Derek. He knows. He knows that I am for real, and the way he looks at Derek makes me think that he most know Derek personally. Without her guards—or rather, my guards—to stop Derek, Cassandra seems paralyzed, unable to say or do anything to stop him. The guards holding me, Zane, Brent, and Uncle Lawrence back don't release their grips, but they don't exactly tighten them either.

In chilling detail, he explains exactly what happened in the mutiny. He shares every detail, exactly as I remember them and some that I don't remember at all, and when I turn and see Captain Wilson nodding, I know it's exactly as he remembers it, too. The more he talks, the more I can see Cassandra shriveling next to me. She knows it's over for her, and while I'm sure that won't keep her from protesting, she has no chance, and she knows it. With every detail that Derek shares, the crowd gets visibly angrier. And while hearing this story with so much detail makes me uncomfortable, I'm so happy to see Derek up here telling it because it means that I've won.

"Cassandra never should have been in power," Derek says. "It always should have been our princess. I'm just glad that my actions and the actions of others did not harm her and that she was able to come back now and free Trilland from this tyrant."

As Derek steps down, most of the crowd cheers, and while it's unclear whether they're cheering for him or for me, the message is clear: Cassandra's reign is over. She tries to say something, the cheers of the crowd drowns her out. The guard holding my arm looks at me, and for a moment, it's like we're the only two people here, like the deafening roar around us is suddenly quiet. He lets go of my arm, bows his head, and says, "Your Highness."

I step forward, nodding my head toward him, and I see that as the others notice his actions, they release Zane, Brent, and Uncle Lawrence. All of the guards except for a select few that seem to remain loyal to Cassandra bow their heads toward me, and the others mimic them. When the crowd notices what is happening, they quiet down and all bow their heads as well.

Cautiously but confidently, I step up to the mic, and Derek quickly steps back out of my way. "Secretary Johnson," I say, "would you mind assisting me in arresting Cassandra Wellington and all of her conspirators?"

"It would be my pleasure, Your Highness," he says with a big smile. He immediately begins ordering a few different officials around. Cassandra screams and protests the whole time they handcuff her and drag her away, but it's done. It's over. We actually did it.

Uncle Lawrence, Zane, and Brent all come over and give me a hug. We look around for Derek, and we find him already off the stage, but he smiles and waves. I didn't think this day would come, but now, here it is. I'm back in Trilland, and Cassandra has lost.

# Chapter 22

Waking up in my old room feels at once completely natural as well as entirely foreign. It's like that feeling you get when you come home after a long vacation. Everything is the same and familiar, but it's like you see everything differently. Somehow, your home feels distant and detached from you. Now magnify that by a year.

For the first time in a year, I'm woken up not by the sound of the waves crashing against the shore but by the whistling of a maid in my room. I'm kind of glad that we're so far up the cliff that we can't hear the waves that well. I never liked that. In fact, I can remember choosing this room in the house as a child because I couldn't hear the waves.

After Cassandra's arrest yesterday, I briefly told the people that I would be back tomorrow, which is now today, to explain everything. I was so overwhelmed and needed to get everything organized. I'd also like to give my first official speech since my return in something other than Ms. Margaret's daughter's rejected clothing.

I shift in my bed, feeling comfortably cold in the pale pink satin sheets. They had to strip my bed of its usual gold furnishings since they had accumulated quite a bit of dust. These sheets are my back-up set, but they're still so lovely. When I roll over onto my back, the maid notices me and smiles.

"I hope I didn't wake you," she says. "I just wanted to do a little cleaning in here before your breakfast is brought up. It's still a little dusty up here."

"Oh, you didn't wake me," I say, even though she did. "Thank you for your help."

"Oh, I'm so happy to help," she says. "I've missed you so."

"Wait," I say, realizing who I'm speaking to. "Jane? Is that you?"

Jane nods excitedly. "I didn't know if you'd recognize me."

"Why would you think that?" I say, feeling the sweat start beading on my palms. I haven't told anyone about my memory loss, but has someone else? Have they figured it out?

"It's just been so long. A year can really change people."

I exhale a small sigh of relief. She doesn't know. "Well, that year has been good for you. You look beautiful. Did you dye your hair?"

Jane smiles and runs her fingers through her curly strawberry ponytail. "I had it highlighted with a little blonde. I thought it suited my skin."

"It does," I say. "But, you know, I was always a little jealous of your red hair."

Jane scrunches her nose. "Psh. Carrot hair."

"Auburn," I protest, and we both laugh.

"My mother is dying to see you," Jane says. "I practically had to restrain her to keep her from waking you up in the middle of the night. She was one of the few people in the palace who heard."

"You mean everyone doesn't know?"

"No. Only the people who absolutely needed to know. You know, those in charge and those likely to come in contact with you. Like me." So, the guards really took me seriously when I said I wanted to keep my return to the palace under wraps. "Besides, not everyone is here."

"What do you mean?"

"Cassandra fired a lot of people after you were gone. Anyone who protested too loudly at her control was removed. They're still in Trilland, but they don't work in the palace anymore. My mom and I stayed quiet so that we could stay close to the palace."

I sit quietly on the bed, rubbing the sheets between my fingers. It hadn't occurred to me that Cassandra would fire everyone. They're all family to me. I have to get them back.

"I need to see Uncle Lawrence. I need to ask him something. Can you track him down for me when you get a chance?"

"Of course, anything for you," Jane says. "Oh Lorraine, where were you all this time? We've been so worried. It's been awful without you."

I shift uncomfortably. I don't really want to explain. Not yet. "I'm going to explain everything, I promise. I'll call a meeting of the house sometime today and tell you all everything. And I'm going to undo all the damage Cassandra has inflicted."

"I just missed you so much," Jane says, a lone tear slipping down her cheek.

"Oh, Jane." I beckon Jane with my hand, she sits next to me, and we hug each other for a good while. I had hoped I would see Jane. Her mother was my mother's favorite hand maid by far. She adored her. Jane and I were practically sisters. Without my parents here or even Elise, I'm glad I have Jane.

"Well," Jane says, wiping her face, "I should go. Your breakfast will be here soon."

"Thank you for still being here, Jane. I needed you to be here."

Jane smiles. "Where else would I be?"

Jane starts to head out the door, but she stops in the doorway and turns around with a smirk. "So, who's that really hot guy you brought with you?"

"Jane!"

"What? He's really handsome. Not the one you kissed. I assume you're dating that one."

"He's just a friend. He helped me get back here."

"Well then I like him all the more." Jane dances out of the room.

~~~

"You want to *what*?" Brent says.

"They deserve to know," I say.

"Our entire goal since the moment we got here was to keep anyone from finding out that you had amnesia. Now, you just want to tell everyone?"

"First of all, I don't have amnesia anymore, so the problem is no longer a problem. And second of all, I don't want to tell everyone, just the employees of the palace, all the old ones that I'm bringing back. They deserve to know where I've been."

"And what if they tell the rest of Trilland?" Brent says.

"Brent has a legitimate concern," Uncle Lawrence says. "I respect your pursuit of honesty and transparency, but it can't be guaranteed that everyone will keep the secret. The people of Trilland are going to be curious."

"I'm going to give a speech to Trilland tonight," I say. "That's already set up. The most important piece of information is that Cassandra tried to assassinate me. That will be enough explanation for the people. But there are many people in this household that I've known my whole life. They are like family to me. I have to be honest with them about what happened to me."

"I say go for it," Zane says. "If they're really family, then they should know, and you should be able to trust them. You do what you think is right."

"I think it's a bad idea," Brent says.
~~~

"The bad idea was not telling Uncle Lawrence what was wrong with me," I snap. "I know you're just looking out for me, but I don't need your help anymore. I know what I need to do."

"Then that's what we'll do," Uncle Lawrence says, standing up. "I'll put in word that you want to have a meeting around one o'clock. Everyone else should be back by then. I've already called them, and they're on their way. Is that a good time?"

"Perfect. Thank you."

"Anything for you." Uncle Lawrence smiles and heads out of my room, followed closely by Zane who is muttering something about fishing.

"Lorraine, we have to talk," Brent says as soon as Uncle Lawrence closes the door. "We can't keep going at each other's throats like this."

"I agree."

"So?"

"So what?"

"You know I didn't mean to hurt you."

"But you did."

"I know," Brent says, ducking his head down. "And you have no idea how sorry I am."

"How could you keep such important information from Uncle Lawrence? I should have had contact with him. I might have remembered sooner."

Brent takes my hands in his. "Lorraine, I really am so sorry. You have to believe me."

"I do," I say. "I do believe you. I just don't feel like I can trust you."

"It's Zane, isn't it? I was just never going to be able to compete with him."

I drop Brent's hands. "Zane has nothing to do with this. How could you even say something like that? This has to do with you, not with him. *You're* the one who deceived me when you were supposed to be helping me."

"I just think that if Zane had done the same thing as me, you would forgive him, unlike me."

"He wouldn't do something like that."

"But what if he did?"

"He wouldn't," I say. "That's the point. Zane would never intentionally hurt me like that."

Brent just stares at me blankly. I think he realizes that he's lost this argument. This was never a contest between Zane and Brent, even though they both saw it that way, which might be my fault. Zane is just Zane. He's been a constant in my life for the past year. No one was ever going to replace that, though I think Brent thought he could.

Brent clears his throat and speaks solemnly. "I did not mean to upset you, and for that, I'm sorry. I hope we can still salvage a friendship out of this."

"However I feel about you right now, you were still an important part of me getting to Trilland and regaining my memory. I'll always be grateful to you for that. I hope you'll stay in Trilland."

Brent smiles slightly. "I will always remain a part of Trilland."

"Well," I say, trying to change the topic and end this painfully awkward conversation, "I have to prepare my speeches for today. Do you mind giving me privacy to work?"

"Of course not. I'll see you later."

~~~

Everyone gathered in the ballroom is buzzing with conversation. The entire staff hasn't been called together since Cassandra took power apparently, and that, of course, was not good news. The staff has expanded since I was last here, especially now that I've brought so many people back. Or maybe it just seems that way because now I have
~~~

to deliver a speech. Either way, there are a lot of people in here, at least forty or fifty. If this makes me nervous, how am I supposed to give a speech tonight to all of Trilland?

"You ready?" Uncle Lawrence asks.

"No," I say.

"Yes you are." Uncle Lawrence gives me a quick hug. "Don't think of it as a speech. Just have a conversation with them. You know a lot of them."

I nod and take to the podium. I stand at the podium, grip the sides, stare at the people expectantly staring back at me, and reconsider. I ask one of the guards to hand me a chair and I sit down on the stage, pushing the podium to the side. Later, I can be professional and deliver a speech from a podium. For right now, Uncle Lawrence is right. I'm just talking to them.

I take a deep breath and begin. "First of all, thank you all for taking the time to assemble for this impromptu meeting. I know the notice was last minute, but I didn't want to leave you all without explanation any longer. I know there's a lot of mystery surrounding my disappearance a year ago. I want to clear things up for you all because the people of this house have always been like family to me. Many of you have known me since I was an infant. I feel you deserve to know what happened.

"Many of you already know Cassandra Wellington tried to have me assassinated. On a routine trip to visit Trilland's provinces, the crew of the ship I was on mutinied against Captain Wilson in an attempt to have me killed. Captain Wilson was overtaken, and the crew tried to steer the ship straight into a dangerous storm, a storm which Captain Wilson wanted to avoid. Captain Wilson sensed the unrest on the ship and planned ahead for my safety. He managed to get me on a lifeboat and directed me toward a nearby island. He succeeded in getting me off the ship before the mutiny was complete, but his ship was taken over, and he was stranded on Gessend."

I take a deep, shaky breath before I say the next part. "Captain Wilson hoped I would make it to an island and be all right. What he didn't know was the reason why I never did return: in the chaos of the storm and the mutiny, I was hit in the head, and I developed amnesia."

There is a collective gasp around the room. I see Jane and her mother both tear up. Several people hold their hands over their mouths in shock and distress.

I press on. "I couldn't remember anything, not even my name. The people on that island took care of me, but they had no way of knowing where I was from. I lived there for a year without any memory at all. Obviously, I knew that to find my home I'd have to leave the island, but where would I start? I had nothing to go off of.

"But a couple of months ago, Brent Grayson, this man to the right of me, arrived on my little temporary island home." I point to Brent, and he blushes and smiles awkwardly. "Captain Wilson had sent him on a journey to find me because he became concerned about my well-being since I hadn't returned. He knew that if I could, and if I knew how bad things were back in Trilland, I would come back, but I hadn't.

"Brent found me, and through a series of events, my memory came back in pieces until, ultimately, it returned completely a couple of days ago."

There is another collective gasp and a few murmurs. I guess people are startled to find out that my memory recovery is so recent. Honestly, in some ways, it still feels really recent to me. In other ways, it's hard to remember a time when I didn't know who I was.

"I realize that this all comes as a shock. I'm still a little shaken myself. But frankly, I don't have time to freak out about it now. Trilland is in distress as a result of Cassandra's destruction. I need to focus on Trilland's recovery right now. I only ask one thing of everyone in this room. I ask that the knowledge of my bout of amnesia remain a secret held only by those in this room. I do not want Cassandra to seize on it, and more importantly, I do not want the people of Trilland to worry. As far as I can tell, my memory is without gaps, and there is no reason for anyone to be concerned. I will deliver a speech tonight to all of Trilland in which I will discuss my return, Cassandra's treasonous actions, and the plan for Trilland's future, but I will keep my amnesia limited to the people in this room. Does anyone have any questions?"

I look around the room, but no one gives any indication that they are going to speak. People seem to avoid eye contact with me or exchange nervous looks with each other. Everyone seems dumbfounded and astonished.

"It's okay," I say, "ask anything you want to know."

After a few moments, a brave young waiter raises his hand hesitantly. I point to him and nod, and he stands, adjusting his jacket back into place.

"Um, Your Highness?"

"Yes, go ahead."

"How did your memory return?"

"A few fragments came back through conversations with Brent and with Captain Wilson, but the whole piece came back when I first entered this palace and confronted Cassandra. I saw a family portrait, and it somehow cleared my memory."

"But how can you be sure that it is entirely back?" the waiter asks.

For some reason, his comment troubles me. I guess I can't know for sure. I mean, if there is a gap in my memory, how would I know if it's there? I wouldn't be able to remember it. This question makes me nervous, but I don't want these people to know that, so I smile.

"I guess I can't be entirely sure, but I know this much. Before, everything was coming together in fragments. When I saw that portrait and looked into my parents' faces, it was like my mind cleared. The world made sense again; I knew who I was. I lost the feeling of uncertainty and anxiety that I've lived with for a year. I can't imagine that I would feel that way if I still had pieces missing."

The waiter, apparently satisfied with my answer, smiles, bows, and sits down. Immediately, another stands up, this time a maid, and bows slightly.

"Do you think you'll ever tell the people of Trilland, or will you keep it a secret forever?"

I consider this for a moment before replying. I hadn't given that any thought. "I can't tell you for sure. If I ever feel it would be advantageous for Trilland to know, then I will tell them without hesitation. For now, it is best that they don't know."

I ask for more questions, and people hesitate again, but then the manager of the house, Lady Vivian, stands, tears glistening in her eyes.

"Your Highness, can I speak for everyone in this room when I say that we are all so infinitely happy to know that you are okay. We all worried so much this past year. No one wanted to believe that you were gone for good."

Everyone else chimes in at Lady Vivian's words, agreeing heartily.

"Thank you." I say. "I hope I can restore Trilland to everyone's expectations."

"We don't care about that," Lady Vivian says. "We care far more about your safety. Thank *you* for returning to us."

Lady Vivian's words bring tears to my eyes, so I rush down the stage and wrap my arms around her. She still wears the same musky perfume, a scent I have smelled since I was a small child but haven't smelled in a year. I hold on tighter, and she whispers in my ear, "I love you dear. Welcome back." Even though I've been home for a day, this moment truly feels like home.

Lady Vivian speaks up so the whole room can hear. "We will keep your secret for as long as you like. You don't need to worry." Everyone in the room agrees audibly.

"Thank you all," I say. "You have no idea how good it feels to be in this room, reunited with all of you. I have missed you all dearly."

I step back onto the stage and compose myself. "Tonight I will deliver my speech to all of Trilland. I hope you all will watch. Thank you for your support in my decisions."

I shake a few hands, hug a few necks, and generally just feel so comforted by the people in this room. This is family.

While I'm talking to a few people, I see Timothy wave from behind her. I guess Uncle Lawrence tracked him down. I thank Lady Vivian again and rush over to him.

"I'm so glad you're back," I say.

"Me, too. It's a lot more fun protecting the princess when it's you. Cassandra was not fun to protect."

Timothy was always my father's favorite guard, and I can see why now. He has a big heart, and I feel safer just knowing he's here. "I'm very glad to see you again, Tim."

"Princess," Timothy says with playful warning in his voice.

"I had to." I laugh. "I hope you'll stay."

"I wouldn't dream of being anywhere else but here. Your father would have been proud of what you did, yesterday and today."

I throw my arms around Timothy and give him a squeeze. He smiles and walks off, and when I spot Annette, I immediately rush to Jane and her mother. She throws her arms around me and sobs into my shoulder.

"Annette, it's so good to see you again." I stroke her graying blonde hair gently.

"In between tears, Annette says softly, "All of Trilland has been waiting for you for so long."

Chapter 23

Disappearing for a year really hampers one's wardrobe. What on earth am I supposed to wear to address the people of Trilland? All of these dresses are years old, and it shows. The ones that still fit are hideous or falling apart, and Cassandra's dresses are worse. She's at least four or five inches taller than me and stick thin. Besides, even if we were the same size, her style is horrendous. She must have trashed my more recent outfits because I can't seem to find anything decent.

"You sent for me?" Jane pokes her head through my door with a smile.

"My gosh, yes. I need help. I don't know what to wear."

"I figured," she says. "Luckily for you, I brought assistance."

Jane and her mother both come in, and Jane starts picking through the few dresses still hanging in my closet while Annette tries to sort through the mounds on my bed.

"This green one is pretty." Jane holds up a chiffon strapless.

"Yeah it is," I say. "It's also about two inches too short and was made when I was thirteen."

Jane giggles. "So no then. These all look kind of small, actually."

"I know, and all the ones on the bed are either too small also or they're just awful."

Annette perks up. "I have an idea. I'll be right back. Jane, could you do Lorraine's hair while I'm gone?" she says and darts out of the room.

"What on earth could she be thinking?" Jane says.

"I don't know, but I don't think I have a better option than to trust her."

"Okay, sit down." Jane plugs in a curling iron and starts pulling a hairbrush through my tangled mess. By the time she gets all the knots out, the curling iron is fully heated, and she starts winding strands of hair meticulously around the iron, crafting pretty, cascading curls.

"Wow," I say.

"What?"

"I forgot how pretty my hair looks curled."

"You never curled your hair in the past year?"

"The island didn't exactly have curling irons."

"Well, that's a travesty," Jane says. "Your hair was made to be curled."

Jane's almost done curling my hair, so she starts playing with the ringlets, stretching them out a little and repositioning them to her liking.

"Do you want it up or down?"

"I don't know," I say. "It's hard to know what to pick without seeing whatever your mom's got in the works."

"Then we'll do both," Jane says, twisting pieces of hair and pulling them back from my face and pinning them. It's really starting to come together, so I pick up an eyeliner pencil and hesitantly line it up with my lash line. The first stroke is shaky, but the second is much smoother, and it takes me hardly any time at all to get my old rhythm back. I avoid eyeshadow for now, waiting until I know the color of the dress.

"I'm back," Annette says, carrying a dress bag. "Now, this might be a little long on you, but it should fit, and I can easily hem it."

Annette unzips the bag, revealing something I hadn't expected to see. It's a beautiful plum satin dress with a sweetheart neckline and a flattering cut. Across the top is a line of beaded rhinestones, expertly adorning the neckline and off-the-shoulder cap sleeves.

"Is that—"

"It is." Annette smiles, tears in her eyes. "When you went missing, and Cassandra took over, I knew you'd want your parents' things if—when—you came back. So, I grabbed as much as I could and hid it all in my room."

"This was one of my mother's favorite dresses," I say.

"I remember. Now, let's see how it looks on you."

I slip into the dress, and Annette is right. It's a little long, but it fits me perfectly. It looks beautiful, and I love it not because I think I look beautiful but because I think I look like my mother.

Annette places a few pins in the dress, I slip it off, and she whisks it away to hem it. After seeing the dress, I decide to leave the eyeshadow off and avoid a necklace, only wearing small stud diamond earrings. Jane's hair turns out to be perfect and flatters the neckline of the dress perfectly. When Annette returns with the dress, and I see the whole picture, I'm stunned. I wish Elise were here. She would absolutely die if she saw me now.

~~~

I smooth the lines in my mother's dress for the fourteenth time and take a deep breath, exhaling slowly, for the fifteenth. Uncle Lawrence gently positions my old tiara on my head, pressing the hair pins into my curls.

"I can't do this," I say.

"Yes, you can," Uncle Lawrence says with a smile.

"No, no I can't. What was I thinking?"

"Calm down, Lorraine. Take a deep breath."
~~~

"Deep breaths aren't helping."

"Lorraine." Uncle Lawrence holds my shoulders gently. "Your entire life, speeches have made you nervous. Every time you ever had to say anything in public, you got like this. And every time, after you finally just gave the speech, your father would pull you aside and say, 'See?'"

"'Your worry was worse than your reality,'"I say in unison with Uncle Lawrence, smiling at my father's memory.

"Just because it's been a while doesn't mean that's any less true," Uncle Lawrence says.

"But I'm out of practice," I say. "What if I mess this up?"

"Frankly, you can't mess this up," he says. "You are Lorraine Everhart, lost princess of Trilland, finally returned to her kingdom. People are going to be ecstatic that you are even alive. Whatever you say after that is just icing on the cake."

I nod and try not to shake—or, at least, not let Uncle Lawrence know I'm shaking.

"Now listen," Uncle Lawrence says quietly, "since you will be speaking live from the balcony, it is very likely there will be a lot of shouting, applause, or anything else. Don't let it startle you. Smile, keep calm, and wait for it to die down. If you let it rattle you, you will stress yourself out. When the crowd calms down, begin your speech. There will likely be more applause during and after your speech. Wait with a smile each time. I'll cut off the cameras at a good time, but remember that when the cameras go off, you're still in front of town square. Smile until we close the doors. Got it?"

"I think so."

"You do." Uncle Lawrence smiles. "Try not to worry. You'll be fine."

He turns and gives a few directions to a few people nearby, and Zane takes my hands in his.

"He's right, you'll be great," he says. "I'm so proud of you."

He kisses me on the cheek and steps back over with Jane and Brent. I'm so glad he's here.

"Everything will be fine," he shouts.

I nod and take my place at the microphone, wishing that I could believe him. I keep trying to remind myself that I already spoke to the palace; this is just step two. But the palace members are family. Talking to family is easier than talking to a kingdom. When I spoke yesterday to defy Cassandra, I was running on pure adrenaline. Now, it's much harder to remain calm. Plus, I can't get the images of the people of Anden out of my head. They were so angry. What if Trilland is angry too?

I position the microphone to be comfortable for my height and smooth my dress one more time. Okay, two more times. The sound guy gives me the "okay," and I plaster a smile on my face while I listen to the feedback from the secretary of state's introduction. But now it's my time. The guards push the doors open, and cameras flash all around me.

Like Uncle Lawrence said, people are stunned. Some stare, mouths hanging open, unable to process what they're seeing. Others immediately applaud. I guess they're happy to see me. Still others, those younger than me, tap their parents on the shoulder, probably asking who I am. Their stunned parents hardly even notice them. I think some of these people must have missed Cassandra's live speech and my interruption. This crowd certainly looks much larger than the one yesterday.

When the noise dies down, I clear my throat and begin. "Good evening, Trilland. I'd like to thank you for taking the time to watch this address. I wanted to greet you all properly. I am Lorraine Alice Everhart, princess of Trilland." I pause and allow the people to cheer, and boy, do they. I know people wanted me back and that Cassandra had made things terrible, but the boisterous response is still jarring.

When the cheering dies down, I continue. "I realize the details surrounding my disappearance are vague at best, so let me begin by clarifying that."

And I do. I tell the entire story, very similarly to how Derek told it just yesterday. It makes me just as uncomfortable to tell it now as it did to hear Derek tell it yesterday, but with more of my own detail. It's also the only memory that still feels just the slightest bit hazy. Maybe it'll always be that way. And maybe I'm okay with that.

I hear a few gasps from the town square. The lie they were told really must have been elaborate and far from the real story. The more I tell the story, the more exasperated the crowd looks.

"Due to a series of unforeseen circumstances, I was unable to get back to Captain Wilson, not knowing where he was since he was stranded on a different island and therefore unable to get back to Trilland. I am deeply troubled over what Cassandra did during that time. I wish I could go back and undo it all, but I can't. I'm so sorry.

"But the past is the past. I'm looking toward the future. I dream of Trilland returning to its former glory, the great country it was when my parents ruled. I think it can be that way again. I think that between you all and me, we can restore Trilland to the way it once was." The crowd below me erupts into cheers, many people hug, all smile.

"But I don't want to stop there. I want to progress. I want Trilland always to look for ways it can be better for its people. For this reason, in a few weeks, I will hold a panel where you all can express your opinions, wants, and needs. I want to know what the people of Trilland want out of their government. I will also hold elections following that panel so you, the people, can vote for the legislature and the people that *you* want. And of course, Cassandra Wellington and her rebels will be tried for treason and attempted murder of the royal family.

"Dear Trilland, I only ask this of you. I ask that you give me time to reacclimate myself to Trilland. It's been a long time, and much has happened in my time away. I need time to readjust and get my affairs in order. I thank you in advance for your patience.

"And, dear Trilland, I thank you again for taking time to hear me speak today. I hope it was a welcome appearance." I smile, letting my face turn a little red, and the people laugh and smile. "I will not hold you up any longer. Thank you, and goodnight to you all."

I watch the red camera light flick off, but I keep a smile, just like Uncle Lawrence said, risking a wave or two to the crowd below, until the guard comes up beside me and shuts the doors. My smile drops the second the doors click shut, and I deflate with relief.

Uncle Lawrence hugs me. "That was great. See? Wasn't your father right?"

I nod. "My father was always right."

"I have to go. I'm going to check in and see what people are saying. Relax. Celebrate, even. You did great."

I watch Uncle Lawrence skip away happily before turning around to Jane who is giddy with happiness. She reminds me of Elise in this moment. I'll have to introduce the two soon.

"That was amazing." Jane gives me a squeeze.

"Thank you."

"I have a question though."

"Yeah?"

"Why wait so long?" Jane says. "Why not go ahead and prosecute Cassandra and start the voting early? You're finally back."

"I know, but I need to go back to the island and get my things, say my goodbyes, that kind of stuff. I wasn't planning on leaving for good when I left. I always intended to come back."

"Is it going to be hard to leave that island?"

"I hadn't thought about it, but yes," I say. "That island has been home for a year. The villagers there are so important to me. I don't really want to leave them, but my place is here."

"Why don't you bring them here? They could live in Trilland."

"No," I say. "Those people love their little island. They'd never dream of living anywhere else, especially a city. I do wish I could help them though. They're pretty self-sufficient, but they could really use some of Trilland's resources. It would help them so much."

"Well what if you annex the island?" Jane says. "Then they could be part of Trilland but still be separate."

"Jane, you're a genius," I say, throwing my arms around her neck. "If I annex them, I can protect them and help their economy, but they can still be independent and do what they want. That's the perfect solution, thank you. I can't wait to tell Zane."

"Zane?" Jane's face breaks out into a suggestive smirk. "So what's the deal with Zane?"

"Uh, just a friend from the island."

"Seems like more than a friend to me."

"Shh."

I look up and see the cameraman eavesdropping on our conversation, so I grab Jane by the wrist and drag her down the hallway, darting into a small parlor room. Like my bedroom, it looks like this room hasn't been used. Probably too small for Cassandra's big head to fit in. It's pretty dusty, and the furniture is covered in sheets, but when I flick on the lights, it still looks like a nice room.

"So?" Jane smiles. "Tell me about Zane."

"He and his mom took care of me when I first got to the island. He's my closest friend."

"Are you into him?"

I shrug and avoid eye contact. "Maybe."

"What does that mean?" Jane shoves my arm. "Does he like you?"

"I mean—he kissed me."

"What?"

"I didn't know. I had no idea that he even liked me, and then one day, he just kissed me out of the blue."

"And he came with you here?"

I shake my head. "He followed me here. We had a huge fight right before I left, but he came to Trilland for me."

"That's so sweet."

"I just don't know what he's going to do now. Obviously, I'm staying in Trilland, but he may want to go back to the island. But I'd hate to be apart from him, especially after everything we've been through."

"Now I understand why you have to go back," Jane says. "So, when are you going over there?"

"I was thinking tomorrow," I say. "Maybe the day after."

"So soon? What about Trilland?"

"Trilland will be fine. I'll speak to Secretary of State Johnson. He can handle the press for a few days. Uncle Lawrence will get me there and back in a matter of days."

"You're not going to tell the people?"

"No," I say. "I just got back after a year. I don't want to worry them, and I don't want them to think I'm abandoning them either."

"Do you think I could come with you?" Jane says hesitantly. "I'm kind of curious to see this island you speak of."

"Of course," I say. "I'd love for you to come."

"I'll go pack." Jane skips off happily, and I follow her example and head upstairs to throw a bag together. Honestly, it shouldn't be that hard. I never really unpacked from the island.

I start walking up the stairs, and I find Brent waiting for me about halfway up the steps. He stands up straight on the landing, back against the wall, but he looks nervous somehow.

"That was a good speech," he says.

"Thank you," I say. "I was pretty nervous about it."

"I hear rumor that you're going back to the island?"

"Who—"

"Captain Wilson," he says. "He was making preparations to sail. I couldn't imagine that he would leave you so soon, so the only explanation is that you're going with him. Can't think of anywhere else you'd go."

I nod to confirm his suspicions, and we both just stand there in awkward silence for a few moments. I'm desperate to end the silence, but I don't know what I could say. Thankfully, Brent is much better at conversation than I am.

"You should have seen him," he says, a small smile on his face. "It's like he's never been happier. He's running around the docks, inspecting all the royal ships, ordering crew members around. He's back in his element."

I smile. "I'm glad he's happy."

"The only thing he's not happy about is the condition of the ships. I guess Cassandra didn't sail a whole lot. The ships are all neglected."

"They're in good shape, I hope. Seaworthy?"

"Oh yeah, they're fine. Just need a little cosmetic maintenance. New ropes, a coat of paint maybe. Nothing significant."

"Good," I say.

"No need to worry. You won't get shipwrecked again."

I let a small laugh escape my lips. "Thank you."

"So, you're going back?" he says.

"Just for a few days. I need to say goodbye to everyone there and collect my stuff. Plus, I want to ask them if I can annex them."

"Really?"

"Yeah. I was upset about losing them, but if I annex them, I can keep them close to me and help them."

"That's a great idea," Brent says.

"Thank you. I thought so when Jane suggested it."

"Do you think they'll be up for that?"

"I think so," I say. "I can't see why not. They can retain any amount of independence they want. I'll let them do whatever they want. I just want to help them. They deserve that."

"So, I guess you'll tell Zane first?"

"Probably."

"Of course."

"Don't do that," I say. "Zane is my best friend, and he's really important to me. You know that."

"I know, I'm sorry," he says, slowly digging his heels into the carpet. "I hope he's happy. I hope they all like the idea."

"Thank you," I say, waiting a moment before asking the question on my mind. "Are you going to join us?"

"No," Brent says, smiling slightly. "I completed my mission. I'll stay here, help keep the palace in order—if that's what you want."

"I would really appreciate that, thank you."

"Then enjoy your trip." Brent steps aside to let me pass upstairs. "I'll see you soon."

Chapter 24

Even though I've only been back at Trilland for a few days, suddenly, the little island I've spent the last year on feels so foreign and distant yet familiar at the same time. I could walk these trails with my eyes closed and still get exactly where I'm going. But this island doesn't feel like home anymore. It will always be special to me, but it used to feel like the only place I belonged. I guess seeing it with old eyes, the eyes that remember who I am, changes how I see this place. Now, I can see it for what it is: a temporary home where I stayed for a year.

I'm excited to annex it as a part of Trilland. I can't imagine anyone here will object, though of course I'll ask them before I do it. I want to annex this little island as part of Trilland not only so I can take care of the wonderful people here who took care of me for so long, but also because I selfishly want to keep it close to me. Even though Trilland is home and always will be, I've missed this island, with its beautiful beaches and its cute little village. Everyone here is one big family, and I want my family close.

It's early in the morning. Zane and I purposely waited until morning to come ashore so we could have a quick moment alone, just the two of us. I don't want to talk to anyone else before I talk to him, but there's something about seeing that house and spotting Harper baking through the window that really makes it feel like I've returned.

She looks happy, like she always does when she bakes, and it makes me smile. I remember waking up to that picture of Harper baking and dancing. I was confused, I had a headache, and I was worried, but seeing her put me at ease. I knew I was safe around someone like that.

We pass the fishermen, keeping far enough away that they won't notice us. I watch them for a few minutes and feel at peace. It's only been a few days back at Trilland, but I had already forgotten how peaceful it is to watch the fishermen. They're hard-working and efficient, but they're also laid back and having fun with their job.

"So, I have to ask the village something. I have a proposal," I say.

"You do? About what?" Zane says, stroking my hand with his thumb.

"You'll see. I want to ask them something as the princess of Trilland."

"I'm intrigued," Zane says.

"It's good news," I blurt out, somehow fearing Zane was thinking the opposite. "I just want to ask everyone before I do anything."

"Well then, let's call a town square meeting." Zane smirks, darting to his left to knock on Gus's door.

It only takes Zane a few minutes to gather everyone, and since he just got back, everyone has a lot of questions. When Zane says something is important, people listen. And besides, as soon as they see me, they all rush over to me, celebrating and hugging me. It's funny: it's like I've been gone for weeks, months even. It's only been a few days, and everyone is so happy to see me again.

Zane borrows a few empty mango crates from Gus and stacks them into a makeshift stage. It's uneven, and I feel like my feet are going to fall through any second, but I can tell that this will be my favorite stage I'll ever stand on.

Zane hushes the crowd for me, and I start preparing a professional speech, but I quickly let that go. I don't need a perfect speech for these people. They don't make me nervous. I just have to talk to them.

"It's so good to see everyone again. You all have no idea how happy I am to be back. I have something to tell you all. You all have taken such good care of me this past year, and I can't thank you enough. I want you all to know, because you've been there since the beginning, that the first day I arrived in Trilland, my memory returned in full."

Everyone breaks out into cheers and hollering. I see Harper wiping tears from her eyes, Gus picking through his mangoes, probably trying to find one for me to celebrate. I spot Elise with the biggest smile I've ever seen, Ms. Flora nodding happily. Of course, I look to Zane, who is smiling, and I've never been so happy to see him smile.

"I'm thrilled that it's back, but I could never forget everything each one of you did for me. Ms. Flora, you took care of me for days, preventing me from getting sicker than I was. Harper, you took me in and became like a mother to me when I desperately needed that kind of care and affection. Elise, you agreed to be the roommate of the weird amnesiac and never let me turn to pessimism about my situation." Elise laughs along with the crowd. "Gus, you always saved the best mango for me because somewhere in my brain, I knew that was my favorite fruit. Tito, you pulled in my boat, and because of your attentive eye to the sea, even saw me in the first place. Daisy, you always provided a laugh for me.

"You all will never know how much you mean to me. For that reason, I want to propose something to you all. First of all, you should know that Brent Grayson, the paddler who appeared a little while ago, was right. Everything he knew about me turned out to be the truth. I am the princess of the country of Trilland."

Several people cheer or applaud, many smile, and only a few look surprised. I wonder why no one is shocked. When I imagined this moment when I finally told the whole village that I really was a lost princess, I expected shock and disbelief. Maybe they always saw something in me that I simply didn't see.

"Obviously, I have to move back to Trilland and begin to pick up the pieces of the country that a rebel tried to destroy, so I must leave the island. I am deeply saddened to leave you all, and I wish there was a way for me to stay, but Trilland is home as much as this little village is. But I have a solution. I wanted to ask you all if you would like to be annexed as an outlying province of Trilland. I realize you all are happy with your way of life, and I wouldn't want to disrupt that. I would let you all have as much freedom and independence as you want. If you want, nothing will change except that your island will get a name and a deed. I will not do anything that you all don't want. But, if there is anything you want, I will be more than happy to provide it. It's the least I can do for this village."

Everyone looks around for a few moments, unsure what to do. I wave my hand in a circle, trying to encourage someone, anyone, to say something, but no one takes the bait. Finally, I look down at Zane who looks confused but bails me out anyway.

"What do you mean 'anything we want'?" he says loud enough for the crowd to hear. "What would we want?"

"Well, you're certainly not obligated to take any offer I give you, but Trilland could help you economically. Gus, you could sell your fruit to the mainland or other islands and make a bigger commission. You all," I point to the fishermen, "could sell your fish as well. Elise, you could come to Trilland and be an apprentice for a chef. Trilland's wealth could help you all build anything you want. Also, and I doubt this would ever happen, but if anyone ever tried to attack this island, you would have Trilland's royal forces to count on. Stuff like that. Or anything else you can think of."

"But we would still be independent?" Harper calls out. "No one would be interfering in our business?"

"Not if you don't want it," I say. "I would make sure that I have exclusive control over this island, so if you tell me you don't want interference, you won't get it. I'll make sure your desires are honored."

"Could we get better medicine?" Ms. Flora says quietly from the front row.

I see everyone strain to hear her, so I answer loudly. "Yes, Ms. Flora, if you want medicines, you will definitely get them. Anything you want."

"Because my job would be a lot easier if I didn't have to depend on some kind of leaf-berry thing from Gus's boy Davie."

"That stuff works just fine, and you know it," Gus shouts, and we all laugh.

"Whatever you like, Ms. Flora," I say. "Any other questions?"

"What about better income?" Eric from the general store shouts. "We don't make much selling to each other."

"You can sell to anyone you want."

"And fishing supplies?"

"Trilland has a huge fishing industry, so I would be happy to get you the best supplies."

There's a silence as people look around at each other until finally Harper shouts, "So where do we sign?"

Tears sting my eyes, and I smile wide. "You mean you all want to be part of Trilland?"

Elise runs up to the makeshift stage and hugs my waist. "We want to be with you. If that means being part of Trilland, then we're in."

I look out to the crowd, and everyone nods in agreement with Elise. I nod happily, unable to say anything. I hadn't realized how afraid I was that they would say no. I'm so glad they want to be a part of Trilland. Now I can help them and protect them forever.

When I didn't remember who I was, I used to fantasize about how I would pay the people here back for their kindness to me. I never could have dreamed then that I would have the resources that I do. I know I'm offering a lot, but it still feels like nothing compared to what they did for me.

"So, what would we name it?" Tito calls out and several shout agreements. "The island I mean. We have to name it, right?"

"Whatever you like," I say.

A few kids start shouting out some silly suggestions like Ocean Island or Beach Island, and the adults laugh, but no one really seems to have a legitimate suggestion. I scour my own brain, but I can't come up with anything. What is this island known for? Mangoes? Mango Island? No, that's terrible. The sand is really pretty, almost like gold. Golden Island? Ugh, that sounds like a cheesy honeymoon destination in a bad romance novel. What else? What's important to this island?

Zane jumps up on the crates next to me, cups his hands around his mouth, and shouts, "What about Maris? Maris Island?"

I whip my head around to shoot Zane a glare, but in the time it takes him to shrug unapologetically, I hear several shouts of concurrence.

"I like it," Old Man Barnes shouts from the back of the crowd.

"Me too," Harper and Elise agree while Daisy smiles under her mother's arms.

"Maris Island?" I say. "You all would name your island after me?"

"Technically, that's not actually your name, so don't get too excited," Zane says, giving me a wink. "And, I mean, yeah. You're so important to all of us. And you're the reason we're even trying to pick a name. Why not you?"

"Are you all really sure?"

"It's settled," Tito calls out. "Maris Island."

"Maris Island!" the fishermen all shout together.

"Okay, then it's settled," I say. "Maris Island."

Everyone cheers heartily, and Zane helps me down from the crates. He keeps his arm around my waist, and he smiles, but I can tell he is not as happy as he wants me to believe.

"What's wrong?"

"So, I guess you're going back to Trilland," he says.

"I have to. It's my home. The people there need me. I have to undo everything Cassandra did."

"What will I do without you here?" Zane holds my hips and looks sadly into my eyes.

"I was hoping you would come with me," I say.

"You were?"

"Zane, you have been my best friend this entire time. You encouraged me when I got down, you stayed by me when I didn't feel well, you argued with me when I said I would never remember, and you loved me even when you and I both pretended we didn't have feelings for each other."

He smiles, blushing a little, and says, "I Wasn't sure you would want me to come to Trilland, but I was hoping you would."

"Of course," I say. "Zane, I can't do this without you. I was hoping you'd come to Trilland with me. Now that the island—*Maris Island*—is part of Trilland, visiting it will be official business that I'll have to do. Please come with me."

"Well, I was thinking that I could show those people in Trilland a thing or to about some real fishing. Seems they're going to need my expertise." When I roll my eyes, he adds, "And maybe I could pick up a few things, too."

"So you'll come?"

"I wouldn't have it any other way, *Maris*." Zane kisses my cheek, and I finally feel at peace.

# *Epilogue*

Finally. I'm finally done with this speech. After days of writing, rewriting, scrapping, and rewriting again, I finally finished this speech. I don't know why this one was so hard. Maybe it's because it is the first time I'm addressing parliament since my return. Maybe it's because financial budgets are just not that interesting, and it's very difficult to make them sound interesting. Maybe I'm just always a nervous wreck.

That's probably the most likely.

But it's officially done, and I don't have to think about it anymore.

I practically run down the hallway and down the stairs and bolt out of the palace toward the parliament building. I still have to deliver my budget proposal to them so they can look it over before my presentation, and I wanted to give them a copy of my speech as well. I'm sure they'll be glad to finally have it; I've been holding it back from them for so long.

"Hello, Diane," I say to the secretary at the front desk. "I've got the budget proposal for you."

Diane smiles brightly and takes the papers. "Excellent news, Your Highness."

"Could you make copies and distribute it to all the members of parliament? I'll also want a master copy eventually to post in the square for people to read."

"Not a problem," Diane says. "I'll get right on that."

"Thank you. I've got to get going now."

"Why the rush?"

"I was supposed to meet Zane nearly an hour ago," I say sheepishly. "I've just been so busy working on this budget."

"Well, get going then," Diane says with a smile. "Enjoy your day, Your Highness."

"Thank you," I say as I bolt out onto the street.

I know I'm late, and I should be hurrying, but it's a beautiful day today. I just can't help but enjoy how pretty the town square looks today. It looks so charming with everyone bustling about. Clearly the weather is making everyone else as happy as I am.

"Good morning, Your Majesty," three young girls say in unison as they pass me.

"Good morning," I say back.

"It's 'Your Highness,' girls, not 'Majesty,'" the mother of one of the girls says.

"Oh that's all right," I say. "I'm hardly going to object to such sweet girls. Enjoy your days."

"You as well," the mother says with a smile.

I get back to the palace and choose to slip in the side door. Maybe I can dart upstairs and change before I meet Zane. I'm so late, he'll surely be waiting for me at the main door. He won't expect me to come in from the servants' entrance.

I open the door slowly, trying to minimize the creak but actually maximizing it, wave to the maids I pass, and slip down the hallway only to run straight into the folded arms of Zane.

"What are you doing?" I say.

Zane smirks. "I knew you'd try to sneak in some other way. Where have you been?"

"I had to take the budget down to parliament. I just finished."

"Well, congratulations, but you could've sent someone to deliver the budget."

"But if I do that, I can't enjoy the town square myself. What's the fun in that?"

"Fair enough," Zane says. "Come on, I've been waiting to show you something."

"What?"

"Just come on." Zane takes my hand, and we walk all the way to the other side of the palace.

"Have you read the budget yet?"

"I'm about halfway. It's dry reading."

"It was dry writing," I say. "Oh, I've got the final papers for Maris Island, too. We should make a trip over there to deliver the papers personally."

"Why won't you let anyone deliver something for you? Do you really want to sail?"

"No," I say, "but I want to see everyone. It's been five months since we left. I miss everyone. Don't you?"

"Eh, I was around them my whole life. I don't need to see them so much. I've seen them."

"You don't mean that."

"If you really want to go visit, we can," Zane says. "I just don't think it's necessary."

"How can it not be necessary?"

In response, Zane throws the doors to the ballroom open where everyone I know, including all the townspeople from the island, shouts "surprise," and confetti cannons fire.

"What—what is this?" I stammer.

"It's a surprise birthday party," Zane says. "Sorry that I couldn't make it a fake surprise birthday party. I tried, but you're not as smart as I am. You didn't figure it out."

"But—but why?"

"Today is your birthday, isn't it?"

"Well, yeah, but I never told you that."

"You think I didn't ask around to find out?"

"Zane," I say, staring at him with tears starting to form in my eyes. I can't believe he did this.

"Well, go on." Zane gestures toward the party. "You're the one who wanted to see everyone."

I walk into the room, and sure enough, everyone is there. Harper, Tito, Gus, Elise, Daisy, Ms. Flora, and everyone else. Jane, Annette, and Brent are there as well. Uncle Lawrence tells me he sailed to go pick everyone up so they could be here today, and I just can't believe it. I can't believe Zane pulled this off.

"You're incredible," I say to Zane when I get a chance to pull him aside.

"I told you someday I would throw you a surprise birthday party. Just following through on a promise."

~~~
~~~

# Acknowledgements

This was the second novel I ever wrote, and it was the first novel I wrote actually feeling like I knew how to write a novel. I wrote it in a span of about a year, edited it, then left it to rot unseen on my hard drive. I loved the story, but I didn't feel like it was the right time to release it. Now that I feel a little bit like I know what I'm doing, it feels right to return to this story that I love and let it see the light of day. It holds a special place in my heart because I remember the outlining process, the drafting, and the realization that I was capable of writing a decent novel. Younger Kristen would be so proud to know that I finally did write a whole novel and published it (along with others)!

Thank you to Crystal Bonano and Elizabeth Kahn for being the earliest readers of this book during my undergrad creative writing program at the University of South Florida. This book changed quite a bit thanks to your input, and I'm so grateful that you were even willing to read this. There are elements of this story that you both first suggested, and now, I can't imagine the story without those pieces.

Thank you to the University of South Florida for being the place where I wrote my first novel, where I found a writing community, and where I realized that I could actually write a book. A special thanks to Dr. Rita Ciresi for your tireless support of my writing ambitions.

Thank you to Emerson College for being the second phase of my journey of learning how to be a writer. A special thanks to Lisa Diercks for inspiring the cover of this book and for being instrumental in learning how to design and publish a book.

Thank you to MockingbirdArtist for designing a wondrously beautiful map of Trilland. You exceeded my expectations.

Thank you to Morgan Brownlee, Laina Strickland, Kristen Christensen, Kelly Layne, and Kayla Tirrell for supporting my crazy ideas when it comes to releasing books.

Thank you to my parents Brian and Sylvia and my sister Ashley for being my most consistent and passionate supporters. I wouldn't have gotten to this point without you.

# About the author

When she's not writing books for YA readers, she's teaching them AP and DE English. Kristen Grafton is a Florida native with an MFA in Popular Fiction & Publishing and an MA in English Rhetoric. She was a triple major in college. She has an unhealthy obsession with her cats and Taylor Swift. She is also the author of *Thank You for Applying* and *Line of Succession.*

To learn more about Kristen Grafton, follow her on Instagram @kmgrafton1 and visit www.kristen mgrafton.com.